Dakota Stories I

Dakota Dawn
Dakota Dream

Books by Lauraine Snelling

One Perfect Day
Breaking Free
Saturday Morning
The Healing Quilt
The Way of Women
The Brushstroke Legacy
Washington
Once Upon A Christmas
Yuletide Treasure

A Secret Refuge
Daughter of Twin Oaks
Sisters of the Confederacy
The Long Way Home

Dakotah Treasures
Ruby   Opal
Pearl   Amethyst

Daughters of Blessing
A Promise for Ellie
Sophie's Dilemma
A Touch of Grace
Rebecca's Reward

Red River of the North
An Untamed Land   The Reaper's Song
A New Day Rising   Tender Mercies
A Land to Call Home   Blessing in Disguise

Return to Red River
A Dream to Follow
Believing the Dream
More Than a Dream

Youth Fiction
What About Cimmaron?

Available at www.dakotabooknet.com

LAURAINE SNELLING

Dakota Stories I

Dakota Dawn
Dakota Dream

Smoky Water Press

Bismarck, North Dakota

Dakota Stories I
2008
Dakota Dawn
Copyright © 1993
Lauraine Snelling

Dakota Dream
Copyright © 1993
Lauraine Snelling

Cover design by Sydney Bren, Clearwater Communications, Bismarck, North Dakota.
Cover photograph Main Street, Almont, North Dakota 1910.

Scripture quotations are from the King James Version of the Bible.

Published by Smoky Water Press
Post Office Box 2322
Bismarck, ND 58502-2322

Smoky Water Press is a division of Capital Communications, Inc.
Bismarck, North Dakota

Printed in the United States of America

ISBN: 978-0-9820752-0-3

DEDICATION

TO TODAY'S SONS AND DAUGHTERS OF THE PIONEERS.
May we always remember those who came before us.

LAURAINE SNELLING is the award-winning author of numerous novels, including the beloved Red River of the North and Daughters of Blessing series. She and her husband Wayne live in the Tehachapi Mountains of California with their basset hound, Chewy. Visit her at her website, www.LauraineSnelling.com.

Dakota Dawn

Chapter 1

Nora Johanson leaned her forehead against the sooty train window. It seemed as if they had not climbed a hill nor traveled through any woods in the last forty years. "Don't be silly," she chided herself. "You haven't been on this train for forty years, it just feels that way." She glanced over at the corpulent man sprawled in the seat across the aisle. She certainly didn't need to worry about her mutterings waking him—snores fit to wake hibernating bears puffed at his walrus mustache.

Besides, he would not have understood a word she said since he obviously did not speak Norwegian and her few, carefully learned English phrases were not understood by most people she met.

She dug a cloth out of her carpetbag and scrubbed at the window, the dirt reminding her of how desperately she wanted a bath. If only she could have bathed in Minneapolis. But she was down to her last few coins and could afford only a small hunk of bread.

What will you do? What will you do? The question beat in time with the clacking train wheels, ever bearing her west. Farther from her beloved mountains and fjords of Norway but closer to the arms of the man she had promised to marry. At fifteen she had been so sure of their love. Now, she could barely remember him. She scrunched her eyes shut to conjure up a picture of Hans Larson, but it was easier to see his handwriting on the letters they had exchanged over the last three years.

She carefully drew off her natural wool, knitted mittens and opened her purse to count the coins that were left. One, two, three, four. *Uff da.* No blessed angel had multiplied them while she dozed. Four pennies—all that was left of the money Hans had sent to her. Her stomach rumbled.

In the last letter, Hans had said it was plenty. But then he had not counted on the overly long, storm-tossed sea passage. Or the tedious wait with the thousands of other immigrants on Ellis Island in this year of 1910. Or the blizzard that stopped the train for twelve hours.

Her stomach rumbled again. Would they never come to another town?

Nora fought back the tears that seemed to hover like persistent bees at the back of her eyelids. She sent a silent plea upward. *Please, make the town hurry.* Or maybe it was the train that should hurry. Whatever.

She leaned her head against the back of the seat. Visions of home danced through her mind. Home—with her family crowded around the white-clothed kitchen table, laughing, teasing, telling funny stories.

A sob caught in her throat. Her sister Clara had promised to come to the new land too, as soon as Nora could send her passage money. And her brother John. When she closed her eyes she could see them so clearly. She shut off the memories with a snap. *Think only of the better times,* she told herself. Remembering her loved ones, all bundled up and waving good-bye at the train station in Oslo, cut too deeply.

She blew her nose and wiped the errant tear away. As Mama had always said, "The good Lord will be with you and guide you when we can't." But right now Nora needed a human hug, one that she could touch and feel, and even hear. She sneaked a peak at the man in the other seat. She certainly could hear him. The train trip had not kept him awake.

She focused her attention again to what was out the window. The snow did not surprise her—it would be weeks yet before spring came to the hills and valleys at home. It was just the unending flatness of the land. The only rises were the drifts that piled against the buildings and sometimes stopped the train. Several times, the railroad men had been forced to dig through the drifts so the train could continue. It would have helped if the men had allowed her to assist them in digging instead of just looking at her as though the wind had frozen her brain. Her brothers would have tossed her a shovel and dared her to outdig them.

She caught a sigh as it was escaping her throat. *Think about Hans*, she ordered herself. *Think of what a fine man he is, how wonderful it will be to have a home of your own and milk cows again. Think of his promise to buy some chickens in the spring.*

Will there be flowers by the house? she wondered, closing her eyes to see them better. *Roses. I'll have pink ones and red, maybe even a scarlet climber.*

Just before she nodded off, she jerked upright. This time through the window she saw the sinking sun fling banners of orange and red, vermillion and gold across the sky. The heaped high, gray clouds were now burnished to shine and glow like the very gates of heaven. As the fiery red sun slipped below the horizon, the clouds faded to lavender and purple—and back to gray.

One thing this flat land does exceedingly well, Nora thought, *is sunsets.* She had never seen such a display—not even over her beloved mountains in Norway. As she watched, she dared not blink in fear that she might miss a single hue.

"I'm sorry, Miss," the woolen-coated conductor said as he paused at her seat. At least he spoke Norwegian. "But we'll be an hour later than I thought." He dragged out his gold watch and peered at its face. "Somewhere around ten, I expect."

"*Mange takk,* thank you," Nora nodded with her words.

"Surely your young man will check at the station, so he'll know our arrival time."

Nora nodded; she seemed to be doing a lot of that. Why didn't she feel the consolation the man was trying to offer? Was something wrong with her hearing? "I. . .I'm sure he'll—Hans'll be there."

Not true, a little voice inside her whispered. *You're sure he won't be there to meet you.*

Nora forced her lips into a smile and thanked the man again. She kept herself from turning around and watching him as he made his way down the length of the car, swaying with the movement of the train. He had boarded the train in Chicago and was beginning to seem like an old friend. The music of her own language cemented that feeling. She had never dreamed she would be at such a loss for words because she spoke only Norwegian.

She started to take out her dictionary but put it back because the light was so dim. She had not been able to concentrate on learning new words for the last two days anyway. Since the Norwegian woman she had traveled with left the train in Wisconsin, Nora had practiced English with no one.

Seeing her reflection in the darkened window, she smoothed a few stray hairs up and tucked them under the thick, golden braids she wore coronet-style. She shook her head. "You really need to brush and rebraid your hair," she whispered to the woman in the glass. "And take a bath." She used her handkerchief to dab at her tongue and rub off a spot on her cheek.

In the reflection she could also see a portion of the car behind her. Polished wood on the walls and ceiling gleamed in the lamplight; the brown fabric of the padded seats was worn in spots; some of the passengers had drawn their window curtains closed against the cold and dark. Not Nora, though—she hated to close herself in any more than was necessary. The car had looked comfortable in the beginning, but these five days of being cooped up had worn on both her body and spirit.

It seemed like another week had passed before the conductor

returned, announcing, "Soldahl. Next stop, Soldahl." He stopped beside her. "You take care of yourself, now." He reached up and swung her bag down for her from the overhead racks. "I've already made sure your trunk will get off when you do. I just hate to see a pretty thing like you..."

Nora could feel her cheeks flame at his compliment. *"Mange takk.* I thank you for all you've done. I...I'm..." She lifted her chin. "I'll be just fine."

While the train slowed, Nora searched for lights. Surely everyone in the town had not gone to bed already. But, as the train huffed and screeched to a halt, she saw only two lights off in the distance—only two. There must be more than two houses in town; Hans had said this was a big town.

She pictured his letter and tried to remember how his voice sounded. "It's a large town for the area. We have stores, a hotel, a Norwegian Lutheran church and..."

She shook her head to keep herself awake. After all, it was ten o'clock at night.

A lone gaslight hung above the door to the train station. Nora paused a moment at the head of the steps leading down to the platform. It had started to snow again; tiny hard pellets rattled on the roof of the metal car. The square window of the station glowed like a beacon against the blackness of the outside peppered with whirling snow.

The conductor held out his hand. "Be careful going down these steps, Miss," he said with a ready smile. Even with his muffler, he shivered in a draft of bitter wind. "Don't appear anyone's here to meet you." He looked over his shoulder as if hoping that someone— anyone—would make a liar out of him.

Nora bit her bottom lip and forced her mouth into a smile. "I...I'm sure Hans will be here. I'll wait for him in the station."

She trembled at the thought of another falsehood. She wasn't sure he would be there at all. In fact, she was terrified to admit the nagging feeling she had that something was not right.

"You better ask Oscar, the stationmaster, to come pick up your trunk. It'll get buried if this keeps up." He motioned to a black square farther up the station platform.

The train whistled, as if impatient for the delay.

"You take care of yourself now." The conductor helped her down the last step. "Get right inside before you freeze." He waved his lantern, picked up the metal stool, then stepped aboard as the wheels of the train squealed back to life. "God bless."

Before she could get her scarf wrapped up over her nose, the pelleted snow stung her cheeks. *If this is what March is like in North Dakota, what will January be like?*

"Please, God, let Hans come soon," Nora whispered as she peered off to the sides of the station building that seemed to hunker down against the swirling snow. Darkness, so black it reached out for her, sent her skidding across ice-coated planks towards the square of light. *"Uff da,"* she muttered as she slipped and slid, barely keeping her feet.

The wind helped her push the station door open, but it swirled her black woolen skirt and tugged at her scarf before it retreated in defeat. She slammed the door shut and leaned against it. Why did she feel like she had just battled and barely won? Her wish had been that Hans would be waiting inside to surprise her. He had liked to do that—surprise her and make her laugh. But, when she stared into the darkened corners of the room, she felt the dream fade and disappear.

The stationmaster certainly did not resemble Hans in any way. Short and thin seemed the best words to describe him, from closely clipped hair, to feet that barely touched the floor when the man sat at his desk. He had not risen to greet her, but Nora realized right away it was not because of bad manners. The man listened to the telegraph with both his hands and ears.

Nora nodded back at him, left her satchel by the door, then wandered over to the potbellied stove near the station desk. She loosened her scarf and let it drape around her neck. While the room temperature was warmer than outside, the heat from the stove failed to reach the door, or the corners, or the benches lining the center of the room.

His tapping finished, the man gave a little hop to get down from his chair and then he limped forward. "May I help you, Miss?" He reached into a back pocket to retrieve a handkerchief. After blowing and wiping his reddened nose, he peered over his metal-rimmed glasses and, starting at her feet, measured her height with his stare.

Nora felt like the giant troll in one of her sisters stories. "I... I'm Nora Johanson, from Norway." His intense gaze caused her to falter. "I…I wired ahead. Hans Larson, my betrothed, was to meet me tonight. I'm. . .ah sorry, the. . .ah train was late." Why didn't the man say something? Anything? She unclenched her hands in her mittens and extended them to the warmth of the stove. Right now her cheeks felt like they had been sunburned.

Maybe he had not understood a word she had said. She pointed to her chest and repeated her name, louder.

"You don't have to shout." The little man backed away.

Nora breathed a sigh of relief—he had answered in Norwegian. "Did you receive my wire?" she asked.

He nodded.

"Did you give it to Hans Larson?"

The stationmaster shook his head.

"Did Hans contact you?"

A nod. "Close to a week ago. Said he'd return in a day or so. Too far out in the country for me to deliver it." The man limped back to his desk and shuffled the papers in a wire basket. He pulled one out. "Here it is."

Nora felt something clench around her stomach and twist. Hans didn't even know she was arriving today. How could he have met her? She licked her dry, chapped lips. What would she do now?

"The hotel's right up the street. I can take you there on my way home." The man returned to the stove and closed the damper. He set the teakettle to the back and peered through the isinglass windows to check the coals. A grunt seemed to express his approval.

"I. . .ah—" Nora could not force the words past the lump in her throat.

"Ja?" He paused on his uneven journey to the coatrack.

"Sir, I have no money for a hotel." Nora felt like crawling under one of the benches. "The trip took much longer than we planned, than Hans planned. Perhaps I can sleep here, until Hans comes, that is. Maybe he'll come first thing in the morning. I won't bother anyone and..." Her voice trailed off.

"Oscar."

"What?"

"My name's not Sir, it's Oscar."

"Ja, *mange takk.* Mister Oscar, I..."

He was shaking his head again. "Not Mister Oscar. Oscar Weirholtz. But everyone just calls me Oscar. You can, too."

"Mange takk. I—" Nora could feel the tears clogging her throat and stinging her eyes. She clamped her lips shut and looked upwards to ward off the waterworks. She would not cry!

Oscar stopped buttoning his coat. "No money at all?"

Nora shook her head. "Four pennies."

"Well that old goat at the hotel won't give a room to anyone who can't pay in advance." He shook his head. "And, no, you can't stay here. Against the rules of the railway. No one can be here without the stationmaster or another employee of the Great Northern Railroad."

Nora now knew how an animal in a trap felt. *Dear God, what will I do?* The prayer slipped past her strangled thoughts in spite of herself.

"I know." Oscar reached for his hat. "I'll take you over to Reverend Moen's house. Mrs. Moen will take you in and she'll know how to contact your young man. You'll like her." He turned down the kerosene lamp, leaned over the glass chimney, and blew out the flame.

"Oh, my trunk." Nora stopped in midstride. "It's still out by the track. I forgot all about it."

Oscar groaned. "Can't it wait…no, I suppose not." He struck a match and lit another lantern hanging by the door. When it flared satisfactorily, he set it on the floor and pulled mittens from his pocket. "Come on, then. You'll have to help me. We can probably skid it on the ice, but best be careful." He grabbed the wire handle and, swinging the lantern, stepped outside into the black and cold.

Nora pulled her scarf up over her nose and followed him. When they reached the trunk, he handed her the lantern and grabbed one of the rope handles. "You push."

After they broke it loose from the ice, the trunk slid easily. Nora followed behind until they came to the step and then she set the lantern down and hoisted along with Oscar. The trunk screeched its way over the threshold.

"We can leave it here," Oscar said, nodding toward the wall.

"One of the men will bring it down on a wagon in the morning."

"Ja, that will be fine," Nora brushed the snow off the top of the trunk so no moisture would seep inside it. Her quilts, hand-embroidered linens, and household treasures painted with rosemaling designs had not left much room for her clothing. She dusted off the last of the white powder from the trunk and then shook her mittens clean. *Mange takk.* Thank you very much. I am sorry to be so much trouble."

Oscar nodded, checked the stove and, picking up the lantern, led the way out the door, carefully locking it behind him. "No, here, I'll take that." He held out the lantern in exchange for her heavy bag.

Nora looked down at the small man and hid a smile; she stood nearly a foot taller than he. As he swung off through the stinging snow, the bag bumped against his gimpy leg. She hurried to keep up with him so the lantern could light both their paths.

When they stepped from behind the station, the wind snatched at her scarf and huffed to extinguish the flickering light. Dark buildings lined the street now carpeted with white snow.

Oscar strode down the center of the road. "Less ice this way," he shouted to be heard above the whistling wind. While the falling snow stung all the skin it could find, each gust of wind made the visibility worse.

Nora knew that this storm was a playful kitten compared to the fierce lions of Norwegian blizzards. Hans had written her of the howling winds and whiteouts of the North Dakota winters of the past, of the cold that cracked trees and killed anyone careless enough to be caught out in it. Her homeland and North Dakota had one thing in common—winter could be deadly.

She shivered at the thought. Was that why Hans had not been back in town? Had there been a terrible blizzard? She shook her head. This new snow was only ankle deep and while snowbanks lined the street, there did not appear to be deep drifts of snow.

Oscar puffed beside her. Nora wished she could repossess her bag, but she hated to hurt the man's feelings. He had been so kind to her.

"Here we are," he said. He opened a gate on their left and walked up a path to a porch that spanned the entire front of the house. Oscar stepped forward and, after setting her bag down, thumped on the door.

Nora felt like crawling over the porch railing and hiding down under the straw banking the sides of the house. How terrible to wake people in the middle of the night like this. And bringing a stranger, at that.

"Don't worry, Miss." Oscar turned to her with a smile. It was as if he had read her mind. "The Moens, they'd skin me alive if I didn't bring you here. You needn't worry about your welcome. And they'll probably know about your young man, too." He pounded on the door again.

Nora flinched at each thump of his fist. A light flickered and gleamed beyond the curtain-covered window.

"I'm coming." A deep voice sent shivers up her spine.

Dear Lord, please make this man willing to take me in. I don't know where else I could go this night. She banished thoughts of "no room at the inn" and swallowed hard. This certainly was not going the way Hans's letters had promised, or like her daydreams on the long trip.

The door swung open and a tall man wearing a dark, belted robe shielded the flame of the candle from the wind. "Come in, come in. You must be freezing out there." He stepped back and held the candle high. "Oscar, whom have you brought us this time?"

"Who is it, dear?" A woman's voice floated down from the hall.

"Hello. I'm John Moen, pastor of the Lutheran church here in Soldahl." He shut the door behind them and extended a hand to Nora. "That voice you heard, that's my wife, Ingeborg. She'll join us in a minute. And you are... ?"

Nora could not decide whether to shake hands with her mittens on or take them off first. She drew off the right one and extended her hand. "I'm Nora Johanson, from Bergen, Norway. I've come –"

"And who is this?" A tiny, rounded woman with her blond hair in a long braid down her back, beamed up at Nora. Her smile removed any doubt of trespassing on their hospitality. "Whom did you bring us, Oscar?"

"I'm sure they'd tell us if you'd give them a chance," Reverend Moen said, with a twinkle in his eye and love in his voice.

Ingeborg laughed, a merry sound that not only invited smiles from those around but made resistance impossible.

Nora felt a sigh start down in her toes and bubble upward to bring a quiver to her bottom lip. "I. . .I'm Nora Johanson, from

Bergen, Norway. My betrothed, Hans Larson, was supposed to meet me at the train, but I suffered all kinds of delays during my trip here. I wired him a message, but—"

"But he didn't pick it up," Oscar finished for her. "I hoped she could stay here until we notify her young man."

"Ja, sure, you know that she can."

Nora intercepted a look between husband and wife. "Only for tonight," she said, feeling a sharp stab of unease. "I'm sure I can find transportation out to Hans's farm tomorrow. I don't want to cause you any trouble."

"No, it's no trouble." Ingeborg shot another look at her husband and reached up to unwind Nora's long knitted scarf. "You give me your coat and come on over by the fire. Oscar, would you like a cup of coffee before you start home?"

"No, no, that's fine. I need to get along. It's late." He turned to leave and paused. "Is something wrong?"

"I'm afraid so." John studied the floor for a moment, then looked at his wife. At her nod, he continued. "You said you were engaged to Hans Larson?"

Nora nodded. A tiny arrow of fear sneaked between her ribs, stabbing her heart.

Ingeborg reached out to take both of Nora's hands in hers.

"I'm so sorry to be the one to tell you this," John paused again as if fighting to get the words out. "But we buried Hans two days ago. He died of the fever."

Chapter 2

It won't be much longer now." Doctor Harmon looked up at Carl Detschman, the pacing father-to-be. "If'n ya can't stand still, get on out to the other room. You men are all alike. You say you want to help and then you make matters worse."

"I'm sorry." The tall man with eyes the faded blue of sunbleached skies tore his fingers through his thatch of wheaten hair. 1 just never—

"That's the problem, you men never—and I never shoulda asked you to help, but Anna here insisted. I shoulda stayed by my rule—no men ever in the birthing room. Go on out and tend your cows or something."

"But this," Carl waved his hand at the woman he loved, the woman who had now been in labor for a day and a night. "How much more can she stand?" Torn between leaving like the doctor said or staying to help if he could, Carl resumed his pacing.

At a groan from his patient, the doctor stopped lecturing the man and turned back to the woman lying limp on the bed, slowly recovering from the small dose of laudanum he had administered to her.

"All right, my dear. You've had a bit of a rest now, so let's get this baby born." The doc handed a dry towel to Carl as the younger man dropped back to the bedside to take his wife's hand.

"Anna, my heart, you must be strong," Carl murmured as he wiped her brow and smoothed back the tousled hair from her white forehead. Fear nearly strangled him at the sight of her slowly opening eyes, now sunken back in her head.

"Carl!" With the attack of another contraction, her hot hands gripped his. Her body arched off the mattress. She bit back the scream that twisted her face in agony. Even in her near-delirium, she kept quiet so she wouldn't waken their three-year-old daughter who slept peacefully in her own room.

"Oh, my God!" Carl said in a prayer. He knew that in spite of his great physical strength, there was nothing else he could do but pray.

"Push! Push!" The doctor shook his head when he realized his words failed to penetrate the fog she swam in. "Prop her up on the pillows. When the next contraction begins, you yell 'Push' at her and give her every bit of strength you have. I can see the head—if you can just give her the strength to make it through this. You understand?"

Carl nodded and placed his hand on his wife's bulging belly. "Come now, Anna, my love. This is the time." He kept up the soothing murmur even as he felt the contraction begin.

"Now," the doctor ordered when Anna's body tightened again.

"Anna! Push, now! Like you've never done before. Push, Anna!" Carl felt her fingernails dig into the palms of his hands. Her teeth ground into the rag the doctor had placed between her jaws. Sweat poured into her eyes and down to her ears. *God, please! Help us!* He was not sure if he had shouted the plea aloud or screamed it in the hollows of his mind but, at that very second, the doctor grunted his approval.

"You can rest now, my dear." The doctor held the slippery infant in his hands. "You have a son."

Carl leaned his cheek down on Anna's forehead. "You did it, my beautiful love, you did it. You wanted a baby boy and now he is yours." He kissed her forehead, then her cheek.

"Come on, little one, breathe." Doctor Harmon slapped the baby on the buttocks. "Breathe!"

"Wha. . .what's happening?" Anna's voice was so weak, Carl nearly missed it.

"Nothing, everything's fine. You just rest now." Carl murmured reassurances, all the while never taking his eyes from the battle waging at the end of the bed.

The doctor turned the baby over and rubbed its back. Finally, he pinched the minute nose and blew into the baby's mouth.

A cough, faint but gurgling. A moment of silence and then a weak, indignant cry.

"Stubborn, just like his father." Doctor Harmon's shoulders slumped. He placed the infant on Anna's chest and proceeded to cut the umbilical cord, all the while murmuring in a singsong voice.

Carl was not sure if the man was comforting the baby, the mother, or him, but he did not care. He finally allowed his shoulders to relax and the tears to flow. They had made it; they had a son. He knelt by the bed and gently touched the baby's head. He wrapped his other arm around Anna's head.

"Is he all right?" Her voice barely stirred the heavy air.

"Ja. He's fine."

Her eyes fluttered open. One hand crept up to lie across the tiny back. "He's so still."

"Resting like you must." Carl stroked her hair back from her forehead.

"Not yet," the doctor said. He picked up the slippery baby and wrapped him in a soft blanket. "Here, Carl. You put him in the cradle by the fire. We, Anna and I, have more work to do here."

Carl pushed himself to his feet and took his tiny son from the doctor's hands. How could anything so small cause such problems for his mother and yet be so perfect?

"All right, now. Let's get this over with." The doctor had no sooner finished saying the words when along with the afterbirth came a bright red flood that drenched the sheets.

No matter what he did, the bleeding refused to slow. No matter how desperately Carl pleaded with her to hang on and railed at the doctor to do something, nothing helped. Within a few minutes, Anna Detschman quietly slipped away. She never woke again to cuddle the son she had wanted so much.

Carl sat numbly by as she breathed her last. A pain—the likes of which he had never known before, clogged his throat, his chest, his very life. This could not be happening. Just yesterday, his Anna had been laughing, promising Kaaren a new baby brother. And now...

"I'm so sorry, son." The doctor leaned his head against the wall. "I don't know what else I could have done." He turned and, bending over, gently pulled the sheet up over Anna's now peaceful face.

Carl folded the sheet back down. "Just leave us alone." His manners caught up with him. "Please."

"Of course." The doctor turned toward the door, then went to the fireplace and picked up the cradle. "I'll wait outside." He left the room, closing the door behind him.

Carl sat on the bed staring at his wife, his love. Only moments ago, she had been there, fighting for the life of their son, and now... now she was gone. Anna, the laughing center of his life...of their home and family. Gone, leaving him and their children behind. With a gentle finger, he stroked her hand and her pale cheek.

"Oh, Anna. How could you leave me? What kind of a God would let you suffer so and then take you away when we need you so desperately?" He raised his eyes to the ceiling. "Why?" Sobs racked his body as he put his arms around her shoulders and clutched her to his chest. Together they rocked as if he could bring back her life force by sheer willpower.

An hour—an eon later—Carl staggered from the room and collapsed into the rocking chair by the stove. A striped gray cat left the warmth of her box behind the iron stove and rubbed against his leg.

"What will you do?" Doctor Harmon asked from the shadows of the other rocker.

Carl dropped his hand from his eyes and peered into the shadows. "Oh, Doctor Harmon. I ... I'm sorry. I guess I forgot you were here." His own voice sounded like it came from a far distance.

"I understand." Before he spoke again, the doctor allowed the silence to lengthen. "Oh, Carl, if only I knew of ways to keep tragedies like this from happening. I want you to know how terribly sorry I am."

Carl nodded. "Ja. I know."

"I know you can hardly think now, but that baby there needs some nourishment and soon. Do you know if Anna had some bottles ready? You know, just in case ... ah ...of an emergency."

Carl lifted his head. The weight of it took all his strength. "I... umm. . ." His breath sighed out like the bellows of a forge. He waited as if expecting someone else to answer. "I don't know."

Just then, a weak wail grabbed their attention.

"See what I mean?" Doctor Harmon touched the cradle with his foot. "Where would the bottles be?" He spoke slowly and precisely, enunciating each syllable as if Carl were hard of hearing.

"In the pantry, there…the door to your left."

"And the milk?"

"Out in the well house." Carl rose from his chair and stumbled to the outside door. He slid his feet into the boots waiting on the rug by the door and lifted his coat from the hook. After pulling a knitted stocking cap over his ears, he turned the knob on the door.

"Don't you need a lantern?" the doctor asked.

"Oh, yes." Carl placed the palm of his hand on the doorjamb and leaned his forehead against it. He felt like he was lost in the dark and someone had just blown out the only light.

"Would you like me to get the milk?" Doctor Harmon left his chair and came to stand by the door.

"No. No, I'll be…I'll get it."

The baby wailed again, louder this time.

"You see to him, all right?" Carl dug a match out of the box and lit the lantern sitting on the shelf. Without another word, he pulled the door open and staggered out into the dark.

Icy pellets of snow drilled his face and swirled about in the lantern's glow. He kicked the drifted snow away from the well house door and yanked it open. Compared to the freezing wind outside, the cool house felt warm. He pulled a bucket of milk from the nearly frozen water and, after latching the door, headed back to the house.

The doctor, with the swaddled baby in the crook of his arm, had stirred the embers of the fire and added more coal to it. "Water from the reservoir's still warm," he said as he looked up to greet Carl. "I think a cup of coffee would do us both good."

Carl blew out the lantern and hung up his jacket. Bathed in the golden glow from the kerosene lamp on the table, the doctor looked right at home. Carl filled the bottle on the table and set it in the pan of water the doctor had placed off to the side of the range.

When the baby began to fuss, the doctor patted his back and crooned a song in rhythm with the gentle swaying of his own body. "Here," he said, when the bottle seemed warm enough. He handed both baby and bottle to Carl and nodded toward the rocker. "Set yourself down. You both need the rest."

Carl settled down and pushed the nipple into the tiny, rosebud mouth. The baby pushed it out and turned his head, searching for a breast. After several more failed attempts, Carl handed the baby back to the doctor. "You try." He flung himself out of the chair and went to stand at the frosted window.

The baby began to cry, a soft sound that quickly grew into a wail. A voice from the back bedroom joined in the chorus. "Pa-a-a. Ma-a-a."

Carl shrugged his shoulders and dropped his hands in defeat. "Coming, Kaaren." He strode down the hall. "It's all right, *liebchen*." He sat on the bed and hugged his three-year-old daughter close.

"There's nothing to be afraid of."

"Where's Ma?" the towheaded child sniffed and rubbed her hand across her eyes. "I want my ma."

Carl hugged her close. "Your ma's busy," he whispered. "You have a new baby brother."

"Ummm." Kaaren nestled into his chest. She popped a thumb into her mouth and, after one pull, relaxed into the sleep of the innocent.

Carl laid her back down. He could still hear the baby crying.

"He refuses to suck on this thing." The doctor waved the bottle in the lamplight. "He won't last long if he doesn't eat."

"Do you know anyone who could wet-nurse him?" asked Carl.

The doctor shook his head and tried again to get the infant to take the bottle.

Carl raked his fingers through his hair until the white-blond strands stood straight up. "What am I going to do?"

The doctor pushed himself to his feet. "How about harnessing up my horse while I rewarm this and try again. I'll get to town right about sunrise and I'll see if I can find one of the women to come out and help you. They're always better at this than I am. Maybe Widow Nelson can help. Naah. She's gone to Fargo to take care of her sister."

Carl ignored the doctor's mutterings and dressed again for the cold outside. Lantern in hand, he opened the door and left, shutting it quickly to keep out the cold.

The barn warmth welcomed him as he slipped in through the small door. The doctor's old bay horse nickered a greeting. Even that simple touch brought tears to Carl's eyes. To keep from throwing himself down on the mound of hay and letting the tears ravage him, he concentrated on each step of the job at hand.

Pick up the harness, settle the leathers in place, buckle the straps, and lead the animal out of the stall. Back the gelding between the shafts. "Sooo now, easy, boy." *Don't think. Don't feel.*

Why was he so clumsy? Because of his gloves? He dashed the back of the knitted fabric across his eyes.

Secure the shafts to the breast piece. Open the main double doors. He continued giving himself orders, as if all this was new to him. Then, he backed the horse and buggy out into the freezing wind. After retrieving his lantern and closing the door, he led the horse up to the house.

He trudged along, knowing he would rather have stayed in the barn. In there, life was as it should be. Life, not death. But duty called him back to the house.

Carl blocked the thought of his wife lying in their bed.

Think of something else. Think of nothing.

The house was silent.

"Shhh." The doctor laid a finger across his lips. He was dressed for the outdoors, his hat pulled down over his ears. "He's asleep." He pointed to the cradle by the stove. "I got him to take a bit. I'll try to find someone for you. In the meantime, try giving he wakes up. If he gets hungry enough, maybe he'll eat."

"Thank you, Doctor." Carl extended his hand. The older man clasped it and covered their joined hands with his other.

"You're welcome, son. I just wish I coulda done more." The man hefted his worn black bag and slipped out the door.

Carl listened to the jingle of the harness as the horse trotted down the lane. Only the whistle of the wind, seeking entrance through tiny cracks, disturbed the silence of the house. The awful silence.

Chapter 3

Nora felt like a glacier pressed upon her shoulders. "Oh, my dear, I am so sorry." Ingeborg guided the younger woman into a chair. "Such terrible news and right off when you first arrive like this." She pulled up a stool and perched immediately in front of her guest so as to hold Nora's shaking hands.

Nora heard the men talking by the door as from a great distance. She forced herself to concentrate on the caring woman before her. What had she said? Anything that needed an answer? Hans had died. He was dead. Shouldn't she be weeping? But the sorrow was more like that of losing a dear friend, not the love of one's life. She was sad. Of course. But it did not seem to touch her—not inside where heart and love dwelled.

Instead, the thoughts that set her body shaking raced one on top of the other. *Whatever will I do now? Wherever will I go? Who will take care of Hans's farm? Could I live there?* She pulled herself back from looking over the precipice of her future and focused on the tender smile of the woman in front of her.

"I. . .I'm sorry, I seemed to have wandered off somewhere." Nora leaned back in the chair and drew in a deep breath. She felt the shudder start at her toes and work its way up until even her teeth rattled.

"Are you cold? Can I get you a blanket? The coffee will be ready shortly." Ingeborg rubbed Nora's icy hands.

Nora heard the door close and Reverend Moen approach. She studied her hands, warmly clasped in Ingeborg's as if to keep the outer world at bay. Her own hands, so large with long fingers and so smooth due to the long weeks of idleness. Ingeborg's hands, small and reddened from the work of her house. Maybe she could help the Moens for a time.

But Hans's cows and the horses. Who was taking care of them since he had passed away? He had said he had no near neighbors.

She reached to unbutton her coat. Here she was, dripping all over the spotless kitchen. What kind of visitor did things like that?

"I'm sorry for dripping snow on your floor. What you must think of me."

"No, no. You mustn't worry. You've had a great shock. Here, let me take that." Ingeborg pulled herself to her feet and reached for Nora's dark, wool coat. "Let me hang this over a chair by the stove so it can dry. Your scarf and mittens, too."

Nora felt like a small child obeying her mother. How comforting. She went through the motions but her mind insisted on darting around like a cornered animal. Hans—her friend of so many years—was gone. When she thought of their growing up together, she felt the tears beginning in the back of her throat. What about his parents? At the thought of their dear faces, the tears overflowed.

She covered her face with her hands, trying to stifle the sobs that shook her shoulders. Oh, the dreams that died along with a loved one. The happinesses that now would never be.

She felt a hand smoothing her hair, heard a gentle voice murmuring condolences. Words that ran together with no meaning, save that of love. She rested in their comfort.

When Nora leaned her weary head against the back of the chair, Ingeborg took a steaming cup of coffee from her husband and handed it to the young woman. "Drink this, it will help. I don't know if you use sugar, but I sweetened it to lick the shock."

Nora nodded her thanks and wrapped her hands around the mug.

She sipped carefully. The aroma seeped into her pores, as the warmth cupped between both her hands and now sliding down her throat overcame the shivers.

"Did you know Hans well?" She looked from one Moen to the other.

Reverend Moen nodded. "We knew him, but we were not what you might call friends. He attended our church a few times when he had first arrived. This is a small community, so everyone knows everyone else."

"Did he talk much about his farm. . .our farm? You see, I'm concerned about the cows and horses, that someone is caring for them." Nora caught one of those looks passing from husband to wife again. An uncomfortable silence thrummed between the three of them. Nora took her courage in hand. "Is something else wrong?"

Reverend Moen inhaled deeply. "You asked about *his* farm?"

Nora nodded. "Hans wrote in his letters about the two-storied house and big barn, three milk cows, and a team of gray horses he'd already purchased. He said that last year he built a windmill so I wouldn't even have to pump water. He said..." Her voice trailed off. She had been babbling like a brook in the spring. She rubbed the smooth edge of the cup in her hand.

"Ach, you poor child." Ingeborg patted Nora's knee.

"Please, tell me." Nora whispered her plea.

Reverend Moen drew up a straight-backed kitchen chair and folded his lean frame down onto it. He shook his head. "I am so sorry to be the bearer of bad news tonight but...well..." He drew in another deep breath. "Hans Larson worked as a farmhand for the Elmer Peterson family, south of town. He lived in their bunkhouse with the other hired hands." He shook his head. "Hans didn't even own the horse he rode."

This is too much. I cannot bear all this. Nora's thoughts weighed her down. She wished she could sink through the leather seat of the rocker and down into the floor. "Are you...you sure? My Hans

Larson was tall, yellow hair, and a smile that broke your heart. He—" She forced her mind to think of something different about him. "He had a scar from a burn on the back of his right hand, from when we were children."

Reverend Moen nodded. "Yes, that's whom I am talking about. The same Hans Larson, from Bergen, Norway. He arrived about three years ago."

The crushing iceberg settled on her again. Nora bit the inside of her lip to keep it from quivering. No Hans. No farm. "Well, then, at least there are no animals suffering from neglect." She attempted a smile in the minister's direction but failed miserably.

Instead, she studied the muted colors in the braided rug at her feet. Anything was better than looking at the faces of the two sympathetic Moens. How could she have been such a fool?

"You mustn't blame yourself...I mean...how could you have known anything else clear back in Norway? You trusted his letter, like you should have." Ingeborg leaned forward from her perch on the stool. "Besides, he was such a charming young man."

That he was, thought Nora. His charm was one reason she had fallen in love with him. Or had she fallen in love with love, with the adventure of coming to the New World? She drank some more of the sweet coffee; its warmth seemed to melt that glacier she felt resting on her. After draining the coffee mug, she glanced around for a place to set it down.

Ingeborg took the empty cup. "Would you like some more?"

Nora shook her head.

"Then, if you'd like, I will show you to your bed. I'm afraid you must share it with our seven-year-old Mary. She'll be surprised when she wakes up in the morning, but Mary loves company."

Nora felt the words flowing over her like a healing draft. She did not have to make any decisions tonight. Maybe tomorrow she would be able to think better. Maybe tomorrow God would work a miracle and take this all away. Maybe tomorrow she would awaken from this terrible dream and be back with her beloved family.

"Good night, then." She nodded to the man adjusting the damper in the great black iron stove. "And, thank you."

"I've already taken your bag upstairs." He clattered the round lid of the stove back into place. "Sleep well. Things always have a way of looking brighter in the morning, even when times seem the darkest."

"Mange takk," Nora followed Ingeborg up the steep stairs. Halfway up she paused to rest. She had not realized how exhausted she was. Each step seemed like a mountain, with her feet so weighted she could barely lift them. She stepped with her right foot, then her left, each dragging the other until she reached the upper hall. Soft light from Ingeborg's candle beckoned from the room on the left.

"If you sit in that rocking chair, I can help you with your boots." Ingeborg turned from arranging the sleeping child in the bed. "Have you a nightgown in your bag?"

Nora nodded as she sank down into the chair. Waves of weary sadness washed over her. She felt like she had been pounded by waves down in the fjord on a stormy day and was being pulled out to sea. Ingeborg's voice came from far away. She felt herself sinking.

"Now, let's just get you in bed before you fall asleep in the chair." A gentle hand tugged her upright. Nora did as the voice commanded. She stood, stepped, turned, and sank into the feather bed that rose up to greet her. She heard her mother's voice, *"Now mind your manners,"* but Nora could not force the required *"Mange takk"* past the sleep that clogged her throat and eyes.

"God bless you, my dear. I'll leave the candle here in case you need it." Ingeborg smoothed the hair back from Nora's forehead just like she had done to her daughter. The feather-light touch was the last sensation Nora felt; she was at home, in her mother's care.

Light, bright as though from a thousand flashing diamonds, filled her eyes. She blinked against the brightness, then slowly opened her eyelids. To the left, sun streaming through the frosted window-pane made her blink again. She turned her head to the right.

A solemn stare from bright blue eyes met her own. In a blur of spinning braids and a voice to wake the deaf, the child fled out the door.

"Ma, she's awake!" echoed in the hall.

Nora stretched her hands over her head and pointed her toes to the end of the mattress. Oh, how good it felt as she rotated her shoulders.

The night before came crashing back. Hans was dead. Hans had lied. What was she to do now? She felt like pulling the covers over her head to blot out the sun and the new day. Instead, she lifted her head and looked around the room. Covered by colorful patchwork quilts, she had not noticed the cold through the night. A small rocker held a rag doll, which kept company with the grownup one. By the bed, a pitcher and matching bowl painted with pink roses sat on top of a dark oak commode. More pink roses climbed trellises up the wallpapered walls. . .the same pink roses she had dreamed of for her new home.

"Enough of that," she ordered herself when she could feel a lump beginning in her throat. "As Ma always says, 'The good Lord has His eye on the sparrow and us as well.' " She threw back the covers and planted her feet firmly on the braided rug of many colors. "This is the day that the Lord hath made. I will rejoice and be glad in it."

She bit back the quiver in her chin. She had said that verse every morning since her confirmation, but today it was difficult to say. So she said it again—more firmly. "This is the day that the Lord hath made." She heard footsteps coming up the stairs. "I will rejoice and be glad in it."

Ingeborg tapped on the door before entering. "What a marvelous way to start the day." Cheeks red from the heat of the cooking stove made her blue eyes sparkle even more. "You must have been sleeping hard since Mary came down without waking you."

"Oh, I did…sleep well, that is."

Ingeborg poured hot water into the pitcher on the stand. "Now you can wash and, when you're ready, there's breakfast waiting."

"Ma…" A young voice floated up the stairwell.

"That's Knute. He's five. You've met Mary…"

Nora nodded.

"Ma-a-a."

"Goodness. With these four of mine there's always something." She turned in a swirl of skirts but paused at the door. "You come down when you're ready now."

Nora pressed a hand to her chest and shook her head. She felt like a whirlwind had just blown through the room. She crossed the room and closed the door. Now, she would finally have a real washing.

In spite of the heating grate in the floor, she shivered in the cold room as she hurried through her bathing. Wishing for clean clothes, she thought of her trunk still at the station. But that would come later. She pulled on her clothes and the long black wool stockings. While warmer, she no longer felt so clean. She shook out her shirtwaist and black wool skirt before buttoning them in place.

With her hair brushed and rebraided, she felt more like a young woman who had boarded the train for a new country. Actually, she was feeling better than she had felt for days. In spite of her difficulties, she hummed under her breath while she made the bed and wiped the water from the oak stand.

As she made her way down the stairs, she could hear young voices. Her stomach rumbled, reminding her of how long it had been since her last meal.

She turned to the right and stopped at the entry to the kitchen. Two children sat at the oval oak table in front of the window, reading their lessons. They looked up when they heard her tread. Nora smiled at them both and then at the picture Ingeborg made. The baby was nestled in her arms while a chubby little girl played with the cat at her mother's feet.

An ache began somewhere in the middle of Nora's heart. This was what she had dreamed of...and now that dream was shattered. She resecured the smile on her face and buried the ache under the ashes of her yesterday. As Ma and the Good Book said, "Weeping may endure for a night, but joy cometh in the morning."

And this was definitely morning—she glanced at the grandfather clock by the door—but not morning for much longer.

"I'm sorry to be such a lazybones, I..."

"Not at all." Ingeborg shook her head. "You needed the rest. Now, I know you must be starved." When she started to get up, Nora laid a hand on the woman's shoulder.

"No, you stay there with the baby Just tell me where things are and I will fix my own. The coffee smells wonderful." She reached into the glass-faced cupboard for a cup. A loaf of bread sat on the counter, next to a crock of jam.

"Thank you, my dear. Everything is right in front of you. We'll be having soup for dinner in about an hour or when Reverend Moen returns. He had some calls to make."

While Nora sliced the homemade bread, Ingeborg introduced her children. "Mary is the oldest at seven, Knute is five, Grace is three, and James here is five months." She dropped a kiss on the rosy cheek of the baby asleep in her arms. The gentle rocking of the chair creaked its own song, in counterpoint with the kettle singing on the stove.

Nora sighed blissfully as she took her first sip of coffee and bite of the jellied bread. She placed two thick slices on a plate and carried her breakfast over to the table. "Do you mind if I join you?" she asked the children.

The two with hair so blond as to be white, hers in braids and his bowl-cut, stared at her solemnly. Mary broke the ice with a grin. "I didn't think you were ever going to wake up."

Not to be outdone, Knute piped up. "Did you like the train ride?"

"He always wants to go on the train." Mary closed her book. "But we never have." She leaned her chin on her stacked fists. "Ma said you went on a ship, too."

Nora set her plate and cup on the table, then pulled out a high-backed oak chair. "Yes, I did. Both a ship and a train." She sat down. "Now, why do you like the train so?" She leaned forward to look Knute right in the eyes.

"It is so big and goes so fast."

"Big and fast. Big and fast." Mary shook her head like big sisters everywhere.

Nora smothered a grin behind her coffee cup. "Someday, I'm sure you'll have a train ride."

"Now, you children go play in the other room," their mother ordered. She rose to her feet and laid the baby in his cradle. "Miss Johanson and I would like to visit."

"Yes, Ma." The two obediently slid to the floor and, gathering their books, ran laughing down the hall.

"No running in the house."

"Yes, Ma." A giggle floated back to the peaceful room.

Ingeborg poured herself a cup of coffee and brought it over to the table. The orange-striped cat followed her and wound herself around Nora's ankles. The toddler followed the cat and tugged at her mother's skirt to be picked up.

Nora felt a tug at her heart. "What beautiful children you have." She leaned over and scratched along the cat's arched back. "It is so wonderful here."

"Thank you." Ingeborg settled little Grace on her lap and leaned back in her chair. "Mary and Knute should be at school, but there have been so many children sick that they closed the school for a time. I thank the Lord each day for keeping us safe and healthy. The fever seems to come like a fiend from the north and before you realize it, people are coughing to death. That's where John is now. Someone else died during the night. And the doctor was at a difficult birthing. But there seems to be nothing he can do for these poor ones. Some get well but many don't."

"We've had those in Norway, too. But not so much this last year." Nora got up and refilled her coffee cup.

"Ach, what a terrible hostess I am," Ingeborg moved as if to get up.

"No, you stay there. This is the least I can do when you take in a stranger like this." Nora sat back down. The cat leaped up into her lap and settled itself for a nap.

"The cat likes you; the children like you; I like you. That means we all agree. You are welcome to stay as long as you need to." Ingeborg stroked little Grace's silky white hair; the little one's eyes drooped closed and a thumb found its way into her mouth.

"You have no idea how much your offer means to me, but I must earn my own way. With all the illness, isn't there someone who needs a strong back and willing hands?"

"I don't know." The older woman wrinkled her brow in thought. "Can you teach school? There is a town not far from here that is looking for a schoolteacher."

Nora shook her head. "I think not. I have no certificate and, besides, I don't speak English. Does everyone around here speak Norwegian?"

"No, there are Germans and Swedes and several Norse dialects. You would have to learn English." She thought awhile. "You're not thinking of returning to Norway then?"

"I have no money."

"None at all?"

"Four pennies. That is why Oscar brought me here last night. I couldn't afford the hotel." Nora sipped her coffee. "Do you suppose they need anyone at the hotel? I can cook and clean."

Ingeborg shuddered. "I know the Lord says not to speak ill of anyone, but we can't let you work there. We'll ask John when he comes home. Surely he'll have an idea of what to do."

Nora stroked the soft fur of the cat purring in her lap. It was true, animals and children always took to her, especially the wounded. Back home she loved teaching Sunday school for the little ones. If only she did not need English to teach school in North Dakota.

The clock bonged the first notes of twelve.

"Oh, my land. John may be home any minute." Ingeborg roused the sleepy Grace and, after a quick kiss, set the child on the floor. "Mary, time to set the table. Knute, the coal bin is nearly empty."

"Let me help." Nora set the cat down in Grace's arms and patted the little girl on the head. She glanced out the window. "Here comes Reverend Moen. He's just opening the gate."

Nora helped Mary set the table and, with everyone flying to do their jobs, the dinner was on the table by the time the father had hung his coat on the coatrack by the door and had washed his hands. The children scrambled into their places, Grace into her high chair, and, when the adults sat down, everyone joined hands for grace.

The familiar words of the table prayer transported Nora back to the warm kitchen of her family's farm. She swallowed a tear and sneaked a peak at the child in the high chair beside her.

Grace murmured her own unintelligible words along with them all. But her "Ah-men" rang loud and clear and her proud grin prompted giggles from the others.

Their father eyed them sternly, but they caught the twitch in his cheek.

Nora tried to suffocate her chortle, but a glance at Ingeborg struggling the same way did her in.

When they all laughed, Grace announced "Ahh-men" again and banged her spoon on the table.

Reverend Moen reached over and removed the spoon from the child's hand. "Ja, that was good." He smoothed her hair back with the back of his knuckles. "Now you must eat your dinner like Mama's good little girl." He looked around the table. "As you all must."

Conversation lagged while everyone devoured the soup, both first and second helpings. When they finished, Ingeborg brought cookies and coffee to the table.

"Now. Did Mary and Knute do all their lessons?" Reverend Moen gazed at each child, then his wife.

"Mostly," Mary answered.

"That's not enough. You go get your books and bring them to the table while we talk. Knute's, too." When the children were settled and the coffee poured, he turned to Nora. "And now, how are you?"

"I'll be all right. This all takes some getting used to."

"Yes, it does. I want you to know you can remain with us as long as you want."

"*Mange takk.* But we, Ingeborg and I, were talking about—do you know anyone who needs a…someone like me to help them? Ingeborg said you might have heard of someone who is sick or a family that needs…well, I can cook and clean, manage a house, a barn." Her voice began to fade away. She took a breath. "I'm not afraid of work."

Reverend Moen leaned back against the chair. He looked up at the ceiling, his brow creased in thought. The clock ticked loudly in the silence. "There are so many that need help but they can't afford to pay anyone. Times are harsh here on the prairie." He rubbed the bridge of his nose with a long finger. "I'll ask Doctor Harmon if I see him this afternoon. We'll be having another funeral in the morning. Old Peder Stroenven died during the night."

"Ach, this is so hard." Ingeborg shook her head. "The young and the old are always hit the hardest."

Nora glanced out the window in time to see a horse and sleigh stop in front of the gate. "You have company."

Reverend Moen pushed back his chair and rose to his feet. "You'd best make some more coffee. Whoever it is will be cold clear through if he's driven far. The cold is fierce even with the sun shining."

He strode to the door and pulled it open before the knock sounded. "Why, Carl Detschman. How good to see you. Come right in."

Nora felt lost immediately. The greeting was in English. She looked up to find frozen blue eyes staring at her. Then the man's gaze flickered back to the pastor. Their conversation continued.

The man handed a well-wrapped bundle to Ingeborg and pushed a very young girl forward also. Then he touched his hand to his forehead and left. The door closed behind him.

"Oh, the poor man." Ingeborg sank down in a chair and began to unwrap the bundle. A tiny red-faced infant emitted a wavering cry. Tears formed in the little girl's blue eyes and ran down her cheeks.

"Pa!" she cried and ran to the door. "Pa!"

"What is it? Can I help?" Nora sprang to her feet.

Ingeborg settled herself in the rocker. "Carl's wife died last night in childbirth and he can't get this mite to take a bottle. John said we'd help. Why don't you bring the little girl here? Her name is Kaaren."

"Now, we'll have two funerals tomorrow." Reverend Moen stood in front of the window. "Dear Lord, when will this cease?"

I wonder if this is the family I am to help, Nora thought as she went to the stove for the coffeepot. *Mr. Detschman is certainly a man with more than his share of troubles.*

Chapter 4

Oh, that poor man." Nora felt her heart break for him. "P-a-a."
Kaaren tried turning the doorknob to follow her father. Tears
streamed down her face as she twisted on the slippery knob.

Nora rose and knelt by the child. "Your pa will come back. Come
here and let me dry your tears."

Kaaren pulled away and wailed more loudly.

Nora sat back on her heels. If only she could speak the language.

Reverend Moen stooped beside her. "Come, Kaaren, you must
give this up now. You'll make yourself sick with such tears." He
lifted the little girl in his arms and patted her back.

"Pa, I...I want my...my pa."

Nora rose to her feet, thankful that the Moens spoke both
Norwegian and English. However would she be able to work for a
family that did not speak Norwegian?

"Mary, you take Kaaren and show her your dolls," John said.
He set the crying child down again and linked the two girls' hands.
"Kaaren, you go with Mary. Knute, why don't you help entertain our
visitor, also?" When the children wandered off to the other room
chattering, he turned back to Nora.

"Carl said he needed to get back to take care of his livestock.
That's why he left so hastily. He also said he'd bring Anna, that's his
wife, in for the funeral tomorrow."

"Oh, that poor, poor man." Nora shook her head. Visions of stern, blue eyes in a strongly handsome face returned to her. So young for such a tragedy. She totally forgot her own situation while praying for his.

"God be thanked that Carl didn't lose his son, too," Ingeborg added.

"That is true. But for right now—" Reverend Moen studied the toe of his boot. He inhaled deeply and sighed in weariness. "I need to go over to the blacksmith and ask him to prepare another box. Then locate someone to ride out and help Carl. He looked about at the end of his tether." Reverend Moen reached for his coat and hat. He paused. "You know anyone besides yourself who could wet-nurse this baby, Inge?"

Ingeborg looked up. "What? Oh dear, I don't know, not right now."

After the man left the house, Nora began clearing the table. Had the good Lord answered her prayer already? Here was someone, literally on their doorstep, who needed help. And he needed help now! Granted, she could not nurse the baby, but maybe she could persuade him to take a bottle. Maybe after Ingeborg nursed him a few times to get his strength up—the thoughts leaped and tumbled over one another.

"There, now," Ingeborg said with a sigh of relief. "The mite finally found out what he's supposed to do." She pushed her rocker into its creaking song. "Who else might still be nursing a baby? We've had no newborns around here for a time."

Nora reached under the sink for a metal pan. After slicing several curls off the hard lye soap bar and into the pan, she poured in steaming water from the teakettle. Then, she added the dishes. All the while her thoughts tumbled on. She could work for Carl Detschman, of course she could. That way she would earn money for her passage back to Norway. She could go home. What kind of wages would he pay? Maybe he was unable to pay like the others that Ingeborg mentioned. What then?

Memory of her mother's voice blew cool reason through the confusion in her mind. *"If you are doing God's will, He will make your path straight." I don't only need it straight,* Nora thought, *I need the bumps taken out and a good road map. What am I supposed to do?*

"There." Ingeborg nestled the infant up on her shoulder and rubbed his back for a burp. "He should feel much better now."

"What did they name the baby?" Nora finished drying the dishes and putting them away.

"Peder. Peder Detschman. Such a strong name. He will have much to live up to." The baby burped in her ear. "There now, little one." She cuddled him in the crook of her arm; the rocking chair continued its song.

Nora heard the beginning stirrings of Ingeborg's baby waking in the cradle by the rocker. She hung the dish towel over the bar behind the stove and, picking up the iron handle, lifted the round stove lid and set it to the side. Red coals glowed in the firebox. She picked up the small, metal scoop on top of the coal bucket and dug out several dusty, brown pieces of lignite, the soft coal of North Dakota, and scattered them over the red embers. After replacing the lid, she dropped the scoop back into place.

The baby in the cradle announced that he was ready to be picked up now—and eat.

"Will you have enough for him?" Nora nodded toward the cradle.

"We'll make do." Ingeborg put both arms around the baby in her arms and made as if to stand. She looked from the bundle in her arms to Nora and then back down. "Here, you take little Peder and lay him in the cradle after I take James in for dry diapers."

Nora leaned over to take the infant from the older woman's arms. As she straightened, she studied the baby wrapped so tightly in his blankets. When his eyelids fluttered and the rosebud mouth yawned, she felt her heart fly right out of her chest and open wide to the tiny baby.

"Oh, you are a darling, baby mine," she crooned to him as she rocked him carefully in her arms. Without a thought, she hummed him a lullaby, learned at her mother's knee. She hesitated to put him down, this mite who was starting life with no mother. He needed her.

If only she had milk for him. But she did not. Her practical side won out, and she laid him on his stomach in the cradle. Peder squirmed and mewed like a newborn kitten. When Nora gently rocked the cradle and resumed her sweet song, his body relaxed and he drifted back to sleep. Nora knelt by the cradle, reluctant to take leave of her charge.

She smiled as Ingeborg returned with her contented baby perched in her arms. James waved an arm and, turning his face, began rooting at his mother's breast.

"Ja, you are hungry again." Ingeborg settled herself back in the rocker. "With two of these young men, I know what a ewe with twins feels like." His sucks and gurgles proclaimed his relief that he was finally being fed.

Ingeborg chuckled as she stroked the baby's round, still-bald head. "This one, he's not shy about letting his mama know when she is neglecting her duty. He seems so big, especially when I hold him right after little Peder." She trailed a finger down the baby's rosy cheek.

His blue eyes concentrating on his mother's face, James waved a chubby fist and reached for his mother s mouth. She nibbled on his fingers and then kissed them.

Nora felt an ache in her heart. If only she and Hans. . . She rose to her knees and then to her feet. As she dusted off the back of her skirt, she dusted away the regrets. Hans was now a memory, and any dreams of him and their life together should be put to rest in the cold ground, like he had been. That sounded so easy.

"Ingeborg, would you like a cup of coffee?" She swept away the thoughts, firmly planting a smile on her mouth, a mouth that would rather quiver.

"Yes, please. Here I am so remiss. What kind of a hostess do you think I am?"

"A very busy one," Nora replied with a smile. "Since I'm not able to perform your special task, let me take over some of your other ones."

"There are cookies in the round blue tin on the second shelf," Ingeborg motioned to the cupboards with her chin. "Why don't you set out enough for everyone and call the children? They have been playing so good. There's milk for them in the pantry."

Nora did as asked, taking a peek at the sleeping infant every time she passed the cradle. He was so tiny. As soon as the table was set, she walked through the sitting room, scarcely taking time to admire the stiff, horsehair sofa and matching chairs. She could hear the children laughing through a door at the opposite end of the room.

"There are cookies and milk on the table," she said, pausing in the doorway.

Smiles greeted her from the two girls sitting cross-legged on a counterpane, surrounded by dolls. Mary cuddled a porcelain-faced doll with curly, blond hair and dressed in blue dimity. Kaaren clutched a rag doll as if it would be taken from her, she turned to look up at Nora.

On the floor, Knute stopped his train rumblings and screechy noises and sprung to his feet. "Cookies, yumm." He brushed past Nora in the doorway.

"Knute, put your train away," Mary called after him.

As he trudged back into the room muttering under his breath, Mary took Kaaren's hand. "Come on. There are cookies and milk." When spoken in English so she could understand, Kaaren smiled and, still hugging the doll to her chest, slipped by Nora in the doorway, careful not to touch her—or look at her.

What does she think I am, the big bad troll? Nora thought while waiting for the hurrying boy to put his toys away. *Just because I talk Norwegian instead of English. Poor little mite, how will she bear it with no mother? I wonder if they've told her yet. How do you tell a little one like her that her ma won't be coming back anymore? How can she even understand...when I don't?*

Nora followed after the children, wishing she could gather little Kaaren close and take away the tears that would be coming.

And come they did, as soon as Kaaren saw Ingeborg nursing her baby, James, in the rocking chair. "I want my ma-a-a." Huge tears spilled from her eyes and rolled down her cheeks. When Mary offered her a cookie, Kaaren pushed it away and continued to cry. She scrubbed her fists into her eyes and leaned her forehead onto the edge of the table.

Nora scooped the little girl up in her arms and sat back down on the vacated chair. She rocked back and forth, cuddling Kaaren against her chest and murmuring words of comfort. She stroked the fine, blond hair and wiped away the tears as they continued to course down the pale cheeks.

"Hush, now," she crooned. "You'll make yourself sick with all these tears. You've cried so many we'll all float away on a puddle."

Mary left her chair and brought one of the crisp sugar cookies to Kaaren. She took the younger girl's hand and placed the cookie in it. "My ma makes the best cookies anywhere. You'll like this." Mary took a big bite of the cookie in her other hand and grinned between chews. "See?"

Kaaren sniffed back her tears and took a bite. As she solemnly nibbled at the rich cookie, she kept her gaze on Mary. Sniffs punctuated the bites.

Nora looked over the little girl's head to see Ingeborg smiling and nodding. The baby had finished eating and was now playing poke-a-finger-in-my-mother's-mouth, a favorite mother-baby game since time began. She could hear him cooing, imitating his mother's sounds and, once in a while, adding a contagious belly laugh.

She continued the soothing rocking motion and laid her cheek against the child's head leaning on her chest. Who would care for this dear little one? Could it be herself? How would she propose this idea of hers? Just step forward and say, "I know you need help with your children and I need work"? She mentally shook her head. Should she talk this over with Ingeborg? But what if she disapproved? Why would she do that? Nora felt like she had two people arguing in her head.

"Mary, why don't you and Kaaren play with James while I start fixing supper? Bring the quilt in from the foot of the bed and all of you can play on the floor." Ingeborg held her baby under his arms and bounced him on her knee. "I could sit and play with you all afternoon and then what would your pa say? He'd like to have supper ready when he comes home." The baby gurgled in agreement.

While the children played on the floor, the women shared the cooking chores. Nora peeled carrots and potatoes to add to the already cooked pot of chicken that Ingeborg had brought in from the pie safe on the screened-in back porch.

"Then, we'll make some dumplings and supper'll be all ready." The older woman glanced at the clock bonging by the door. "We have time to make applesauce cookies. Would you like to help me?"

"Of course." Nora rinsed off her hands and bent over to check the cradle where Peder was making the squeaking noises of a baby awakening. She set the cradle rocking gently with the toe of her shoe. "Hush now, little one. You must sleep longer."

"Ja, so I have more milk for him." Ingeborg set a tan earthenware bowl on the table and began adding ingredients. As she measured and stirred, she kept up a running introduction of the residents of Soldahl for Nora's delight and amusement.

Nora felt like she would be able to recognize her prospective neighbors just from Ingeborg's mimicry. "What can you tell me about Carl Detschman?" Nora asked, after giggling at another of Ingeborg's tales of life in Soldahl.

After sliding a sheet of cookies into the blackened oven, Ingeborg paused. The creak and slam of the oven door snapped her back in motion. "Ja, that poor man. He has his hands full now. And it is so hard for him to ask for help." She shook her head, like so many other women who wish they could do something but did not know what.

Nora waited, continuing to drop the cookie dough onto another flat baking pan.

"We've known Carl since he arrived in Soldahl six years ago. He was just starting out after buying old Mr. Einer Peterson's farm. Einer had died that summer from the consumption. He'd been sick a very long time."

Nora had a hard time to keep from interrupting. She did not want to hear about Einer Peterson.

"Carl came from Minnesota, somewhere down by St. Paul, so he has no family around here. He was already betrothed; that was such a disappointment to the young ladies in our church. You could just see their eyes light up the day he walked into services. Such a handsome young man."

Nora could agree with that even though she had seen him when he seemed frozen in the middle of an ice chunk.

"And the voice of an angel. When he sings those hymns—why he just lifts the rest of the congregation and leads us into heaven." Ingeborg winked at Nora then picked up the full sheet of cookies and slid it onto the bottom rack in the oven. With one ringer, she touched one of the cookies on the top rack to see if it was done. When the cookie indented rather than springing back, she turned the cookie sheet around 180 degrees and closed the oven. "Now, where was I?"

"About what a voice Carl has," Nora reminded her.

"Oh yes, and such nice manners. You know his ma taught him well. He brought Anna to meet us when they returned after the wedding. They were married at the end of harvest. It was a very good year, I remember. He'd ordered a new wagon to drive her home in, painted all red and green with shiny yellow wheels. That wagon was really a sight."

Nora did not want to hear about the wagon, either.

"He's a hard worker, that Carl. Einer, because he was so sick, had let the farm run down. But by the next year, Carl had painted the barns and even the house. I said Carl is a hard worker. Well, his Anna was, too. It was a shame they didn't get more acquainted with the community. But they worked from dawn to dark."

Ingeborg opened the creaky oven door and removed the top sheet, placing it off to the cool side of the range while she moved the bottom sheet to the upper rack.

"Oh, Ma, those look so good." Mary and her three shadows lined up by the table, ogling the cookies as her mother lifted the fragrant goodies from the pan to the table.

"Wait until they cool a bit." Ingeborg pushed away an inquisitive finger. "My, they do smell good, don't they?" She sniffed appreciatively.

Nora agreed. The apple-cinnamon aroma filled the room. She dug a finger into the dough and, after putting the dab in her mouth, sucked her finger clean. She looked up, guilt evidenced in the heat coating her cheeks when she saw Ingeborg watching her. "I know, I'm setting a bad example for the children as my ma always said, but..."

"No buts, child. I usually can't resist myself. But here, why don't you try this instead?" She picked up a hot cookie and brought it over, along with the empty pan. "You eat this and I'll finish." She turned back to the table. "Go ahead, children. Just be careful you don't burn yourselves." The three did not need a second invitation.

"Thank you," they chorused and joined James back on the quilt.

"No! No! He's too little." Nora flew across the room to scoop the baby up, safe from the cookie Kaaren was going to shove into his mouth.

The little girl burst into tears that turned into wails. "Ma-a-a. I want my ma."

Realizing he did not know who the strange person was who had snatched him up, little James joined Kaaren, puckering up and letting loose with a wall-shaking howl.

Mary and Knute stared from one to the other, forgotten cookies clutched in their hands.

Ingeborg dropped the spoon of cookie dough and, in the process of spinning around to help Nora, bumped the cradle with her toe.

With both the noise and motion, Peder yowled almost before he awakened.

"There, there." Nora tried to quiet the screaming baby in her arms with one hand and comfort the little girl with the other.

"Whatever is going on in here?" Reverend Moen stepped through the door. "I could hear the noise clear out to the street."

Ingeborg gathered James from Nora and hid her laughing face in the baby's chubby neck. James quieted immediately.

Mary patted Kaaren on the back, trying to comfort her but to no avail.

Nora looked from the little girl to the baby yelling in the cradle. Whom should she go to first? When Reverend Moen squatted down in front of the two little girls, Nora picked up the screaming infant. She put him up to her shoulder, joggling him and crooning comfort at the same time.

"What's for supper?" John asked after calming Kaaren and picking her up. Together, they leaned over the fresh cookies on the table.

Nora and Ingeborg stared at each other—supper was not ready.

Ingeborg threw her hands into the air and laughed. "Chicken and dumplings but, even with two cooks, it'll be a while."

"I can fix the dumplings since I can't take care of this one's needs." Nora continued swaying with the still-snuffling baby.

"Good." Ingeborg turned to her husband. "And, if you'll take care of your young son here, we can proceed. Mary, why don't you and Kaaren set the table?"

"Oh, the cookies." Nora reached for a pot holder as she handed Ingeborg the baby. The smell of burning chased the cookie fragrance from the room. All the cookies on the back corner of the pan had changed from light brown to smoky black.

"I'm so sorry to burn—" Nora felt her cheeks flame again.

"Oh, well. The birds needed something to eat, too," Mary said over her shoulder as she led Kaaren and Knute from the room.

Ingeborg chuckled. Nora bit her lip. John grinned from one woman to the other, his eyebrow arched above his right eye. Laughter filled the room and bounced off the darkened windows.

Just like home, Nora thought. *Oh, how I've missed the laughter.*

Ingeborg settled herself in the rocker and started to nurse the baby. She flipped the baby's quilt over her shoulder and set the chair rocking.

John pulled out a chair and, after sitting down and bouncing James on his knee, reached across the table for another cookie. "How good to come home to such a happy place." He took a bite of cookie and closed his eyes in bliss. "Now, if only I had a cup of coffee to wash this down." He looked his young son in the eye, as if asking his opinion. "Wouldn't that be about right?"

Nora leaped to grab a cup and fill it to the brim. If she wanted to hire out as a housekeeper or helper, she had better begin to anticipate what a man arriving home would want.

"I hope that is hot enough." She placed it in front of him. She watched him with anxious eyes as he sipped then nodded. "Good. Now I start the dumplings."

On her way back across the kitchen she stopped to check the fire and added more coal. After moving the cooking pot to the hotter part of the stove, she raised the cover and gave the contents a stir with the wooden spoon that rested in a saucer on the warming oven.

While she mixed and stirred the dumplings, Nora listened to the conversation between the pastor and his wife. Thanks to Ingeborg's delightful descriptions, she recognized many of the people John talked about. The conclusion of both doctor and pastor: No one was available to nurse this new baby. Also, they had not talked to people about hiring Nora.

"Maybe tomorrow, after the funerals, I'll have a better idea for you," Reverend Moen told Nora. "In the meantime, we are grateful to have you here."

"Especially since all I seem to be doing is feeding babies." Ingeborg lifted baby Peder to her shoulder and patted his back.

Nora took her bowl to the stove and, after raising the lid of the steaming kettle, plopped the spoonfuls of dough onto the bubbling chicken. "There now." She resisted the habit to taste her cooking and set the kettle farther back on the range so it would simmer.

That evening, after a dinner lightened with laughter, the family remained gathered around the table for the father to read from the Bible and lead family prayers. Nora relaxed against the back of her chair, caught up in the rhythm and beauty of the Beatitudes.

"Blessed are they. . ." The words rolled off Reverend Moen's tongue and brought a lump to Nora's throat. It was so easy to picture herself back home and pretend this was her father reading. "Blessed" was one of her mother's favorite words.

Nora opened her eyes to lock herself into the present. These people—this family—were indeed the merciful. To take her in as they had and make her feel so much a part of them. "Thank you" hardly seemed sufficient for all the gratitude she felt.

When he prayed for Carl Detschman, she joined her thoughts and prayers with his. And for little Peder, sleeping so soundly and blissfully in the cradle at their feet. Kaaren nodded on Nora's lap, as did Grace on Ingeborg's. But, when the "Amen" came, all the little ones joined right in.

"I'm going to take Peder to bed with me so we can keep him warm enough. Nora, I'm sorry to ask this, but will there be room for Kaaren with you and Mary? Grace is still using the crib and I dislike making a pallet on the floor in case she throws off her covers."

Nora hugged the little one on her lap even closer. "No, that will be just fine."

"Come on, Kaaren, you get to sleep with me." Mary bounced to the floor and, grabbing the little girl's hand, dragged her up the stairs.

"Me, too," Grace wailed, trying to scramble down from her fathers lap.

"All right, all right." Ingeborg threw her hands over her head. "You go on up with the others." After Grace trudged partway up the stairs, Ingeborg whispered, "We'll bring her down to her crib after they all fall asleep." She gave Knute an extra hug and sent him up after the others to his room across the hall. "I'll be up in a bit for prayers."

Nora rose to her feet and began clearing the table. "Maybe I should have Mary teach me English," she said as she stacked the plates. "She switches between English and Norwegian like she's speaking one language. I know the Bible says not to envy, but I wish I knew two languages like that." She carried the dishes to the sink.

"Ja, and Kaaren speaks some German since her mother and father speak both languages. These little ones learn quickly." Ingeborg dipped water from the reservoir to fill her dishpan. "Tomorrow, we'll all begin teaching Nora English. You'll help, too, won't you, John?"

Reverend Moen looked up from his Bible and the papers beside it. "I'll be happy to, after the two funerals." He rubbed his forehead with the fingers of one hand. "So many we are losing. And this isn't even what you'd call a bad year."

"Did you talk with Carl again today?" Ingeborg crossed the room to rub her husband's neck and shoulders.

"No. I asked Einer, who works down at the feedstore, if he could go out and let Carl's neighbors know he needed help." He leaned his head forward. "That feels so good."

Nora took Ingeborg's place at the sink and continued with the dishes. She bit her tongue against asking if she should go out and help Carl. When he came for the children, that would be the right time.

After they had shuffled all the sleeping children into the right beds, Nora studied the faces of the two girls sleeping together. Kaaren's hair was darker, more like honey than towhead white like Mary's. Freckles dotted Kaaren's turned-up nose, and the trace of a tear still lingered on one pale cheek.

Poor little lamb, Nora thought as she lifted the covers and slipped into the bed. So young to be left without a mother. No wonder she cried herself to sleep. Nora snuggled down into the feather bed and tucked the quilt around her shoulders so no cold air could sneak in.

How long would it take her to earn passage home to Norway? Could she be there by Midsummer's Eve? At home she shared the bed with her sister Clara, not two little girls who looked enough alike to be sisters.

"Dear Lord," she whispered, "please let Carl Detschman hire me so I can go home soon." But her last thoughts were not of home. Instead, a tall, blond farmer walked through her dreams and the land he strode was flat.

Chapter 5

By noon the next day, Nora had a headache. "You're trying too hard." Ingeborg patted the younger woman's shoulder as she walked by. "You can't learn to speak an entire new language in one day. Even with all of us helping you."

"But I feel like. . .like as soon as I have a word locked in my head, it takes off like a lamb running from the barn up the hill after its mother." Nora rubbed her aching head.

"Well, the table is set and dinner is all ready, so why don't you sit down with a cup of coffee and close your eyes a few minutes? Both babies are sleeping and I'll read a story to the others in the parlor." Ingeborg suited actions to her words and left Nora sitting in the rocker in front of the stove.

Nora tipped her head forward, stretching the muscles as far as she could, then leaned it back against the rocker. With one foot she set the chair in motion. The hum of the fire and the creaking-rocker song were as soothing as a cold compress on her forehead.

The fragrance of bread, fresh from the oven, and the stew simmering on the stove, mingled with the bite of the lye soap with which they had washed diapers. Strung on a line behind the stove to dry, the diapers added their own peculiar odor.

The cat meowed at her feet then leaped up in her lap and arched its back against the palm of her hand before circling three times to find its comfort spot. As Nora stroked its back, the cat's rumbling purr added harmony in bass to the kitchen quartet.

The drumbeat of her headache left her temples and escaped up the chimney pipe.

After several minutes of comfort, she heard boots scraping snow off on the step, then a fist knocking on the door. Nora swept the cat to the floor and rose to answer the summons.

Up close like this, Nora realized how tall Carl Detschman really stood. Even with the difference of the porch and house floors, he towered over her by nearly a head. Tongue-tied because she could not speak his language, Nora just stepped back and motioned him to enter.

At his "Guten tag, "Nora bobbed her head. She was amazed. It sounded so much like Norwegian. Would they really be able to communicate?

"Come in, come in." Ingeborg and the children joined them at the door.

"Pa!" Kaaren threw herself into her father's waiting arms. She locked both arms around his neck as if defying anyone to try to remove her.

Carl Detschman stood and took off his hat but refused to venture farther into the room. He pointed to his snowy boots and shook his head. "Is Reverend Moen here?"

"Any minute now," Ingeborg shooshed the other children back. "He had another funeral this morning and then a call to make. How may I help you?"

"I…that is, Anna…"

"Ma? I want my ma!" Kaaren placed her hands on both sides of her father's face and turned him to look at her. "Please, Pa."

Nora did not need to speak English to understand what the little girl was saying—the look on Carl Detschman's face said it all.

"Can you keep her. . .them. . .until after the funeral?" Carl asked after shushing his daughter.

"Of course. We'll talk more then. But why don't you come in

and sit down to wait for Reverend Moen? What will you—"

"I can't." He drew himself straight, hugged his daughter, whispered in her ear, and handed her to Ingeborg. "I just can't." He turned and yanked open the door, the cold draft sending the women's skirts back against their legs.

The look on his face imprinted itself on Nora's mind. *Lost and angry. What a heavy burden,* she thought.

"Why didn't they have both funerals this morning?" Nora asked after they had settled the children again. Kaaren sniffed back tears once in awhile—and hiccuped.

"Because Carl and Anna are German," Ingeborg snapped, "and some people in this town are hateful." She hid her mouth with the back of her fist. "Forgive me, I didn't—I shouldn't even think such things. But, much as Reverend Moen preaches to love thy neighbor, some people think that doesn't include anyone who isn't Norwegian." She shook her head. "Sometimes, being the pastor's wife isn't easy, let alone being the pastor."

"So, will anyone come to mourn with him?"

"Ja, a few."

"Why don't you go and I'll stay here with the children? Just being with you is a comfort, and I know he needs that."

"Ja, that is a good idea. Thank you." Ingeborg used the edge of her apron to wipe something from the corner of her eye. "I should have fed Peder by then, and I won't be gone long if James wakes up. Now I know how difficult it would be to feed twins."

Everyone ate dinner with serious faces and little talking.

"Mary, you help Miss Johanson with the dishes," Ingeborg reminded her daughter as they all rose from the table. "We won't be gone very long and I'm depending on you to show what a helper you can be."

"Yes, Ma."

"We'll bring Carl back for coffee and maybe others who attend the funeral. So would you please set out the coffee and cookies?" Ingeborg pressed a forefinger against her lips. "I have some *søtsuppe* in the pie safe also. You could bring that in and thaw it out over the stove. That, warmed, will taste good."

"Oh, I haven't had that for so long." Nora continued to clear the table. "My mother uses all kinds of fruit in hers."

"And we have cream to pour on top." Ingeborg lifted her black wool coat from the wooden coat tree and pinned on her black veiled hat while standing in front of the mirror. "Now, you children be good for Miss Johanson." She bent and kissed each one, including Kaaren. Then, waving her fingers, she went out the door.

When Kaaren started to fill up with tears again, Nora lifted the little girl in her arms and spun her around. Laughing together, they all trooped into the kitchen. She handed each of the children a dish towel and as she washed each dish and cup, she handed them one at a time, to each child. Mary led the game of naming every item in English with Nora repeating the word each time. After the dishes were done, they continued the game by naming things around the room. When Nora forgot the word for table, they chorused it together; when she remembered stove and oven, they cheered.

After setting the table again and finishing the preparations for company, Nora sank down into the chair and, lifting Grace to one knee and Kaaren to the other, gathered Mary and Knute as close as she could. *Oye* was eye and *toyebryn*, eyebrow. The game continued just like teaching a baby he had a nose and mouth.

They were all laughing over nothing when the door opened with a blast of cold air.

"But you must have some help," Reverend Moen was saying as they stamped snow off their feet and entered the house. "You can't take care of all your livestock and the children, too. How will you manage?"

"I don't know. I..."

"Here, now. See how nicely Nora has prepared things for us. Let's just sit down to eat and talk things over." Ingeborg helped the younger man off with his coat and hung it up with her own. "You can't go off without something warm in your belly."

Nora flew to set the coffeepot on the table and dish up the *søtsuppe.* Mary carried the cream pitcher and set it in front of her father.

"Pa!" Kaaren attached herself like a limpet to her father's leg.

"Is no one else coming?" Nora asked Ingeborg in a voice only they could hear.

Ingeborg shook her head. "It was getting late and they needed to get home before dark."

Nora finished the comment in her mind. *Or so they said,* whoever "they" were.

"Why don't you leave the children here for a few more days," Reverend Moen suggested after everyone was served. "Peder is getting stronger, but we haven't found a wet nurse for him, yet. And Kaaren is doing fine here. What do you say, son?"

Carl glanced over at Ingeborg as if asking her permission.

"Ja," she said with a nod. "I feel that is best, too."

"I appreciate what you are doing, but I—"

"No buts, then. It is settled." John clapped a hand on Carl's shoulder.

Nora refilled the coffee cups and wished she knew for sure what they were saying. In a moment of silence, she took all of her courage in hand and announced, "I could go out to help Mr. Detschman with the house and the children. If we get Peder to take a bottle, there wouldn't be any problem." She stopped to look at the Moens' faces, took a deep breath and continued. "You said there wasn't anyone else and. . .and this way I could earn my passage money back home...to Norway...that is...if Mr. Detschman can afford...ah..." This time she could not pick up the words again.

"Certainly not!" Reverend Moen shook his head. "Why he couldn't—you couldn't—"

"What he means to say is that you're not married," Ingeborg interposed softly, "and if you, as an unmarried woman, went out to work for Carl, your reputation would be ruined. No one would ever marry you."

"But...but..."

"Thank you, Miss Johanson." Carl answered after Reverend Moen translated the conversation for him. "But they are correct."

Nora tried to remember the good reasons she had thought of earlier but, in the face of their unified disapproval, she fell silent. She had thought things might be different here in the new country, but the old customs still held sway.

"I just thought this might be a way out of a difficult situation for both of us." She raised her chin and sat up even straighter. "I need work and you need a worker." She thought she saw a ghost of a smile soften his mouth and eyes, but she must have been mistaken—when she looked again, the glacier had taken over his eyes and voice.

"I thank you for all your kindnesses. I'll return on Sunday for church and to pick up the children, if that will be all right." Carl whispered in his daughter's ear and set Kaaren down on her feet. When she clung to him, he gently disengaged her fingers. "I'll see you on Sunday and then we'll go home," he promised.

"Thank you again, Miss Johanson." He nodded in her direction and, after shaking hands and thanking the others, he shrugged into his wool coat and bent over to plant a kiss on his daughter's wet cheek. "You be a big girl now."

"Pa!" The forlorn child leaned her head against the door after it closed after him. "Ma-a-a. I want Ma."

Ingeborg scooped the whimpering child up into her arms. "Your ma has gone to live with Jesus in heaven, little one." She kissed away the tears and crooned soft words until Kaaren quit crying.

He never even looked at the baby, Nora thought, as she and Mary cleared the table. *And I still think mine was a good idea.*

Up in her room that night, before falling to sleep, Nora carefully penned a letter to her family. When she told them about Hans's passing away, she did not mention the lies. She described the trip and the Moens. And said she would be looking for work.

She fell asleep thinking of eyes the blue of a glacier ice cave, shimmering in the sun. But the eyes were so sad as to bring tears to her own.

Saturday, the entire house had to be cleaned and the food prepared for Sunday. Nora and Ingeborg worked with a rhythm that showed how close they had become. The naming game continued with new words thrown in to make sentences.

"This is a table," Nora said as she waxed the shiny surface. Kaaren and Mary clapped their hands. "This is a chair." Big smiles. "This is a..."

"Rug," the girls chimed. "This is a rug."

"And it needs to be shaken. Take it out on the back porch," Ingeborg told her daughter. The two little girls picked up the corners and carried the woven rag rug out the back.

Nora raised her hands in the air and shrugged.

Late in the afternoon, Ingeborg sat nursing baby Peder and Nora had the children gathered around her, telling them a story of trolls. Even Kaaren laughed at the funny faces and voices Nora used for each character. When the story was finished, Nora hugged each of them and set the two littlest girls off her lap.

"You will make a wonderful mother," Ingeborg said after the children trooped off to play. "You are so good with the little ones. And what a help you've been to me. I'm spoiled already."

"Thank you. You make me feel like one of the family."

They rocked in companionable silence. Little Peder burped once into the stillness and continued his soft nursing noises.

"What will happen to Carl?" Nora finally asked, softly. "How will he manage?" She knew she should refer to the man as Mr. Detschman, but he could only be Carl in her mind.

"I don't know." Ingeborg leaned her head against the back of the rocker and stared up at the ceiling. "He has family in Minnesota, but he doesn't think any of them can help. His sister is still too young to come out here and the others all have families of their own."

"What about a bottle for Peder?"

"We'll start him on that tonight. I wanted to give him as much breast milk as possible." She lifted the baby to her shoulder and rubbed his back. "Since he's so much stronger now, I think he'll be all right."

"Then I can feed him." Nora looked across the dimming light to her friend in the other chair.

"That you can. He'll have two bottle-feedings before we go to bed and then I'll nurse him in the middle of the night." She chuckled softly. "God certainly knew what He was doing when He created mothers and babies. This one is such a love." She trailed a finger across the baby's closed fist. Her sigh seemed to come from deep within her heart. "I love babies so." She kissed the baby's cheek and looked up. "Here, you hold him for a while and I'll get the supper going."

Nora accepted the bundled infant and settled him into her arms, like Ingeborg had done in her arms. She watched the baby's eyelids flutter and the perfect little mouth pucker and relax. "He is so beautiful." How could one do anything but whisper in the face of such a miracle?

Several hours later, she felt the same awe but only more so when she got the baby to take a bottle. While he fussed at first, he finally sucked on the nipple and settled down to feed. Nora felt like she had climbed the highest mountain near the farm at home.

Sometime later, in the middle of the darkest night, Nora awoke to the sniffling and tears of Kaaren, crying for her mother. Nora gathered the sobbing child into her arms. With hands of love, she brushed the straggles of hair from Kaaren's face and wiped away the tears.

"I...uh...want...my...ma. Why doesn't she come?"

Nora murmured responses in her own language, wishing she could say the things in her heart to this grieving child. Ingeborg had told her that her mother had gone to be with Jesus. That she was not coming back. But how could such a little one understand that?

Softly, so she would not wake Mary, Nora began to sing. "Jesus loves me. . ." As the words and love in the song crept into that silent night, she felt the child relax against her shoulder. Jerky, leftover sobs that racked the small body tore at Nora's heart. "Yes, Jesus loves me..." She finished the song on a whisper and removed her arm from under Kaaren's neck.

"Heavenly Father, comfort this family," she prayed. "Bring back the love they've lost and, if You want me to care for them, please find a way. Amen."

Forgotten were the tears of the night as the two girls bounced up to greet the sun sparkling around the feathery frost patterns on the windowpane. They ran, giggling, down the stairs, leaving Nora to stretch and twist her body from one side to the other in the softness of the deep feather ticking. When she heard a baby crying, she leaped from the bed, put on her wrapper, and made her way downstairs.

Ingeborg was jostling James on her hip while warming a bottle for Peder, who was crying in Mary's arms in the rocker.

"And a good morning to you, too," Nora said with a laugh while relieving Mary of her squalling bundle.

"Good. Now I can take care of this one," Ingeborg sank gratefully into the other rocker. "He thinks his mother should drop everything the minute he cries. What a spoiled little boy."

Nora tested the warmth of the bottled milk on one of her wrists and then sat down to begin the feeding. Peder fussed a bit, not quite willing to take the bottle. "Come now. We did this beautifully last night. Ingeborg isn't going to be here to feed you anymore."

Peder looked up at her as if he understood every word she had said. When she prodded his closed lips with the nipple again, he took it and began to suck like she might take it away before he could fill himself.

Nora chuckled. What a precious baby. And smart, too, she could already tell.

"Mary, you set the table. We'll have mush as soon as I finish here, so put the cinnamon and cream on the table."

"Where's Pa?" Mary asked as she handed the bowls, one at a time, to Grace and Kaaren.

"Starting the furnace at the church. Then he's planning to work more on his sermon. I told him it was too cold over there and that he should come home to finish."

"And?" Nora set the chair rocking.

"And he's over there in the cold because he says he can't work with all the noise around here." Inge's glance around the kitchen included the chattering children as all four went about their chores, Mary firmly telling each one what to do. The teakettle sang merrily on the stove and, up until a few minutes ago, there had been two babies crying. "I just don't understand why he thinks this is noisy." Her eyebrows nearly met her hairline.

Nora laughed along with her friend. "This is the way homes are supposed to be. Someday, I want one just like this." She put the baby up to her shoulder and patted his back. "Just like this."

"With two babies at a time?"

"Well…maybe one by one."

The clock bonged eight times.

"We must hurry if we don't want to be late to Sunday school.

Here, Mary, you take James while I finish making the breakfast. The table looks lovely."

While Ingeborg was giving out assignments, Reverend Moen let in a blast of cold air as he came through the door. "What a beautiful day we have," he said as he hung up his coat and hat. "Why it's ten degrees above zero and getting warmer. Pretty soon, the chinook will come sighing across the plains and, before you know it, spring will be here."

He rubbed his hands together, warming them above the stove. "Wait until you see spring here on the prairie, Nora. It is like no other season."

Nora, like a good guest, kept her doubts to herself. What could possibly be beautiful about this flat country? Now, spring in Norway—that was sight and sound to behold. The cracking thunder as the rivers broke loose from their winter dungeon and the logs cascaded down with the ice floes. The birds returning in flocks to darken the sky and the masses of green bursting forth from the soil as the sun shone longer each day.

The ache of homesickness caught her by surprise. To stem any tears that threatened to overflow, she swallowed the lump in her throat and rolled her eyes upward. Better remember that Old Man Winter still held her beloved homeland in his icy grip.

"I. . .I'll take Peder with me while I go get ready. Unless you need me for something else first?"

"No, no. You go on." Ingeborg shooshed her away with fluttering hands. She went back to stirring the mush that was thickening under her watchful eye.

"I'll hurry." With the baby in one arm and the pitcher of warm water from the reservoir in the other, Nora went up the stairs. She propped the infant against the pillows and continued talking with him as she washed her face and hands. Before she was half done, he had fallen asleep.

With Reverend Moen encouraging haste, they finished eating

and cleaning up in time to be bundled up and out the door, arriving at the church as the first of the other families were hitching their horses to the rails.

It felt like home to Nora and yet she felt strange and out of place. This was the first time in her life she had worshipped in a church other than the one at home. While people were speaking Norwegian around her, none of them were her relatives. At home her aunts and uncles and cousins, besides brothers and sisters, made up half of the congregation.

Nora smiled as each person was introduced. But she kept waiting for one man, Carl Detschman, to appear. He had said he would join them for church but he still had not arrived as the organist played the opening songs.

They had settled in the front pew. Nora rocked the baby in her arms, Kaaren was beside her, and Mary next. Ingeborg was shushing Grace and Knute. What a pewful they made.

Nora did not realize until the closing hymn how much she had been waiting for a tall, broad-shouldered farmer to join their group. She kept hoping he had sat in the back and, when they turned to leave, she thought she saw that familiar blond head leaving before anyone else. He had said he would join them for church. If it was him, why did he leave so quickly?

Peder had slept through the service, much to Nora's relief, but, when they stood for the benediction, he began whimpering. By the time she could get out the door, he had progressed into the demanding stage.

"I'll take him home and feed him," Nora whispered to Ingeborg as she passed the Moens in the greeting line at the front door. At the top of the three wooden stairs, Nora stopped for a moment to look again for Carl Detschman. Was that Carl driving his sleigh down the street?

"Don't be silly," she scolded herself on the short walk back to the parsonage. "It doesn't matter one whit to you if the man came to church or not. Once he picks up his children, you probably won't even see him again. Ingeborg said he was unpopular—an outcast—because of his German heritage. So just put a smile on your face and enjoy the day. You won't have to worry about whether this darling bundle of baby eats or not. It's his father's problem."

So, then, why did her bottom lip feel like it wanted to quiver? And what was that stupid lump in her throat? How could she let these babies go without someone there to take care of them?

She hurried through the door of the parsonage and slammed it shut behind her. In the time it took her to warm the bottle and settle down to feed the crying infant, the remainder of the family arrived home. They were chattering and laughing about their chores when a knock sounded at the door.

"Welcome, Carl." Reverend Moen ushered the visitor in. "I was happy to see you come to the service. Let me take your coat and hat."

"Thank you."

Kaaren made her usual beeline for her father's legs.

"Dinner is almost ready," Ingeborg said while bending down to remove the roast from the oven. "You're just in time."

Nora clutched little Peder tighter. *How have I gotten so attached to these two children in such a short time?*

"Miss Johanson, Reverend, Missus, can we talk for a few minutes? Right away?" Carl ducked his chin, then squared his shoulders. "Please?"

Ingeborg wiped her hands on the dish towel she had slung over her shoulder. "Of course. Mary, you take the children into the other room to play. Nora, Peder can go back in the cradle now."

Nora shook her head. She could not lay the baby down, not when he was to be taken away from her so soon. "I…I'll just rock him. He was fussing a moment ago."

"No—I mean, please, could you join us?" Carl motioned to a chair at the table.

Nora stood and, after laying Peder in the cradle as asked, walked to the table and sank down on one of the oak chairs. With the tip of her finger, she smoothed a spot on the table. Something strange was happening here.

"Miss Johanson, Nora, would you marry me?"

Chapter 6

Nora felt her chin drop—clear to her chest.

"I know this is sudden, but let me tell you what I am thinking. As the Moens said, you cannot come live at my farm without marriage. It would not be proper. But, if we were married, your living there and caring for my children would be all right. I will advertise for a housekeeper in the Fargo and Grand Forks papers and, when we find one, then we will have the marriage annulled and I will pay for your passage to return to Norway."

He waited while Ingeborg finished translating.

I can go home to Norway was Nora's first thought. *I would have a place to work* was her second, and *I won't have to give up these babies* was the third. *At least not for a time*, she amended. She closed her eyes, the better to think. *But marriage! An annulment?*

Her gaze flew to Reverend Moen's face. "Will this work?"

John rubbed his nose with the index finger of his right hand. "A marriage can be annulled only if it is not consummated."

Nora felt her cheeks flame at the thought. Surely Mr. Detschman understood that…that they would not share a bed.

"You and the children will share the big bedroom downstairs, where it is warm. I will fix a bed for me upstairs." Carl ducked his chin and stammered over the last words. "I mean, this marriage would be because. . .to. . .ah. . .save your reputation." His voice deepened to a growl. "That is all I have to offer."

Nora nodded that she understood. And what he was offering was enough for her. Since Hans had lied and died, she wanted nothing to do with North Dakota farmers. She would dream of returning home. This seemed to be a sensible solution.

"What do you think, Ingeborg?" Nora risked looking at her friend.

"I don't know." She looked from her husband to the man still standing, his hand now resting on the back of a chair. "You and the children can stay here for as long as you need."

When Carl understood her response, he shook his head. "I cannot lay such a burden upon you. You have already been good to me beyond duty."

"Let us eat our dinner and think about this plan of yours," Reverend Moen said. "You have not proposed an easy thing."

Nora let the conversation at dinner flow around her like a river around a big rock. It wasn't that she did not understand half of it, she just needed the time to think.

What would her mother say? *Surely I would be home almost before they could send a reply. All I need tell them is that I am caring for two small children for a farmer here who lost his wife. An annulment is like the marriage had never been.*

And I can go home soon. Back to the mountains, with green forests and white rushing rivers. Back to my family. . .Clara and Einer, Gunhilde and Thorliff. And little Sophie—she won't be all grown-up before I see her again. She pictured each of them in her mind.

Halfway through the meal, Peder began his waking whimpers. By the time Nora had a bottle warmed, he had progressed to red-faced demand.

Nora picked him up and whisked him off for a diaper change. Then, she took her place in the rocker and silenced him with the nipple. As the baby sucked, she let her mind roam back across the ocean again. But it refused to stay in Norway.

Instead, she thought of the baby in her arms. If she did not stay, who would care for him? And little Kaaren. She was still waking at night, calling for her mother. Would her father be able to care for her...and do all his farming, too? Spring planting would come and then how would he manage?

Her mind flitted to the man himself. He was so stern. Was this his usual way or was it due to his great sorrow? His children needed some love and light in their lives.

Of course, he could leave them with the Moens, like Ingeborg had suggested, but what if Nora went to work somewhere else? How could Ingeborg handle her home and all the children by herself?

After letting her thoughts race like a fox after rabbits, she tipped her head back. *Father God, what would You have me to do?* Her thoughts quit their scampering. She had prayed earlier for Him to work something out, hadn't she? Was this it?

When Peder finished eating, she rose and walked back to the table. "Ja, I will do this." She nodded as she spoke. "Carl Detschman, I will marry you."

"Today?"

She stared at him. Had she understood? She looked to Ingeborg for confirmation.

"I don't see what the rush is," Reverend Moen said, shaking his head. "Next week—"

"No. If we are going to do this, we will do this now." Carl kept his gaze on Nora's face.

Nora took a deep breath and let it out, along with all her hesitations. "Now."

"Let me warm up the church first." Reverend Moen rose to his feet and reached for his coat.

"No!" Nora cried, then repeated more softly, "no, we'll be married in the parlor, not the church. Since this wedding doesn't count anyway, I do not want the ceremony to be performed in the church."

"If you are certain." John hung his coat back up.

Nora nodded. She kept her gaze on the part in Kaaren's hair. She could not look up at Carl, not right now.

Although the ceremony was spoken in Norwegian, Nora heard the words with only the top part of her mind. The rest of her floated in a fog. She gave the proper answers when the Reverend Moen asked her to, but she never looked above the Bible clasped in his hands.

"I have no ring," Carl said, as he held Nora's hand. "But if you like, I will buy one the next time I come into town."

"No. That is not necessary." Why was there a lump in her throat? After all, this ceremony meant nothing. They really were not married—were they?

Carl and Reverend Moen loaded Nora's trunk into the wagon while the women gathered up all the children's things. Nora repacked her carpetbag and carried it downstairs to the front door.

"I can't believe this is happening." Ingeborg took Nora's cold hands in hers and held them together. "If you need anything, remember your big sister is always here to help you."

Nora tried to smile around the quiver in her chin—Ingeborg was anything but big. Leaving here was almost as hard as leaving home.

The women wrapped Peder in his blankets and then an extra quilt before following the men out the door. Carl had spread hay in the back of the wagon and, with extra quilts, made a nest for his family. Nora placed her hand in his and, using the runners for a step, joined Kaaren in the box. Ingeborg handed Peder in to her.

Carl swung up on the high board seat and unwound the reins from the whipstock. "Thank you, for everything." He tipped his hat to the Moens, who stood by the side, arms around each other.

"Come and visit when you can." He clucked to the team. With a flick of the reins, the horses started forward, the iron sled runners creaking in the snow.

The good-byes rang on the clear air. Nora waved from her shelter. Kaaren waved one last time, then snuggled down into the warm nest of quilts. She leaned her head against Nora's arm and, tipping up her face, smiled broader than Nora had yet seen.

The smile sent angels of joy dancing in Nora's heart. Surely she had made the right choice. She smiled back, then tucked the quilts more closely about them with her free hand. With the sun on its downward slide, the temperature was already dropping. She edged the long scarf draped around her neck up and over the hat she had pinned so securely in place. Hats like hers may be fashionable, but they were not worth anything in a snowstorm.

Carl hunkered down in his seat, offering little of himself to the wind. He flicked the reins again, bringing the team up to a smart trot. The way the sun was sinking, they would barely be home just before dark. He had not planned on spending so much time at the Moens'.

Oh Anna, he cried in the confines of his heart, *have I done the right thing? Little Kaaren needs you so desperately and so do I. The house is empty without you. I'd rather sleep in the barn where at least there is some noise with the animals.*

He covered his nose with the red scarf wrapped around his neck. "Come on, boys. Let's get home." The harness jingled soprano while the hooves thudded bass. The runner creaked in counterpoint, but the symphony was lost on the man hunkered on the driver's seat. He wandered in a frozen, desolate land where music and laughter were outlawed.

How would he talk with this woman he was bringing home? Granted, he had learned some Norwegian since coming to Soldahl, and Norwegian and German had some similarities, but she had to learn English—he would insist. His daughter would grow up speaking English—no people would laugh behind her back. He remembered the cruelty of children, especially at school.

He shivered against the cold. But the cold within him was deeper than any weather could bring.

Nora, snuggled down in the bed of the wagon now turned sleigh, was nearly asleep when a halt jerked her upright. A dog leaped and barked beside them. They were stopped in front of a square, two-storied house, the kind that dotted the prairie like toys tossed out by a giant hand. A snowdrift reached like a dragging scarf clear up to one second-story window. She craned her neck around the rumps of the steaming horses to see the red hip-roofed barn, silo, and other outbuildings. A tingle ran up her spine. Mr. Detschman owned a fine farm.

Kaaren stirred from her sound sleep. "Are we home, Pa?" "Yes, little one, we are." He leaned over the edge of the box and lifted his daughter out. "Here." He handed her a parcel. "Bring this into the house."

When Nora held out the quilt-wrapped baby to him, he took her arm instead and steadied her as she clambered down to the shoveled walk to the house, the infant clutched to her chest. She would have liked to have taken a few moments to look around, but dusk was on them, tinting the snow the bluish gray of eventide. She hurried up the path to open the door for Kaaren.

When she glanced back, Carl was throwing robes over the horses. *He must plan on unloading my trunk right now,* she thought. *I should go back and help.*

Peder squirmed in her arms. No, the baby came first. And it would not be long before the entire world would know that it was feeding time. Maybe the water in the stove's reservoir would still be warm enough to heat the bottle.

"Ma! Ma?" Kaaren yelled into the stillness of the empty house as soon as the door opened. "Ma, where are you?" She ran from room to room, calling, until she collapsed against the bed in the room off the kitchen. "Ma-a-a-a. I want my ma."

Nora felt like joining in the little girl's tears. How could she help this precious little one? And the baby who needed her, too—right now, if his utterings were to be quieted.

Where in heaven's name was their father?

She followed Kaaren into the bedroom and laid Peder in his quilts in the middle of the bed, unwrapping him only enough to allow him to breathe easily. Then, she scooped Kaaren up in her arms, holding her tightly while she cried. While she could not speak the language, words loaded with love and comfort could be felt by anyone. Could she be the mother they needed?

When Kaaren's sobs turned to sniffles, Nora set the child on the bed and, taking her hand, patted Peder's chest. "You do that," she said, depending on sign language. "Be good to your brother. Good, good." She nodded and smiled her approval as Kaaren gently continued the patting. "Keep on, more." Nora backed from the room, all the while smiling and nodding, and headed for the stove.

The reservoir water was still plenty warm, so Nora searched through the lower cupboards to find a small pan. She filled it half full with water, then went back into the bedroom for one of the baby's bottles of milk she had brought from Ingeborg's.

Nora could tell Peder was tired of being patted. His whimper had turned to a howl, so she picked him up. While rocking him in her one arm, she set the bottle into the warm water with the other hand.

"I do not know how all those women managed with just one arm for so many years," she muttered as she continued to lift the stove lid, add coal, replace the lid, open the damper, and comfort the hungry baby. "Your supper will be ready soon. Shhhhh." She swayed with the soothing rhythm that had been passed down through the centuries from woman to woman.

Kaaren wandered into the kitchen and hid her face in Nora's skirt, clinging to the fabric as if that, too, might be taken from her. Nora patted the little girl's hair with her free hand.

Where was their father?

With the baby finally nursing contentedly in her arm, Nora relaxed in the rocking chair. Kaaren stuck to her side like a barnacle on a rock. *I suppose I should make supper,* Nora thought as she rocked, *but what? You would think Carl would be here to show me where things are. That would be the decent thing to do.*

She looked around the room. *We could eat eggs if he has chickens. Is there any bread? Even toast and hot milk would be enough, at least for Kaaren and me.* She studied the white painted cupboards, the sink with a bucket below to catch the water. A red, long-handled pump was bolted to the outer edge. How wonderful, to have water piped into the house.

Lace curtains with red tiebacks brightened every window, both the smaller one above the sink and the double-sashed one on the other side of the round oak table. As in all homes, the large, black, cast-iron stove took up much of the space.

If the remainder of the house is as comfortable as the kitchen, Nora thought, *I'll love working here. And soon, I'll be able to take the ship back to Norway.*

With the baby fed, burped, changed, and put to bed in the cradle by the bed in the other room, Nora picked up the kerosene lamp she had lit, took Kaaren by the hand, and went exploring. The parlor, with both doors closed, was freezing, as was Kaaren's small bedroom in the back of the house. The little girl picked up a rag doll, hugging it to her.

"Come along, let's go back to the kitchen where it is warm."

To keep from wasting the heat, Nora closed all the doors behind them. Back in the kitchen, she found a door in the stair wall with a well-stocked pantry on one side and stairs down to the cellar on the other.

Kaaren stood in the doorway, one finger in her mouth and dragging the doll with her other hand. But she never took her gaze off the woman opening drawers and doors.

"Bread, good" Nora nodded as she talked to herself. "Jam." She gathered the items in her arms. "Butter." She opened a door on the end wall that was screened to the outside. "Ah, milk. But it's frozen." She handed the bread to Kaaren. "You carry this." Then she picked up the jug of milk. "Supper will be coming soon."

She set the milk to thawing in a pan of water on the stove while she sliced bread and set it in the toaster racks she had found hanging on the back of the warming oven. Then, opening the lid on the stove, she laid the rack over the burning coals. By the time the bread was browned, Nora felt toasted as well.

With the milk that had thawed and some toast with jam, Nora and Kaaren set themselves in the rocking chair and started to eat. Nora began the game. "This is... ?" She pointed at the bread.

"Bread. This is bread." Kaaren nodded and took a bite.

Nora pointed to the rich, red jam. "This is... ?"

"Jam." They grinned at each other as they chewed and swallowed.

First, they named the milk, the cup, the plate; and each time, Nora repeated the sentence. When they were finished eating, they remained in the chair, rocking slowly. Nora began humming a song her mother used to sing. When she was humming, she did not have to think about Carl Detschman or to where he had so rudely disappeared. If he was out doing chores, as was most likely, he could have come in the house first and showed her where things were kept. Kaaren settled back against Nora's chest and soon closed her eyes. Before long, the small body slumped in sleep.

Nora had almost drowsed off when the thud of boots, kicking off the snow against the steps on the porch, startled her awake. She started to get up then thought better of it. If Carl Detschman wanted any supper beyond bread and milk this night, he would just have to sing for it.

Chapter 7

Peder demanded to be fed every two hours—all night and all the next day. By the third morning, Nora felt like she had been trampled by six teams of horses. If Carl had heard the baby crying, either night or day, he ignored it. That might be possible at night, since he was sleeping upstairs, but during the day? Granted, he was never in the house except for meals but...

The day before, Nora had passed the disgusted stage and now she was bordering on anger—if only she had the strength to even spark. She leaned her head against the door of the cupboard. Kneading bread took more power than she had thought—anything took more energy than she could summon.

Right now, the baby was sleeping. If she could only get Kaaren down for a nap, then she could sleep, too.

The thought of sleep nearly overwhelmed her. "But first you must finish the bread." Lately, she had found herself talking to herself more often than not.

She and Kaaren still played the naming game, but it was not the same as having a real, live, grown-up to talk with. Mr. Carl Detschman, though, spoke only in grunts; and language between them was not a barrier—there just wasn't any. How would she ever learn enough English this way?

She slammed the dough over on the floured surface and pressed it hard with the heel of her hand. Roll the dough in, press and turn, roll the dough in, press and turn. The rhythm continued.

At night, the temperature would fall to well below zero, so she kept both Kaaren and Peder in bed with her to keep them warm enough. During her nocturnal feeding forays, she would dream of warmer weather and how nice it would be if she could sleep straight through to spring.

She thumped the bread one last time, molded it into a round, and poked the dough with her finger. When the dough sprang back, she placed it into an earthenware bowl, covered it with a dish towel, and set the bowl on the warming oven to rise. After stirring the beans that were baking in the oven, she removed her apron and slung it over a chair.

"Come, Kaaren." She reached over to take the little girl's hand. "We're going to take a nap, you and I." She put her finger to her lips. "And we must be very quiet so Peder can sleep longer, too."

Kaaren put her finger to her lips and silently climbed up onto the bed. She scooted over to the other side, then sat on her knees. "Sing?"

Nora shook her head. "Sleep." She lifted the quilt and motioned to Kaaren to get under it. Kaaren flung herself back onto the pillow and lifted her feet, shoes still buttoned on, into the air.

"This is a shoe." Her eyes sparkled with anticipation.

"No. Sleep, not play."

Kaaren spoke more insistently. "This is a shoe."

Nora put her finger to her lips. "Shhhh. Ja, this is a shoe but now we sleep." She snuggled down and tucked the quilt around their shoulders.

Kaaren lay flat on the pillow, her eyes wide open.

Please, little one, Nora pleaded silently, *go to sleep. I am so tired my eyes won't stay open.* Under her breath she began to hum a song her mother used to sing.

Nora felt the warmth of the quilt steal over her. The little body next to her relaxed, along with hers. Her hum grew jerky until it faded away to nothing.

Somewhere in another world she heard a door close.

"Pa!" Kaaren flew out from under the covers and slid to the floor. "Pa!" Screaming voice, thundering feet.

Peder set up his own welcome, also at the top of his lungs. Nora lay there with her eyes closed. Maybe Peder would go back to sleep. Maybe Carl would take his lively daughter outside with him for a while. Maybe. She was too tired for any more maybes.

She pushed back the quilt and swung her feet over the side of the bed. Head in her hands, she waited for Peder to settle down again, but his demands grew louder.

"I'm coming." She slid her feet into her carpet slippers, pulled herself to her feet, and walked over to the cradle to pick up the hungry baby. With the baby in one arm, and pushing a strand of hair back into her braids with the other hand, she entered the kitchen to find Carl pouring himself a cup of coffee.

"I'm going into Soldahl," he said in German, slowly so she could understand. "Don't worry about the cows if I return after dark. I'll be as quick as I can."

"I go, Pa? Please?" Kaaren wrapped both her arms around his leg, her face raised in supplication.

"No." He shook his head. "It's too cold outside for a little girl like you."

Nora stopped her bottle preparations and turned to look at him. He had spoken more words in the last two minutes than he had done in the last three days.

As he made his way to the door, Kaaren still clung to him. "Now, be a good girl. You can watch out the window." He stood her on the chair so she could see out.

Her lower lip quivered. A tear stood like a bead at the edge of one brilliant, blue eye. "Pa-a-a." The one word held all the woe of a little girl left behind.

Nora dug a cookie out of the jar. "Here. Your pa will be home soon." She placed the cookie in the limp hand and caught the child in a hug. Together, they watched the driver and team trot down the lane. Peder's cries increased in volume.

After feeding the baby, Nora punched down the risen bread dough and placed it on the cupboard where it would not rise so quickly. Then, she set the boiler onto the stove to start heating some water to wash the diapers. She could barely keep up with the baby's clothes. Once the diapers were boiling merrily, she set the boiler to the cooler side of the stove and, taking Kaaren by the hand, headed back for the bed. This time, there would be no interruptions.

Kaaren scrubbed a fist across her eyes to rub out the last of her tears and then turned onto her side and was asleep before Nora had finished settling the quilt.

"Thank you, Heavenly Father." Nora breathed the prayer as sleep claimed her.

By the time Carl returned from town, dusk had blued the snow. Nora was slicing bread when she heard the jingling of the harness. Was that joy she felt leaping in her midsection, just because the lord of the manor was home again? Well, maybe not leaping but more like stretching.

She shook her head at her silly thoughts. Her mother's words echoed for her. "Of kindness there is no equal." Calling Carl Detschman lord of the manor might not be kind, but it was true—wasn't it? The way he gave orders and without a smile—not even for his little daughter who needed love and laughter so desperately. But perhaps he had never been a smiling person. Many Norwegians were like that, too. Handsome, yes, but smiling, no.

She pinched off a small piece of crust and put it into her mouth. *I wonder what it would take to make Lord Carl smile?* The thought lasted until Carl entered the house, bringing in cold air, a sack of supplies from the store, and—

"There's a letter for you." Without even looking at her, he handed her the envelope.

"Mange takk." Nora's eyes devoured the handwriting—a letter from her mother. An ache in her chest made Nora press her lips together. She ignored the burning behind her eyes and tucked the beloved envelope into her apron pocket. She would save it for later, when she could read it alone. For now she must get supper on the table quickly so Carl could do his chores.

That night, after Carl had gone up to bed and the children slept, Nora poured herself a cup of coffee and sat down at the table where the light from the kerosene lamp was the strongest. With trembling fingers, she slit the envelope open and withdrew two sheets of paper.

She was almost afraid to begin reading. What if it was bad news? She shook her head and took a sip of coffee.

Dearest Nora,

I take pen in hand to tell you how much we love you and miss you.

Nora put her head down on the table and allowed the tears to flow. The ache had grown to a roaring pain that tore at her heart and soul. How she missed those beloved faces. She could see her mother at the kitchen table, writing so carefully on the precious paper.

When she was able, Nora dried her eyes with her apron and read on. All were well. Her older brother, Einer, was courting one of the Kielguard daughters. They had all been out skiing. Father and the boys had been up in the forest cutting wood. Ice fishing had been good. How were she and Hans? Did she like North Dakota?

Nora wiped another tear from her eye. How surprised they would be when her letter arrived—shocked would be more like it. She read the letter again and sighed. Life took strange turns and twists—and when you least expected it.

Nora tried to catch a yawn but, instead, it nearly dislocated her jaw. If only she could stay awake long enough to write back. But, there was as much chance of that as a fox turning down a juicy chicken. She adjusted the stove damper, blew out the lamp, and made her way into the bedroom.

Please, Peder. Sleep longer. This had become her consistent prayer and plea, and tonight was no exception. She knelt at the edge of her bed and tried to pray, but even in so cramped a position, she nearly nodded off. Nora was asleep as soon as she pulled up the quilt around herself.

❧

For the next week, Peder continued his demand for being fed every two hours and sometimes he screamed instead of sleeping between feedings. Nothing Nora did made him content. While he was not sick, he was not content, either.

"Hush, hush, my little one," Nora crooned one night in the wee hours when she would have much preferred sleep. She had tried singing to and walking the colicky baby, rubbing his back and then trying the rocker for a time. But she had been so tired that night she had even fallen asleep in the rocker with him and woke up in the morning, cold and stiff, when Carl came down the stairs to head for milking.

"I. . .I'm sorry," she whispered as she rubbed the sleep from her eyes.

He glanced her way but without looking into her face. With a barely perceptible nod, he turned back to the stove, added coal from the bucket, and opened the damper to bring up more heat.

She watched as he made his way out the door, looking like he carried a ten-ton load of coal on his shoulders. *"Uff da,"* She shook her head. "What will become of him?" Even she, who did not know him, could see that the light in his eyes had gone out.

Nora stiffly stood with Peder in her arms and carried him to the bedroom. Together, they went to bed and—Peder started to whimper.

By the end of the next week, Nora could concentrate only on putting one foot in front of the other. Feed the baby, prepare a meal, wash the diapers, feed the baby—when would she be able to add sleep to the routine? At the same time, Kaaren grew fussy, her temper popping out in unexpected places.

Carl had just come in the house for dinner when his daughter tripped over the edge of the rug and banged her knee. *"Uff da,"* she said with a scowl.

"Speak in English," Carl ordered over his shoulder. He turned from the sink with dripping hands. "We speak English here."

"Nora doesn't." The little girl stomped her foot.

Nora hid a grin in baby Peder's blanket. She had understood what was said that time.

"Nora?" asked Carl.

"Ja." She turned to Carl with a look that dared him to say more.

Carl changed his mind. "We'll talk later," he spoke in German, slowly.

That will be a change, Nora thought as she filled the soup bowls at the stove. When she leaned over to help Kaaren with her bread, she heard the little girl muttering very, very softly.

"Uff da, uff da, uff da." Her bottom lip stuck out and her eyebrows met each other in a line that Nora knew meant trouble.

"Nora, can I speak with you in the parlor?" Carl spoke slowly and nodded to the closed room.

With his back poker-straight and his hands clenched, Carl led the way into the freezing room. "Now." He stepped around her and closed the door. "Kaaren must speak English. No Norwegian."

Nora crossed her arms across her chest. She could feel her jaw tightening. She straightened her tired back and suddenly she did not feel quite so weary. "Ja!"

"You must learn to speak English."

"Ja!" Nora shook a finger in his face as all her mother's preaching against the evils of her daughters temper flew right up the chimney with the smoke.

"Ja! You tell me to speak English! How I would love to; if only I could! Who is there to teach me? A three-year-old who is just learning to talk?" Nora tried to slow her words down so he could understand her, but it was like stopping a freight train. "I thought you would teach me—ja, you do not even talk. You don't talk to me. You don't talk to Kaaren. Maybe you talk to your cows!" With that, she spun around, yanked open the door to the kitchen, stomped through, and slammed it shut in his face.

The resounding crash woke Peder, who began to wail. Kaaren stared at her, eyes wide and chin quivering.

"Uff da!" Nora picked up the baby and carried him off for a change of britches. She heard Carl leave, gently closing the door behind him.

She sank down onto the bed, the fury draining away as quickly as it came. What had she done?

Silence hung in the air that night at supper and Nora could feel Carl watching her. Now she knew what a mouse stalked by a cat felt like.

Every morning Nora promised herself she would write to her family. At the end of each weary day, though, the letter still lived only in her mind.

One night, it seemed like she and her unhappy burden paced all night. Finally, she collapsed into the rocking chair. When she awoke, a quilt swaddled her from neck to toe. *Carl. He did this,* she thought. Warmth beyond that of the quilt seeped clear to her fingertips.

But her head ached, her nose dripped, and her eyes felt like they were glued shut. When she put Peder down in the cradle so she could begin the mush for breakfast, she started coughing.

The next morning, both Peder and Kaaren had runny noses and whiny voices. Nora coughed, Kaaren coughed, Peder coughed—and wailed.

By the next morning the baby's throat was so scratchy he could hardly cry. Nora had the kettle steaming on the stove. But, when she leaned her head over it and tried to inhale deeply, her coughing cut her off. If only she had some of her mother's special cold mixture.

The dog, barking outside, drew her to the window in time to see a horse and sleigh pulling to a stop in front of the door. Who could be calling?

Nora looked around the room. Dishes were still on the table; diapers were simmering on the stove; there was nothing in the house to serve with the coffee; her hair was not combed; the children were sick. She looked down at her dirty apron. What would they think of her?

While she took off her apron with one hand, Nora tried, with the other hand, to tuck some loose strands of hair up into her braids. She had finished neither when the knock sounded on the door. Reaching out with a trembling hand, Nora turned the glass knob.

"Oh, Ingeborg, I—a-a-achooo." The sneeze blew so hard it plugged her ears. She reached to get her handkerchief from her apron pocket, but the apron was dangling over the back of a chair. "Cub ind." She tried to smile but instead, at the sight of a smiling, friendly face, Nora collapsed into tears. She shut the door, groped in the pocket of the apron, then, in desperation, held the entire apron to her face.

"Oh, my dear, my dear. You look done in. How long have you been sick? How are the children?" All the while she murmured soothing sounds, Ingeborg patted Nora's heaving shoulders.

Kaaren stood, wide-eyed, in the center of the tumbled room.

"Here, now. You sit down in this chair and I'll get you a cup of coffee." Ingeborg pushed Nora down onto the chair. On her way to the cupboard, she removed her hat. With two cups of coffee in hand, she sat down in the chair next to Nora. "Now, tell me all that's happened." As Nora talked, Ingeborg removed her heavy wool coat and beckoned for Kaaren to come sit on her lap.

Nora poured out her miseries—the baby's eating every two hours, the colds, and, because of the coughing, her fear of the fever.

"And what about Carl?" Ingeborg smoothed the strands of hair off Nora's flushed, hot face.

"Him? I never see him. Only at mealtime. He never says anything. Only scolds me when Kaaren does not speak English."

"Me say 'Uff da.'" Kaaren nodded solemnly.

"Oh, you sweetie." Ingeborg hugged the child and kissed her cheek. "I could eat you up."

Kaaren smiled until a cough choked her.

"Well, I know what you need." Ingeborg stroked Nora's arm. "Bed. You wash your face and go crawl into bed. I can stay until late afternoon. I think some rest without worrying is what Dr. Harmon would order."

"Are you sure?" Nora croaked around the lump in her throat.

"I'm sure." Ingeborg slid Kaaren to the floor and then stood up. She took Nora's hand and pulled her upright. "Go, now."

Peder... ?"

"I can see where you have things. We'll do fine. Now, go."

Nora did not need to be told a third time. She poured water from the reservoir into a basin, washed her face and hands, and stumbled into the bedroom. She took time to put on her nightgown and then crawled under the covers.

"Thank you, Lord," she mumbled before sleep claimed her.

The next thing Nora heard was a woman's voice singing. She blinked her eyes, wondering where she was. And who was that singing? She lifted her head and looked around the now-familiar room. What was she doing in bed at this time of day? She lay back down, her eyelids too heavy to hold open.

Next, she heard a baby crying. "Peder, I'm coming." She sat up and pushed back the covers. This time she felt awake. This time she remembered that Ingeborg had come to visit—and she was sleeping away their precious minutes together.

"Just in time for a cup of fresh coffee." Ingeborg greeted Nora's entrance into the kitchen with a wide smile. "You sit right here," she pointed to the rocker, "and we can talk some before I have to leave."

"Kaaren and Peder?"

"Both sleeping. You're right about that little one. He does not eat much at a time but he wants his bottle every two hours." She handed Nora the steaming cup. "Maybe it's the cow's milk that does not agree with him. Carl says he cries a lot."

"How would he know?" Nora felt ashamed as soon as she had said the words.

"Tell me, dear, how are things between you and Carl?"

At the kind words, Nora swallowed back the tears that threatened to flow. She rubbed a finger around the rim of her cup. "He won't even look at little Peder. He hardly talks to Kaaren but then, when could he? He's never in the house. I do not know where he keeps himself all the time. Has a lot to do down at the barn, I suppose."

She leaned back in her rocking chair and, with a push, started the soothing rhythm. "Ingeborg, what am I to do?"

"Well, one thing I know. The only thing worse than a stubborn Norwegian is a hardheaded German. Right now, I'd say the man is grieving for his young wife and angry at God for taking her." Ingeborg sighed. "I think death is harder for our men than for us. They feel helpless, like they failed. And what can anyone do?"

"Ummm."

"Give him time and love."

Nora stopped the rocking with a thump. "Love? Remember the agreement? I'm going back to Norway as soon as I can."

"Now, now. I'm talking about the kind of love God asks us to give any suffering being. You have an abundance of that kind of love. I've seen it in all you do."

"Oh." Nora again pushed with her toe.

"Can you do that?" The question came softly.

Nora aimed a halfhearted smile at her friend. "It would be easier if he were around more."

"True. But perhaps that will change." Ingeborg pulled herself to her feet. "Well, supper is in the oven and the bread will have to go in pretty soon. I hung some of the diapers outside so they can freeze overnight."

"How can I ever thank you enough?"

Ingeborg took both their cups to the sink. "Just get better. Everything else will work out in God's good time."

The dog barking and a jingle from a harness announced a visitor.

"That must be my John now. He wanted to visit some of the members that live out in the country and that's why I could come today."

"How ashamed I am. I never even asked how you came to be here."

Ingeborg smiled and patted Nora's cheek. "Let's just give God the thanks that He brought me here for you."

After Reverend Moen and Ingeborg left, the special glow that Nora felt around her heart remained. What a good friend she had. The special feeling stayed through the suppertime and after feeding Peder. Carl even played with Kaaren before Nora put the little one to bed. When she came out of the bedroom, he was sitting at the table, reading in the lamplight.

He cleared his throat. "Nora." His voice broke. He cleared his throat again. "Would it be possible that I teach you English? Here... in the evening? When you get to feeling better?"

Chapter 8

The break came a week later. Nora felt like she had been given a priceless gift. Peder slept for four straight hours in the afternoon and again that night. And he smiled at her when she bathed him. This little round face with the button nose that was usually screwed up in either anger or pain, now opened its mouth and let the sides flutter upwards.

Nora lost her heart. She felt it wing from her chest and join with the baby's. She dried him, between each precious little finger and toe, all the while murmuring love words and praising him when the smile came again, broader this time.

Nora wanted to tell someone. Kaaren? No, she was asleep in a much-needed nap. Carl? He should be the person to rejoice in his son's first smile. But he was out working on the farm someplace—who knew where—and, to this day he had never even peeked into the baby's cradle. He never asked about the mite or even said the baby's name.

She would have to settle for writing to her mother as soon as Peder fell back asleep. Her mother would understand the joy Nora felt. It was as if this little life were her very own. Her son. Her Peder.

Nora put a hand to her heart. A pain stabbed at the thought. No, she was only the housekeeper and, in only a few months, she would be returning to Norway. Another would see Peder crawl and take his first step. Carl would marry again and his new wife would take over the care of this home and this family.

The words she said to herself made so much sense. After all, they were the truth and the plan Carl had proposed. Why then did they hurt so much?

That night, when Nora and Carl sat down at the table for the English lesson, Nora found it difficult to concentrate.

First, Carl laid their earlier lessons on the table and they reviewed them. Then, she wrote something in Norwegian and, after making sure he understood what she wanted, Carl wrote the English word beside it. Then, he read it to her. She read the words and they repeated them until she said them correctly.

After the lesson, Nora gathered her courage. "Peder smiled at me today," she said slowly as she wrote the words in Norwegian.

Carl took the paper, read the words, and wrote them in English. After he said them in English, he waited for Nora's response. There was no smile, no change in inflection. Nothing.

Uff da, Nora thought. What an impossible man. She repeated the words aloud, but now they were just words—the magic she had felt with Peder's first baby smile was missing.

Why? Nora wanted to scream at him. *What is the matter with you?* But, instead she watched his hand. The hairs on the back of his hand glinted white in the golden glow of the lamp. They were strong hands with long fingers and hard callouses. How would they feel... ?

"Nora." The tone snapped impatience.

"Ah, ja?"

"The lesson? If you do not want to continue, just tell me. I have other things I could be doing."

She lifted her gaze to his.

Eyes stern, he repeated his words. "Peder smiled at me today."

"Ja, and his father might try the same," Nora said in Norwegian as she shoved back her chair and rose to her feet. She finished in English. "Good night, Mr. Detschman."

As she swept into the bedroom, she thought she heard a chuckle behind her, but she refused to turn and see. No, she shook her head, it must have been the wind.

The next morning, after waking only once during the night to feed the baby, Nora felt more like herself than she had for weeks. She had diapers washed and hung out before breakfast. There was a johnnycake baking in the oven, and Kaaren was giggling at Nora's funny faces.

When Carl walked in the door with a basket of eggs in one hand and a jug of milk in the other, Nora greeted him with a sunny smile. "Good morning, Carl. Would you care for your coffee now?" She spoke in English.

He brushed past her to set the eggs and milk in the sink and grunted.

No "Thank you." No "Congratulations." Not even a smile. Nora knew just how Kaaren felt whenever she stamped her foot. Only now she would prefer having a certain large, booted foot underneath her stamping. His grunt must have meant yes.

When she wrote to her mother that morning, Nora had a hard time thinking of anything good to say about her employer. She corrected her thoughts—"her husband." What a joke!

So, instead, she told them of March in North Dakota, of the Moens, about Peder's smiles, and Kaaren's antics. She did not write about the weeks of walking the floor and wiping runny noses; of no one to talk to; of the ache in her heart for Norway and home; of a little girl who cried at night for the mother that would never return. Of Carl…she said nothing.

A few days later, Nora woke to the sound of dripping water. She slipped out of bed, picked up her wrapper, and, while shoving her arms into the sleeves, went to stand at the window. Dawn had just cracked the dark gray of the eastern sky, tinting the clouds with a promise of gold. The icicles, hanging in dagger points from the roof, now dripped onto the snowbanks below.

Nora cupped her hands around her elbows. She could see the cottonwood trees bending before a wind, a warm wind—if her ears really heard dripping water. The chinook had arrived. Carl had told her about the warm wind that came unannounced from nowhere and melted the snow away. Spring was coming to North Dakota.

That morning, she hurried about her chores. Maybe for a change she could wrap up Peder and take the children for a walk down to the barn. She was so tired of staying cooped up in the house.

"Today, I'll be free," she sang to Peder as she fed him. After all, they were all healthy again. And the fresh air would do them good.

"I'll be going to Soldahl today," Carl announced at the breakfast table. "If you have your letter ready, I will mail it for you."

Nora nodded. She held her breath. Maybe he would ask her and the children to go with him. She watched as he ate his mush with rapid bites. The toast disappeared the same way. Nothing was said about their going.

"Carl, I—" Her words stumbled to a halt. She should not have to ask.

"Ja?"

"Ahh, nothing." She handed him her letter. "Thank you."

She and Kaaren waved in the window, but he never even turned his head. With a fluid motion, he stepped up into the wagon-turned-sleigh and flicked the reins. The harness jingled into the distance.

"Silly goose," Nora told herself. "What difference does it make if he is here or gone to town? You do not see him anyway." But the heavy feeling hung over her shoulders like the wooden yoke she used to carry two buckets of water to the garden.

While washing the dishes, she stared out the window. The sun still shone, the warm wind tickled the trees—nothing had changed. When she put the last cup away, the thought hit her. *You wanted Carl to show you around his farm.* She nearly dropped the cup.

"Who needs him!" She hung the dish towel over the line behind the stove. "Come along, Kaaren. We're going down to die barn."

"See cows?" Kaaren scrambled to her feet. "Horse?" She ran to pull her coat off the rack. "Pa's barn?"

"Ja, little one. Pa's barn. You must wait for me. We have to get Peder ready, too."

By the time they were all dressed and out the door, Nora could hardly keep from running down the carefully shoveled path. She wanted to fling herself into the snow and teach Kaaren how to make snow angels. Brownie, the cocoa-and-white fluffy dog, picked up on her exuberance and bounded over the snow, his tongue lolling. His sharp barks made Kaaren laugh, then made Nora laugh, then set a big black crow cawing from the top of the windmill.

"Bird." Kaaren pointed toward the sky.

"Ja, this is a bird." Nora agreed. "A—what is it called in English?" *Oh well,* she shifted Peder into her other arm and guided Kaaren before her. *On to the barn.*

Nora inhaled deeply when they stepped through the door into the barn's dim interior. She stood for a moment, letting the aromas wash over her. Cow and hay, grain and horses, manure, leather, all the odors so familiar, be they American or Norwegian.

One of the red-and-white shorthorn cows turned her head in her stanchion and lowed at the newcomers. Nora counted four milking cows. Walking farther, she saw the horse stalls. Overhead, a cat meowed and peered down through the open hayloft door.

The animals and barn showed Carl's good care. The manure had been forked out, hay was in the mangers, and the aisles were swept clean. Even with their dense winter coats, the cows showed evidence of having been brushed and curried. Harnesses hung in perfect order on pegs in the wall. Nothing was out of place.

Nora put the bundled baby down onto a pile of hay and, taking Kaaren by the hand, walked up to the first cow. "So-o, boss," she murmured to reassure the cow who turned friendly eyes their way.

She reached through the boards of the stanchion and scratched the cow under the chin.

"See, Kaaren, this is how cows like to be petted." She took the little girl's hand and together they rubbed the cow's silky throat. The cow stretched her nose way out, the better to enjoy the caress. Squatting in the straw, cheek to cheek with her charge, Kaaren and Nora giggled together as the cow closed her friendly brown eyes in appreciation.

A bay gelding nickered when they came to his stall. He turned his head, pulling against the rope tied to his halter.

Nora looked around and saw the wooden grain bins against one wall. Together, she and Kaaren lifted a slanted lid to see the golden oats half filling the bin. Nora pulled her mittens off and scooped out a handful of the grain. "For the horse." Grain clenched in her fist, she motioned Kaaren to stand still while she eased her way past the horse's huge body to reach his head.

The horse lipped the grain from her hand and whiskered her palm, begging for more. Nora smoothed his forelock and rubbed under the halter behind his black-fringed ears. "Oh, you beautiful thing, you. You must be lonely with your friends gone. I wonder what your name is." All the while she talked, she rubbed and stroked. When she inhaled, the smell of horse reminded her again of home. Some things stayed the same, everywhere.

Sure now that the animal was gentle, she went back out and, taking Kaaren in her arms, brought her up to pat the horse, too. Her big hand guided the little one.

"Pa's horse." Kaaren giggled when the animal blew in her face. She wrapped her arm around the back of Nora's neck and leaned against her, cheek to cheek.

Peder began to whimper on his hay nest, so Nora gave the horse one last pat and left the stall. Down the aisle she found another stall, this one with two white hogs. She lifted Kaaren up to see over the wall.

"Pa's pigs," Kaaren announced.

By the time Nora picked Peder up again, he had switched from whimper to demand. "Hush, now. We'll go feed you, but you must be patient." They left the barn and dropped the bar into place behind them.

The windmill squeaked and turned in the wind above the low building that must be the well house. Off to the side of the barn other buildings waited to be explored, but Nora walked quickly between the snowbanks. Peder had been so good he deserved to eat right away.

Under the onslaught of the chinook, the snow quickly melted. Nora watched the calendar as Easter approached. One day after serving fried pork chops for dinner, she made a decision.

"Carl."

He stopped drinking his coffee and looked at her over the rim of his coffee cup.

"Is Easter soon?"

He nodded.

"We go to church?" Nora hated to stumble over her words, but she knew he wanted her to speak English whenever she could.

He pushed his chair back and set the cup carefully down on the table. Jaw tight, he grabbed his coat and strode out the door.

"That must mean 'No.'" She stared after him. At least he could have answered. She had said the words right—hadn't she?

In spite of the thundercloud that seemed to have taken up permanent residence on Carl's forehead, Nora went ahead with her spring housecleaning. Her home must be shiny clean for the risen Christ. Laundry danced on the clothesline, rugs took their beating without a murmur, windows sparkled and welcomed their clean curtains.

On Saturday, while Carl was in town, she poured water into the washtub in front of the stove and, after giving Kaaren a bath, took one herself. She left the tub of water for Carl to use and disappeared into the bedroom with the children.

The next morning, the tub was gone. Nora wished Carl had rinsed away that stern look when he had washed his hair.

"Christ is risen, He is risen indeed." Nora whispered the words to the sun on Easter morning. "Thank You, Father, for loving us and sending Your Son to die. And rise again. He is risen."

When she thought of missing church, the organ, and the hymns, the joy of Easter dimmed. So, Nora refused to let the thoughts of what she was missing bother her.

Instead, in her mind, she repeated the words over and over, *Jesus Christ is risen today.* Even Carl's scowl when Kaaren spilled her milk failed to drown out Nora's inner chorus.

That evening after supper, Nora and Kaaren sat at the table reading a schoolbook Carl had brought back from town. Nora read the English slowly, but Kaaren did not mind. She pointed a chubby finger at the pictures, naming each object. When she got bored, she slid to the floor and ambled off to the bedroom. A few minutes later, she came back, dragging her doll. She pulled on Nora's skirt. "Ma."

Nora felt her stomach fall clear to her knees. She focused hard on her book, hoping and praying that Carl had not heard. She scooped Kaaren up onto her lap. But the deed was done. She did not have to turn to see his face—his thudding footsteps on the stairs told her what he was thinking.

Kaaren put her tiny palm on top of the book, now closed, on the table. "Ma's book."

"Auntie Nora's book." She covered the small hand with her own.

Kaaren shook her head. She peered up at Nora with eyes the blue of a summer lake. "Ma's book."

With a shaking hand, Nora pressed the dear little head to her chest. What would she do about this latest folly? Did Carl think she taught Kaaren to say that? Didn't he know that she would never do such a thing? She leaned her cheek on the top of Kaaren's head. But then, what did Carl really know of her at all?

Nora crawled into bed that night with a heavy heart. How could a day that began with heavenly singing end on such a sour note?

Chapter 9

Two days had passed and he had not spoken to her. Nora felt her temper simmering like a kettle about to boil over. She stifled the urge to slam the lid of the stove back in place—or the oven door. In fact, she knew if she stepped outside after the sun went down, her cheeks would freeze in the smile she forced past her clenched teeth.

She heard her mother's soft voice. *"Ah, Nora, do not let the sun go down on your anger."* But Nora knew that that had referred to keeping a happy marriage. And this. . .this contract she was caught in certainly could not be called a marriage in any terms she knew of.

But this is what you agreed to, the cool voice of reason reminded her. *So you could go back to Norway, remember?*

"Talking to myself, hearing voices. You think my mind is going?" The gray-striped cat in her lap looked up and yawned, showing white dagger teeth and a raspy pink tongue. She stretched her front paws way out, claws digging into Nora's knee, then curled back up and resumed the rumbling purr that could probably be heard across the room.

Nora set the chair to rocking, letting her thoughts fly back over the last few weeks. Whenever she thought of Carl, his anger came to mind. Had she done anything to make him mad? Well, she tried not to, that was for certain, but he either snapped at her or ignored her. *No, that's not all true,* she corrected herself. *The English lessons have mostly been peaceful times.*

Was it his sorrow that made him so. . .so. . .she searched for the best word. Angry, yes. But lost? She stroked the cat's back. Lost, yes, but more like an animal that has been wounded and strikes out at anyone who tries to help. She nodded.

So, what do I do? She let her mind float again, like a thistle seed caught on a summer's breeze. The answer came strong and clear. *Pray for him. Pray for him daily. Pray for him when he spitefully uses you.* A verse from her confirmation time, part of the "blesseds" that she so loved.

Silence reigned in the kitchen, a peace that gilded each chair and shelf, that glistened on the stove, and sparkled in the window. Even the cat's purring ceased. Nora felt that peace slip into her heart and fill it to bursting. "Bless this poor hurting man, oh my heavenly Father. Bring healing to his broken heart and bring him back to You." She whispered the words, as if loud sounds might disturb the moment.

A meadowlark sang from the fence, its song fluting on the morning air.

Nora lifted the hem of her apron and wiped the corner of her eye. "Thank You." The words had to squeeze past the lump in her throat. "I promise to pray for Carl every day. Amen."

After supper that evening, Nora brought out her books and paper and put them on the table. When Carl came back into the house after having checked on the animals, Nora met him with a cup of coffee.

"Please." She nodded to the chair she had already pulled out and extended the cup with both hands. "English lessons I want."

"Nora, I'm really tired, I..."

Nora held the cup and threw all her heart into the smile. "Please."

"Oh, all right." Carl took the cup and sat down at the table. He took a sip and set the cup down on the table. "Let's see where we were."

Nora sent another "Thank You" heavenward and slipped into her own chair. She took up the pencil and wrote, "When do the roses bloom?"

Carl looked at her with a question in his eyes. "Roses?"

Nora nodded. "I love roses." She repeated carefully the word he had used.

Carl shook his head. "No roses here. Wild roses in June."

Nora shrugged her confusion. What did he mean?

"Let's review what we've done before." He pulled out pages they had written on in the past and pointed to the sentences. Nora had been practicing. She said them all correctly.

"Good." He nodded. One lock of golden hair fell over his forehead.

Nora had the urge to reach out and brush it back. Instead she pulled herself to her feet and went for the coffeepot to refill their cups.

Nora sat down and wrote another sentence. "I want to plant a garden."

Carl wrote the English and together they repeated the words.

He nodded. "Soon. I'll plow up the garden, soon."

That night, as she knelt by her bed, Nora remembered her promise. She smiled to herself as she slipped between the covers—praying for the man wasn't so difficult when she didn't feel like pouring coffee on his head.

One morning, Nora had another surprise. Brownie's barking announced company and, when Nora threw open the door, the entire Moen family waved from their light buggy. Reverend Moen reined his horse to a halt and, after climbing down, helped Ingeborg and the children to get out

Nora flew down the steps and met them on the walk. "Come in, come in. Oh, you do not know how happy I am to see you." Her words tumbled over each other like puppies playing in the sun. She hugged Ingeborg and reached out to shake hands with Reverend Moen. "Come in."

"You look wonderful," Ingeborg said as she tucked her arm into Nora's, "And how is that man of yours now?"

"Carl's out riding the fence line to make sure none of the cows can get out." She turned to Reverend Moen. "I'm sure he will be so happy to see you."

"Good. I'll return to gather my family later this afternoon. Maybe he'll be back then." Reverend Moen set a basket on the porch and turned to leave. "You all have a good visit now."

They waved him away and walked into the house. "I brought you some things." Ingeborg handed baby James to Nora and went back outside for the basket. "If the coffee is hot, we can share the cookies right now." She plunked the basket on the table and began removing her gifts. "Jam, bread, *spekemat*, and cheese. One of the church members brought me this the other day. I thought you might appreciate it, too."

"Oh, like home." Nora sniffed the wrapped piece of strong-smelling cheese. "Thank you."

"And sour cream cookies. Mary cut them out for me."

"I put the sugar on," said Knute. "Come on, Mary. Let's play ball on the porch."

Kaaren took her finger out of her mouth long enough to shove her hands into her coat sleeves and followed the others out the door.

"Stay out of the mud," Nora reminded them. "Kaaren, you hear me?"

While a "Yes, Ma," trailed back, Nora looked at Ingeborg and shrugged.

"And here's the best gift of all." Ingeborg drew an envelope from the bottom of the basket.

Nora reached for the letter. "From home. Oh, thank you." She slipped it into her apron pocket to be read and savored later.

With baby James unwrapped from his quilts and lying on another one on the floor and Peder still sleeping, Nora and Ingeborg sat down with their coffee to catch up on the news.

They talked until it was time to fix dinner and continued to talk while preparing the meal. They were both feeding their babies when Nora heard Carl out on the porch, talking with the children.

"All right if these funny people I found on the porch go down to play in the hayloft after dinner?" he asked as he came in the door.

"That would be wonderful," Ingeborg replied.

Nora could not say a word—shock locked her tongue.

Dinner was a lively affair. And quick. Carl even gave up his second cup of coffee to take the children down to play in the barn.

"I have a favor to ask," Nora said when she and Ingeborg sat down again.

"What?"

"Will you write the English words to 'Jesus Loves Me'? I want to teach Kaaren to sing it, but Carl insists we speak English. So many things I can't give her because I speak Norwegian."

"Of course I will. But you are learning some?"

"Ja, Carl and Kaaren, they teach me." She went on to describe her evening lessons.

"And Kaaren calls you 'Ma'?"

Nora nodded. "Carl was not pleased, but I've tried to tell her where her ma is. And he will not talk with her about it. He hardly talks to her at all."

"What a shame." Ingeborg laid her hand on Nora's arm. "He used to have a wonderful smile—Anna would tease him into smiling and laughing. They were happy, those two."

"And now he says nothing. He works himself into a stupor. You should see the barn. I think he has scrubbed the walls and even the floor. I'm sure the machinery is the same. Every buckle on the horses' harnesses shines."

"Men are like that. Sometimes I think God gave us heavy work so we can live through life's sorrow. And men more so than women—they can't cry."

Nora nodded. She picked up her cup and sipped the cooling drink. "But crying and laughing again makes the sorrow easier to bear."

"Ja. That and praying."

The silence, sweet and comfortable, lengthened. The clock on the wall ticked away the moments. A robin sang from the cottonwood tree beyond the fence. Coal whooshed as it sank in the firebox.

Ingeborg roused herself first. "Now, to 'Jesus Loves Me.' Do you have paper handy?"

By the time Reverend Moen came to retrieve his brood, Nora had most of the English words to the song locked in her heart. And, to refresh her memory, the carefully written words. After they left, she studied the letters. Maybe this new language was not so ugly after all.

That night, as she brushed the hayseeds from Kaaren's hair, she hummed the song. Kaaren chattered away about the hayloft with Nora listening carefully to pick out words she knew. "Pa's barn" and "hayloft" she understood, and giggles were a universal language.

Later, after the English language session was finished, Carl brought a box from the pantry and set it on the table. "Go ahead," he said with a motion. "Open it. These are seeds for the garden. I will plow tomorrow."

"Plow?" Nora tasted the strange word.

Carl wrote it down so Nora could look the word up in the dictionary. More and more she was able to find the words she needed by referring to the dictionary. She read the meaning. "To turn the soil with a tool."

"Then we plant?" She gestured to the seeds.

"After the ground dries. Then the harrow. Plant next week."

"Thank you." She turned her attention to the packets of seeds. While she could not read the labels, she did not need to. Peas, beans, corn, pumpkins—all were easily recognized. She held up one packet of very small seeds.

"Carrots." Carl identified it as well as the others. "Turnips, rutabaga, lettuce. Potatoes are down in the cellar. I'll buy onions when I go to town."

Nora nodded. Her fingers picked through the packets as if they had a delicate life of their own. Her own garden. She would plant and weed and water and they would have fresh vegetables. And some to preserve.

After her prayers for Carl that night, she slipped into bed with a smile still on her face. Her last thought wiped it away—by the time the garden was ready to eat, she would be on her way back to Norway.

She could not bear to remain in the house the morning Carl brought up the team hitched to a plow and started turning the soil. Rich black curls of dirt folded over in perfectly straight lines running north and south. She reached down and picked up a handful of loam, clenching her fist and then letting the dirt crumble back to the earth. She breathed in the aroma of the rich soil, the promise of spring and of rebirth.

"Easy, now," Carl sang out to the team as they turned another corner. The harness jingled and the horses snorted as they leaned into their collars.

Nora watched when they started back toward her. Sun glinted off Carl's bright golden hair, the one lock falling over his broad forehead.

Like her, he raised his face to the sun, then brushed the strand back with his forearm. His shirt sleeves were rolled back, exposing skin already turning pink from the sun.

"Ma?" Kaaren tugged on Nora's skirt.

"Ja?" Nora left off gazing at the man on the plow and bent to see what Kaaren wanted.

"See?" Between two careful fingers, Kaaren held up an angle-worm she had rescued from the turned earth. Nora held out her hand and Kaaren placed it on the flattened palm.

What is the English word here? thought Nora as she joined Kaaren in oohing over the creature.

"Show Pa?" Kaaren looked up, her eyes dancing with delight.

"Ja." Nora nodded. "And maybe he'll tell me what to call it," she smiled. Who could keep from smiling on a day like this one?

"I'm going into town," Carl announced the next morning after breakfast. "You need anything?"

Nora thought quickly. Kaaren needed new dresses and they were nearly out of sugar. How she would love to go along and visit with Ingeborg. Maybe he would ask her.

But Carl only wrote down the things she listed for him, including cloth for new dresses. When he drove out of the yard, he was by himself. She and Kaaren were left on the porch, waving good-bye.

"Come, little one. We'll bake some cookies and go down to the barn to see the new calf."

Kaaren stared wistfully at the barn. "Go in the hayloft?" She raised hopeful eyes to Nora. "Jump in the hay?"

"We'll see." Nora turned back to the kitchen. "Cookies, first."

Later, Nora wrapped bread and jelly sandwiches in one napkin, fresh cinnamon cookies in another, and poured milk into a pint jar. Then she wrapped Peder in a blanket and the three of them started for the barn.

The new red-and-white calf bawled from his pen as soon as they swung open the door to the otherwise empty barn. The cows were out to pasture, Carl was driving the horses, and the pigs could be heard rooting around in their lean-to at the side of the barn.

"Up." Nora pointed to the ladder, slanted from the floor to the door in the ceiling to the hayloft. She gave Kaaren a boost and stood beside the ladder until the little girl scrambled out of sight. Nora climbed up halfway and laid their lunch on the smooth boards of the hayloft floor. When she, with Peder in one arm, reached the upper floor, she stopped a moment just to look.

Rafters met in the peaked roof, high and dim in the dust-laden light. Much of the grass hay had already been fed to the livestock, but the densely packed fodder still covered about half the floor to a height of several feet. A pitchfork stabbed into the hay stood erect just like an empty flagpole.

Kaaren ran across the floor to the hay and slipped and slid until she perched on top of the mound. Then, she sat on the edge, legs straight in front, and, like sledding down a hill, slipped down the incline. She landed with a thump, giggling and calling, "See, Ma. Come, slide." She turned and scrambled back up. This time, she lay back flat and slid down again.

"Well, this hardly makes up for the hills in Norway, but we'll make our fun where we can," Nora muttered to herself as she laughed and encouraged Kaaren. When Nora left Peder on the hay and slid down the hay pile, Kaaren laughed and raced back up.

Nora lay back on the hay and looked up at the dust motes dancing in the light streaming through the high window. On the other end of the barn was a square door. It took up most of the wall and was meant to be opened to bring in the new hay. What a wonderful place to have a dance. When she thought about it, she missed the dances at home. People laughing, whirling, and tapping to the music. One thing Norwegians knew how to do—dance and have a good time.

Kaaren plunked down beside her. When Nora did not get up, the little girl snuggled down and laid her head on Nora's shoulder. "Hungry, Ma. Eat now?" She patted Nora's cheek with her grubby hand.

"Ja, we'll eat." With Peder propped in her arms and Kaaren sitting cross-legged in perfect imitation of her, they devoured their dinner. Between bites, Nora sang the first line of the new song she had learned. "Jesus loves me, this I know" rose to the rafters and echoed back to form a heavenly chorus.

When Carl returned home that evening, he brought in the

supplies. One little sack he handed to Kaaren.

She carefully opened the top of it and squealed. "Candy. Yummm." She plopped down on the rug and stuck one piece in her mouth. Sucking on it took all her concentration.

Nora opened her package carefully, too. "So much?" She held up the light blue cotton material with small, dark blue flowers.

"You need a summer dress, too."

"Thank you." Nora held the fabric up to her cheek. "It's beautiful."

"You're welcome." He continued to move packages around until he pulled something out from behind the flour sack. He set the burlap packet on the table in front of Nora. "For you." He spoke like he had a rough patch in his throat.

She stared at him, wondering what else there could be. Carefully, she folded back the edges of the burlap. Inside, the roots still planted in a clump of moist soil, was the start of a rosebush. Tiny red nubbins, ready to sprout into new growth, glowed on three dark green, thorny stems.

Tears filled her eyes and blurred the gift. "Thank you." With the back of her hand, she dashed away the falling drops. When she raised her gaze to Carl's, he dropped his.

The silence vibrated between them like a fine piano wire tapped by the hammer. Unheard, unseen—the music crept into their hearts.

Carl cleared his throat and the silence tinkled to the floor to lie in quivering fragments. "Uhhmm." He started to say something but had to clear his throat again. "I'll be putting the horses away... and milking... If you could have supper ready later?"

"Ja, I will." Nora whispered, never taking her eyes off his face. While there was no smile, she realized the lines between his eyebrows had smoothed away.

The next day, while Nora dug a hole by the front porch and planted her rosebush, Carl readied the garden spot. Now the soil was loose and flat, clods breaking down as the team and harrow cut pass after pass across the land.

"You can plant now." Carl reined the horses in and stepped off the harrow to stand in front of Nora. "The hoe is in the cellar." He made hoeing motions with his hands and pointed to the cellar door slanted against the side of the house. "After dinner, I'll begin plowing the fields." He pointed off to the east. Stubble from the previous fall lay gray on the land. "Wheat first, then oats, and finally corn. Maybe potatoes, too." He took off his broad-brimmed, black hat and the teasing breeze lifted his hair.

Nora stood transfixed. He glowed—burnished by the sun and the wind—his love for the land, part and parcel of his soul, shining from his eyes.

She looked out across the fallow land, flat as her eyes could see. A meadowlark soared and sang above them, its notes trilling down like bits of sunlight to be caught in her heart.

Later, serving the dinner, Nora laid one hand on his shoulder while she set a plate on the table in front of him. The need to touch him, to feel the strength of this man, welled up from that same place within her that hoarded the sunbeams. How right it felt.

"Thank you, Nora, for the good food." Carl pushed back his chair. "See you tonight."

Nora stared after him. Was God working His miracle?

Nora stacked the dishes in the sink and fed Peder. Then, taking a shawl, she settled him in it crosswise and, knotting two opposite corners together, formed a sling that she lifted over her head. She tied another shawl the opposite way and now the baby was clasped snugly against her chest.

With her hands free, she picked up the box of seeds. On the porch waited the hoe that Carl had brought up from the cellar. "Come Kaaren, we are going planting."

The sun had passed the midafternoon mark when Nora looked up from her labors at the sound of the dog barking. She shaded her eyes, looking off to the west where the sound came from. Two men strode across the field.

"We have company," she announced to Kaaren, who was busily digging a trench with a stick she had found. Nora watched them come closer. Dark hair, long, held back with a band. Dark faces, tattered shirts, leather leggings. One carried a rifle.

"Indians." Nora clutched the baby to her. All she had ever read and heard of the thieving, murdering, American savages flooded her mind.

Chapter 10

God, help!" Nora leaned over and grasped Kaaren by the hand, jerking her to her feet. The Indians stopped at the edge of the garden. They stared at her.

She stared at them. Her heart pounded in her chest, loud enough she was sure that they could hear. "You must welcome strangers." Her mother's words could barely be heard over the bellows of her lungs.

Nora tried to swallow. Not even enough juice to spit, let alone swallow—or talk. What good would talk do anyway? What language did they speak? Certainly not Norwegian. She stepped forward like she had a board stuck to her spine. "Hello."

Black eyes did not blink. The taller one surveyed her from the crown of her braids to her boot tips that peeked out from under her black skirt and back up again, slowly. When he muttered something, the shorter one shrugged.

Welcome strangers, welcome strangers. What do you do when strangers come, especially if they are the type that might take your hair and scalp with them when they leave? She clamped her teeth against the bile that rose from her stomach, threatening to make her disgrace herself. *What do you do with company like this?*

Offer them food, of course. "You, eat? Drink?" If that slight motion of the tall one's head was agreement, Nora needed no second response.

"Come." She clutched Kaaren's hand and strode across the planted rows, girl in tow, head high. "Never show fear," was her father's advice for dealing with both strangers and animals. Nora fought to hang onto those words of wisdom.

"Sit." She motioned to the porch steps and, without looking back to see if they obeyed, strode with Kaaren across the porch and through the door, letting the screen door slam behind her. She untied the sling contraption from around her shoulders and laid Peder in his cradle. Back in the kitchen, her hands shook so much she could scarcely pick up the knife. She sneaked glances at the door, sure that it would slam open at any moment and they would come to. . . She sliced bread and poured milk into cups. With bread, milk, leftover chicken that she had planned to have for supper, and cookies on the plates, she paused at the door.

The dark-skinned men sat on the stairs like she had ordered, leaning against the posts with their arms draped across their bent knees. One carved on a piece of wood with a knife that glinted in the sun. The gun rested against the outside of the porch, right near the owner's leg.

Please, God... Nora never finished the prayer as she pushed the door open and crossed the porch. "Here." She handed each of them a plate, then dug into her apron pocket for forks. When she held the silver out, they ignored her and ate with their hands.

Nora eased her way backward and, fumbling with her hands behind her, opened the screen door and slipped inside. She stood watching them through the screen.

The taller man scraped his plate clean with the bread and raised his cup in her direction.

"M-more?" If she could just quit stuttering.

He nodded.

She brought the jug out and refilled both their cups.

When they drained the cups, they set them and the plates on the floor. Slowly, they stood. The tall man picked up his gun. The shorter

106

one slid his knife back into its sheath.

Nora now knew what the rabbit felt like when facing a fox.

"Thank you, Carl's new woman." The tall man spoke in better English than she did. He nodded—once. Their long strides eating up the ground, the two Indians headed east.

Nora felt a gurgle of laughter churning in her middle and pleading to be let out. She stepped out onto the porch and bent to pick up the plates. As she stood again, she looked out across the land. The taller Indian raised a hand high in the air—and waved.

When she told Carl the story that night after dinner, she watched his face carefully. His lip twitched, his eyes crinkled. He had a dimple in his right cheek. When she repeated the Indians "Thank you, Carl's new woman," Carl bent over double. The laughter exploded from him like a shot from a cannon; the kitchen echoed with his chortles.

Kaaren giggled along and banged her spoon on the table.

Nora sat back and let the music of his mirth flow over, around, and through her. She was not sure which she was laughing at more—her story or his enjoyment of her story.

When he wiped his eyes with the heel of his hands, she said with a lift of her chin, "He say better English than me."

Carl dug into his back pocket for a handkerchief, then he blew his nose and shook his head, laughter still quivering in his shoulders. "The tall one is called One Horse and his shorter brother is Night of the Fox. They've been walking through here ever since I bought the farm. Sometimes, I find a deer carcass as a gift. Sometimes, they sleep in my barn. You could say we've become friends the last few years." The grin split his face again. "All Indian stories you've heard, that was long ago."

"Next time I'll know."

The corners of his mouth remained tipped up all through the English lesson and while Nora tucked both Peder and Kaaren into bed. When Nora returned to the kitchen, she took her place in the rocker and picked up the pieces of blue-flowered material she had cut out for Kaaren's dress. In between stitches, she sneaked peeks at the man caught in the circle of lamplight. His smile had faded but so had the lines from his nose to his mouth and those in his forehead.

"Thank You, Father," she prayed that night on her knees. "He is so beautiful when he laughs." She rested her chin on her clasped hands. "But, next time, maybe he could laugh with me instead of at me." Her lips curved up at the thought. "But thanks, no matter what. I'm not choosy."

Before she drifted off, the rest of a Bible verse her mother used to recite floated through her mind. *"Be not forgetful to entertain strangers: for thereby some have entertained angels unawares."*

Funny looking angels, she thought. *And I was so scared.* She pictured the scene in the garden again. *But, it was worth it.*

Within a week, Nora had her garden planted. New growth on her rosebush jutted out several inches with more new leaves unfolding every day. When she looked toward the horizon, newborn grass sprouted, cloaking the unplowed land in green velvet.

"When you look across the prairie," she wrote her sister Clara, "you can see clear into next month. While I miss the mountains and fjords, I can see the beauty in this part of God's creation, also. It is not a forgotten land as I had first thought."

When Carl drove into town one day, he took her letter and returned with another. This one was in answer to his advertisement for a housekeeper.

"Bah. She can't speak English, either," he growled after dropping the letter onto the table. He flicked the paper with his fingers. "Why did she even bother to write? I said specifically that the woman must speak English."

When Nora brought out her papers for their lesson, he waved her away. "I'm too tired to concentrate on that tonight." He heaved himself out of his chair. "Good night."

Nora could hear his weariness in the measured tread with which he climbed the stairs.

Sitting under the lamplight, stitching away on Kaaren's dress, Nora searched her heart. Was it joy she felt when he said the woman would not work out? Surely not. Her dream was to return to Norway, and she would not be able to do that until Carl found someone to take her place.

Each day Peder seemed to do something new. He not only smiled now, but laughed when Nora blew on his round tummy. He waved pudgy arms and, when he reached for an object, sometimes he got it. When Nora laid him on a quilt either on the floor pleading or outside on the grass, Kaaren would dangle a rubber jar ring or the bright red stuffed dog Nora had sewn for him. Hearing them laughing together always made Nora smile.

Carl ignored them.

"How can he?" Nora fumed one night after seeing him take a wide track around the two little ones on the floor. Kaaren was on her tummy, legs waving in the air while she and Peder laughed and chattered, her mimicking Peder's cooing.

One evening, Nora sat rocking and feeding Peder his bottle when she heard a thump, bump...silence...and then a scream to strike fear in any mother's heart.

Carl leaped to his feet, picked the screaming Kaaren up off the floor at the foot of the stairs, and tried to comfort her.

"No!" She arched her back and screamed louder. "Ma-a-a! I want my ma!"

Nora could see blood streaming from a wound above Kaaren's right eye. She stood, handed Peder along with his bottle to Carl, and took the little girl over to the sink. With a cold cloth pressed to the site to stop the bleeding, Nora murmured words of comfort. She turned to see Carl, wooden-faced, holding the baby stiffly in his arms.

Peder began to whimper, wanting the remainder of his supper. Without looking at his son, Carl walked into the bedroom, laid the bundle on the bed as if it were no more than a package from the store, and stalked out the door.

Nora struggled between vexation and pity. She wrapped a bandage over the tiny cut above Kaaren's eye. Then she retrieved Peder and resumed feeding him, still petting and comforting Kaaren.

Vexation swelled into fury. *That man! That insufferable, hardheaded, coldhearted*—she ran out of words harsh enough to describe him. *Who does he think he is anyway? Other people in this world lose their loved ones and they still love those left. How could he not love such a darling baby as Peder?*

"I will not pray for him tonight." She knelt by the bed, hoping to hear Carl's footsteps returning but was almost glad when they did not. "God, You don't *really* want me to pray for him, do You?" She listened to the silence. Outside somewhere, an owl hooted in its nightly hunting forays. The breeze fluffed the lace curtains at the open window.

She started to climb into bed. "Oh, fiddle." She knelt back down and scrunched her eyes closed, her teeth snapping together between words. "Please bless Carl and help him get through this time of sorrow. Make him love his sweet little son and. . ." She stopped to think. Nothing more came. "Amen."

She climbed back into bed and pulled up the covers. "So there." The silence crept back into the room. Was that God chuckling on the breeze? Nora turned over to sleep, a smile curving her lips.

With May, the beans leaped from the ground. Carrot feathers waved in their rows and the potatoes pushed up corrugated leaves to find the sun.

Nora leaned on her hoe, pride in her handiwork evident in the smile on her face. She pushed back the straw hat she had found in the cellar and wiped the sweat from her forehead. What her garden needed now was a slow-falling, soaking rain. She eyed the gray clouds mounding in the west. A lightning fork stabbed the sky.

"At least a storm can't catch you by surprise here," she said with a shrug. "And here I am talking to myself again. Better start giving myself orders, too. So get over there and take the wash off the line. It's been wet once today. It doesn't need to be wet again." She suited actions to her words and paused only long enough to watch rain fall in gray veils across the land. She dashed to the house with a full basket just as the first drops pelted the dust.

Carl galloped the team up to the barn, the harrow left in the fields. Nora stood on the porch. "What happened to him?" Brownie whined at her feet.

"Are you all right?" she yelled above the rising wind.

At his wave, she turned back into the house. Expecting him to come up for coffee, she stoked the embers and added coal to the fire. Maybe she should start an early supper. Even though the clock said four, the sky said dusk.

She crossed to the open door and through the screen door watched huge, fat raindrops pound the earth. She shook her head. "Doesn't this country ever do anything gently?"

"Ma?" Kaaren meandered out of the bedroom, rubbing sleep from her eyes. She leaned against Nora's skirt until Nora picked her up and set the little girl on her hip.

Lightning forked beyond the barn and in a few moments thunder crashed. Nora stood in awe at the heavenly display. She heard the rain gurgle in the downspouts and into the cistern under the house. Lightning lit the sky again.

"Pretty." Kaaren leaned her head against Nora's shoulder. When the thunder boomed, she flinched, then giggled. Nora could already hear that the storm was moving to the east of them. Now, the rain fell in billowing skirts, gentle and kind. The cool breeze felt good.

She left the doorway and finished grinding the dark beans for coffee. By the time Carl stepped onto the porch, the aroma of coffee brewing floated out to meet him.

"Smells wonderful." He sniffed appreciatively and hung his hat on the rack.

"Pretty lights." Kaaren pointed out the window. "Big boom."

Carl tousled her hair with one hand before picking her up. "Did you like it?"

She nodded, her blue eyes grave. "Hungry, Pa?" At his nod, she smiled. "Me, too."

"Sit down. I have cookies. Supper will be soon."

This time, when Nora rested her hand on Carl's shoulder, she felt a tremor go up her arm—he had leaned into her gentle pressure. She finished pouring the coffee and took her own chair. When Carl smiled at her it was as if the skies had parted and the sun beamed down to melt the frost that had stilled the heart.

"Thank you," was all he said but, with the smile, it was enough.

Nora rejoiced in the moments Carl spent with Kaaren. Though few and far between since he was in the fields at dawn and did not return to milk the cows until dark, the little one now met him at the door with a welcome grin. Even though he was so tired he would fall asleep at the table, he took time to listen to Kaaren's chatter and admire her new dress.

Of Peder, he never questioned or mentioned.

One afternoon, Nora moved the rocker and cradle out to the porch so she could sew and enjoy the sun at the same time. For a time, Kaaren played quietly at her feet but soon demanded a song and a story. Nora stuck her needle into the material of the bodice for her new dress and set it in the basket at her feet.

"Here we go." After hoisting Kaaren up onto her lap, Nora picked up the Bible written in English that she had in the same basket and turned to the Gospel of Matthew. Slowly, she read the story of Jesus and the children. Softly, she began singing, "Jesus loves me, this I know." Kaaren joined in and together they finished the chorus.

"More." Kaaren leaned back against Nora's shoulder and Nora closed her eyes. They sang it again. "Yes, Jesus loves me, yes Jesus…"

"What are you doing?" Carl's voice cut like a knife.

Nora felt like she had been stabbed. Her eyes flew open to clash with his, limpid pond against glacier. Confusion to fury.

Kaaren stuck her finger in her mouth and whimpered, her chin quivering as she stared from her father to Nora.

"Pa-a-a!" Her wail floated on the breeze spun up by his leaving.

"Shhh." Nora comforted her. "You sit here in my chair and take care of Peder. I will come back."

At Kaaren's nod, Nora rose to her feet and set the little girl back in the chair. Then, she gathered her skirts and ran down the path to the barn.

Carl had the horses backed up on either side of the wagon and shaft and was hooking the traces when she stopped in front of him.

"Why are you angry?" She stumbled over the words, wishing she could use Norwegian instead of English.

He ignored her, continuing the harnessing.

"Carl!" She might as well have been talking to the barn door.

When he lifted a foot to mount the wagon, she placed a hand on his arm. "Carl, what did I do?"

He spun around, reins in his hand. "Do? The Bible. That song. How can you sing and worship a God who kills innocent mothers and children?"

Chapter 11

But your son lived!" Carl stepped forward, towering over her in his fury. "But his mother didn't! She died and he might as well have."

"What are you saying?" She clenched her hands in the sides of her skirt. She would rather be pummeling his chest.

"I'm saying I don't want you teaching my daughter those songs and filling her head with lies about a God who loves her."

"But Jesus—God loves us all. He will help you, if you ask."

"I don't need His kind of help."

"But, Carl." She placed her hand on his arm.

He threw her hand off, the wind of it whistling by her cheek. Leaping up onto the wagon, he flicked the reins. "Ha, boys." Without a look back, he drove down the lane.

Nora stared after him, tears burning behind her eyes. "Oh, God help you, poor, poor man." She bit the knuckles on her right hand, her left pressed against her throat. "Only God can help you. Father, please take away Carl's bitterness. Bring him Your love. Restore his faith. Father, forgive me. I cannot do what he asks."

Dust from the wagons churning wheels hung in the still air. It smelled like despair.

Nora opened the barn door and wandered inside. Clean floors, harnesses draped over pegs in perfect order—all showed a man who cared about his farm. Outside, the fat cows switched their tails in the shade of the barn, a newly replaced fence post anchored a gate that swung smoothly on oiled hinges. She wandered over to the pigpen. The sow and her piglets lay on a pile of straw under a roof to keep off the hot sun. Carl loved his animals.

On the way up to the house, she thought about him…tossing Kaaren in the air to make her laugh…of his sitting with the chattering child, answering her myriad questions. Yes, he loved his family…the fields, green and growing…the rosebush he had brought her. Here was a man with love locked away in his heart, with wounds deep in his soul. Where was the key to that lock? What salve would heal his hurt?

Back in the chair with Kaaren on her lap, she rocked and thought—and prayed.

May flowed into June and Carl continued working from before dawn until long after dark. With the fields planted and up, the cultivating began. Endless hours of riding the metal seat of the cultivator pulled behind two sweating horses, their heads bobbing in time to the plodding of their hooves.

Nora walked everywhere with Peder in the sling and Kaaren clutching her hand or running ahead. One day, they found wild strawberries along a fencerow. She made preserves from the berries and baked biscuits for shortcake.

Carl only grunted when served the treats.

Nora was not sure if the grunt meant "Thank you" or "Give me more." She didn't.

The temper she had prayed so earnestly over for so many years, simmered and, once in a while, spit.

Haying season began. One evening, Carl drove the team up after dark and found Nora milking the cows. Kaaren was playing in the aisle; Peder was sleeping peacefully on a mound of hay.

"I didn't ask you to do this," he said.

Nora continued to squeeze and pull, the milk singing into the bucket. "I know." She kept her forehead against the cow's red flank.

"Take the children up to the house. I will finish."

"Carl Detschman, you are the most stubborn, bullheaded, prideful man I have ever had the misfortune to know." Nora reverted to Norwegian. She did not know enough of the right words in English. She pulled a bit too forcefully and got a mouthful of cow's tail.

"Nora."

"No, *you* take Kaaren and your son Peder to the house. Maybe you'll have time to soak your head before I get there." She stripped the last of the milk from each teat and, setting the bucket aside, rose to her feet. "I have one more cow to milk."

Carl stepped back before she could trod on his feet.

Nora picked up a clean bucket and her stool and plunked them down beside the next cow. "So-o-o, boss." She settled the bucket between her skirted knees and her head into the cow's flank. With the same easy rhythm, she squeezed and pulled, ringing the milk into the bucket.

She refused to look up when she heard Carl leave. She did not tell him her hands and arms were cramping either. When she peeked over her shoulder, the quilt where Peder had lain was gone.

Nora hid her smile of relief in the warm sweet cow smell, the fragrance of fresh milk foaming in a bucket. Maybe what he needed was to be stood on his ear once in awhile.

So, Nora added the evening milking to her chores. And caring for the gray-and-white barred chickens, as well as the garden and the house.

One day, with the hay cut and cured, Carl wrestled the high racks for hauling hay onto the front and back of the wide wagon bed.

Nora wished for her brothers to come help him. Why didn't he share the haying work with some of his neighbors? The answer came to her immediately. He was too proud to ask for help. And, as Ingeborg had told her in the spring, Norwegians did not always take kindly to superior-acting Germans. That Carl could act superior, she knew for a fact.

"Why do you care?" she asked herself one hot afternoon. She sank into the rocker with a jar of water in her hand. Some she sipped and some she dripped onto a cloth to cool her forehead—she had been hoeing the potatoes.

Down at the barn, Carl had parked the hay wagon under the four, cast-iron prongs that would lift the hay into the steadily filling hayloft. She could see his weariness in the slump of his shoulders. Climb up onto the hay wagon, set the forks, climb down, go around the barn, have the horses pull the rope toward the pile. Trip the prongs and begin all over again. He needed some help.

Nora put Peder in the sling. A jug of water in her one hand, she took Kaaren's small grubby paw in the other. Down to the barn they strolled.

"Hi, Pa." Kaaren announced their presence.

Brownie lay panting under the wagon, his feathery tail fluffing the dirt. Kaaren crawled under with the dog and giggled when he licked her face.

"Here." Nora held out the cool water. Carl wiped his forehead and reached for the drink.

"Thank you." This time she understood his answer.

Carl chugged the drink and, when finished, wiped his mouth with the back of his hand.

"I will help you."

"You would do that?" Carl stared at her over the rim of the jar.

Nora nodded.

"Even after the way I've been acting?"

She nodded again. "Just tell me what you want me to do. I've driven horses before at home and I've also helped with gathering the hay." She tipped her head back, the better to study him from under the straw brim.

"But you have the baby."

She patted the sleeping form in her shawl slings. "He's fine. Peder likes being close, being carried like this."

"All right. But you'll tell me when. . .if—" His gaze dropped to the sling and flicked back to her face.

"His name is Peder."

"I know." He sighed deeply. "When Peder needs you, he comes first." They heard a giggle from under the hay wagon and a smile flitted across Carl's face.

"Would you please go around the barn and drive the team forward when I tell you to? I'll tell you when to stop, also."

Nora nodded. She leaned over and peered under the wagon. "Come, Kaaren."

Like Mary in the Scriptures, Nora pondered these things in her heart. For a German man to admit he had been wrong was like... like...

She could not think of anything to compare it with. And he had finally said his son's name—for the first time in a long while.

Thank You, Father. Thank You. Her heart sang.

Dusty, thirsty, and with sunburned cheeks, Nora waved as Carl left for the hay field and his last load of hay. They would hoist it into the hayloft in the morning. Now, she just had the cows to milk and supper to fix. Peder whimpered and twisted in his sling—and a baby to feed, first of all. She turned and trudged up to the house.

"Nora. Nora." The call carried on the evening breeze.

Nora shaded her eyes, staring after the wagon. Carl stood on the front rack, waving his arm and yelling at her.

"What?"

"Leave the cows for me to milk."

She waved back in agreement. "Your pa is a good man," she said to Kaaren in particular and the world in general. The words sounded puny compared to the chorus in her heart.

Each Sunday, Nora felt tempted to beg Carl to take them to church, but each time she remembered his anger at her Bible reading. How she would love to visit with Ingeborg. And hear the organ playing in church, Reverend Moen preaching in Norwegian, and people visiting after the service. On Sundays, she missed home and her family the most.

The first Sunday in August burned so hot even the birds hushed their singing. Nora spread a blanket out in the shade of the cottonwood trees. She sat propped against the tree trunk, her Bible in her lap, fanning herself and singing to Kaaren. Peder lay beside her, entranced by the shifting leaf patterns.

Between songs, Nora eyed the western horizon, praying to see the mounds of black clouds that brought the cooling rain they so desperately needed. Hauling water to her garden used every bit of energy she could find. But, she reminded herself, *Sunday is to be a day of rest, the good Lord said so, Himself.* She turned away from thoughts of Carl cultivating the corn.

When Kaaren's eyelids drooped, Nora took the most recent letter from Norway from her pocket and read the beloved words again. When she closed her eyes, she could hear her mother saying the words she wrote. How far away Norway and the life there seemed now.

Her eyes must have been closed longer than she thought. She jerked awake. No, everything was the same. Kaaren slept, sprawled like a puppet with broken strings. Peder lay on his tummy, cheeks pink from the heat, his breath even and deep.

What bothered her?

She scanned the horizon again. A flat, black band separated the green prairie and the blue sky. Flat, not piled and puffed up like the life-giving clouds. She read her letter again. The black band grew wider.

Go to the house, an inner voice prompted.

"Don't be silly," Nora argued with herself. "The children are sleeping better than they have for days. It's cooler out here than anywhere else. There's nothing to fear."

The black band darkened, spreading now across the entire western horizon.

A grasshopper flew onto her skirt.

Nora brushed it off and bit her lip.

The band, no longer flat, undulated like a blanket settling onto a bed. A fat, green grasshopper crawled over Peder's back. Still asleep, Kaaren brushed one off her face. The action woke her. She sat up, whimpering and rubbing her eyes.

A sound like nothing Nora had ever heard seemed to come from the widening river of black.

A wave of fear brought Nora to her knees, scrambling to gather their belongings. "Kaaren, run to the house." She set the little girl on her feet and pushed her in the general direction.

"No-o-o!" Kaaren wailed and wrapped her fist in Nora's skirt.

Nora clutched Peder to her chest with one arm. With the quilt flung over the other and the basket in her hand, she had no hand for the whining girl. She stared over her shoulder.

The apparition flowed nearer. The sound, like the buzzing of angry bees, filled her ears.

She looked down at her skirt. Three grasshoppers had landed there. She could feel another in her hair. Were they, too, afraid of the approaching menace?

"Kaaren, help me carry the basket." She bumped Kaaren's arm with the handle.

In spite of her blue eyes welling with tears, Kaaren obeyed. She grasped the basket with a chubby hand.

"Now!" Nora forced a smile on her face and a lilt in her voice. "Let's run."

In the past, she dreamed of running and never getting to her destination. Now, it was so. With the baby bouncing in her arm and the basket thumping her thigh with every step, Nora felt like she was running through a quagmire. Instead of coming closer, the house seemed farther away every time she looked up.

After an eternity, they collapsed on the porch. Kaaren held up her arm and giggled at a grasshopper with iridescent wings and bobbing feelers.

"See, Ma. Big bug." She poked him with her finger. Instead of hopping off, he flew away.

Nora looked from Kaaren to the porch posts. Bugs had landed all over, their wings whirring and clicking. They crawled onto her skirt, the quilt, and Kaaren's dress. She brushed several off Peder.

"Ugh." She looked up at the sky now dusky with flying insects. "Kaaren, brush them off and go inside. Now!" Her tone allowed no chance of resistance. She brushed the marauding insects off the baby's things, her skirt, and apron. When the door closed behind them, she grabbed one from Kaaren's shoulder and threw it outside.

She laid Peder on his quilt on the floor and returned to stand at the screen door. Where was Carl? What was happening?

The cows bellowed from the pasture by the barn. As she watched, they stuck their tails straight in the air and the animals charged off across the pasture.

Should she go down and let them into the barn?

She looked out at her rosebush—its stalks writhed like living things. She bit her knuckles to keep from crying out. The bush was buried in gnawing, buzzing creatures.

Clouds of insects turned the day into dusk. Was the sun, too, being eaten alive by the invading hoard?

Her garden!

"Stay here!" She cracked the order and pointed to the quilt. Wide-eyed, Kaaren sat down by the baby. Nora grabbed another quilt off the bed and, clapping the straw hat onto her head, stormed out the door.

She ran to the garden, waving the quilt then, using it like a club, to beat the bugs crawling over her plants. She shook it in the sky and screamed at the avenging hoard, but they kept coming. The crunch of their feeding filled the air. They covered her hat, her arms, her face. She spit out the one that was crawling in her mouth.

Her arms ached from brandishing the quilt. "Fire. I'll burn them out."

She turned to the house. Kerosene, a torch of kerosene, would that work? How to get it burning? Would smoke drive them away? But what would she burn?

Hay! She ran to the barn with her tattered quilt in hand.

Slipping in with the door open only a crack, she spread the quilt on the floor and forked hay onto it. Then gathering up the corners, she half-carried, half-dragged it back to the garden. Her side ached; her legs quivered. She did not dare open her mouth to draw in the deep breaths she so desperately needed—the thought of swallowing a grasshopper made her gag.

She staggered to the house, grabbed a kerosene-filled lamp and the matches, and dashed back outside again. "Stay there, Kaaren," she panted as she closed the door behind her.

She unscrewed the top of the lamp and poured the kerosene on the pile of hay. She scraped the match across the sole of her shoe and tossed the flaming bit of wood into the hay. The fuel caught; smoke rose in tendrils, then billowed up. Grasshoppers fell. But when the fire dimmed, the horde resumed as if nothing had happened.

Carl found her, kneeling in the dirt, now bare of the beans nearly ready to pick and the corn that had been starting to tassle. Rivulets of tears streaked across her skin darkened by smoke and dirt.

He picked her up and gathered her into his arms, brushing a kiss across her cheek.

Nora sobbed against the wall of his chest. "I...I tried so hard." She hiccuped between words. "N-nothing stopped them."

"I know. Shhhh, now." He murmured comfort, but Nora was beyond hearing.

"I worked so hard and this flat land—it hates me. My garden gone—my family—no one." She thumped a shaking fist on his chest. "I want to laugh again—and dance—and see my friends. There's nothing left. Not-h-i-n-g."

"I know." Carl picked her up in his arms and carried her back to the house. He brushed the crawling insects off the porch steps and sat with her in his lap.

"Pa?" Kaaren stood inside the door, peeking through the screen.

"You be a good girl and stay there." Carl stroked the hair back from Nora's eyes and laid her head on his shoulder.

"But Ma's crying." Her voice quivered with tears.

"I know. Ma's sad." Carl continued to rock Nora in his arms. "Go see how Peder is."

"Pa, I want my ma-a-a."

Deep in her own fog, Nora heard the cry of her child. She sat up, only then realizing the comfort and strength of the arms that held her. She hiccuped again and wiped her eyes with the edge of her tattered and filthy apron.

Oh, to be able to sink back and let herself float on that sea of calm that follows a cleansing cry. To stay wrapped up in arms so warm and safe. To listen again to the heart that thumped in perfect rhythm beneath her cheek. His two-day growth of beard scratched the tender skin of her cheek. How good it felt.

"M-a-a-a-a!"

Nora stood. When she swayed, Carl caught her around the waist. She looked up into his eyes so close and lost herself in their shimmering blue depths. With a sigh, she leaned her head against his chest again. This was home.

"M-a-a-a."

She could hear the rumble of Carl's answer to his daughter through his shirt. She took another deep breath and stepped back. "Let's go in. She needs us."

With Nora still supported by his arm, they walked up the steps and opened the screen door.

Kaaren hurled herself at their legs.

Carl picked up his daughter and patted her back. Kaaren reached for Nora and wrapped her arms around them both.

"Big bug."

Nora looked up to see Kaaren picking a grasshopper from her father's hair.

"Here, Ma." Kaaren dropped it into Nora's hand and giggled when Nora made a face and threw the insect out the door.

After feeding Peder, Nora took a pan of tepid water into the bedroom, closed the door, and took off her clothes. The water on her skin raised goosebumps, but with each swipe of the cloth, she felt closer to being herself. When she had dried herself and changed into clean clothes, she bundled her dirty ones, tempted to stuff them into the stove and burn them.

She shook her head. All they needed was a good washing. She tied on a clean white apron and, picking up the pan of now-black water, reentered the kitchen.

Carl, too, had washed. Moisture darkened his sun-bleached hair to deep bronze. When he smiled, his teeth gleamed white against the tan of his lower face. That stubborn lock of hair half covered the white line across his forehead left by his hat.

Her fingers itched to brush that lock of hair back into place. Instead, Nora emptied her pan of water into the sink and dipped new water into a pitcher. She unclasped her hair and leaning over the sink, poured the water over her scalp. With the last of the rose-scented soap she had brought with her from home, she washed her hair.

"Let me help." Carl removed the pitcher from her hand and

poured the water over her hair to rinse it.

Nora twisted her head from side to side so all the soap could be rinsed away. How wonderful it felt to have someone help her like this. How wonderful to have Carl, stern Carl, rinse her hair. She felt a warmth pool in her middle and spread upward to her heart.

"Thank you." She wrung her hair out and, with the towel she had laid beside her, began drying her waist-length tresses.

"I...I think I'll go get started on the milking." Carl backed away. The urge to reach out and touch that rippling mass of gold caught him by surprise. He had only offered to help her. What was wrong with that?

As he brought in the cows, the questions remained in his mind. When he poured their feed, he stared at the flowing grain. Would there be anything left to harvest? What would he feed the livestock this winter? While he had had a good hay crop, hay alone was not enough. The pigs and chickens could not live on hay.

He thought back. The flood of Nora's tears weighed him down until he felt like his shoulders dragged on the floor. Was she really so unhappy here? She had never said so. But why would she? When had he encouraged her to talk with him, other than to learn English?

He picked up his stool and started on the second cow. One bad thing about milking, it gave you too much time to think.

When he had finished and let the cows out again, one resolve shone clear. He had promised to send her back to Norway and that he would do.

He picked up the brimming pails. But, if he paid for her ticket, how could he hire a housekeeper? Where would he find the money to buy grain for his cows, food for his household?

He knew what life was like after the grasshoppers came. They ate everything in sight. Only those vegetables below the surface were saved. But his potato field was not mature enough to have set potatoes yet.

"God, help me, I don't know what to do," Carl did not realize he had uttered a prayer. He poured the milk into the skimming pans in the cool well house, keeping half a pail out for the house.

He stopped with one foot on the porch steps and looked up at the heavens. Stars peeked out through their windows in the black velvet of the sky. A breeze rattled the bare branches of the cottonwood trees.

He listened carefully. The whirr and crunch of the invading horde was no more.

He walked into the kitchen and set the milk bucket in the sink. "I'll go into town tomorrow and telegraph reservations to New York for your ticket back to Norway."

Chapter 12

Bᵤt I don't want to go," Nora said.

"I will live up to my word," Carl answered. "When we married I promised you could return to Norway."

Nora could feel her mind running like a crazed thing caught in a maze. "B-but, you have no housekeeper for my...the children."

"I will work something out." He turned from her and went to stand at the window.

God, Father God. Please help me. Why does he bring this up now? The prayer continued as she dished the baked beans onto their plates.

The ticking of the clock was the only sound in the silence. She had hurried to put the children to bed. And now she wished they were here to need her. Didn't Carl need her? Who else would love his children, his house, and, yes—his entire farm—like she did?

She nearly dropped the plate of molasses-laden beans. When had love come into her heart?

"Your supper is ready," she called as he stood looking out at the blackness.

Carl sighed as he sat down. He studied the food on the plate before him.

Nora watched him. "Do you want something else?" She jumped up. "I forgot the bread." Returning to the table, she set down a plate of sliced bread and slipped back into her chair. She cast around in her mind for something to say to break the silence.

"The cows.. .they are all right?"

Carl nodded. He scooped a fork of beans and ate them.

"They will still give milk?

He nodded again. "The grasshoppers didn't bother them, just ate all their feed. Thank God I got the hay in before this happened."

Yes. You must thank God, Nora thought. When you can thank Him again all will be right with you. She forced herself to eat. Put the beans on your fork . . . chew and swallow. A bite of bread. . . chew and swallow. Swallowing was the hard part. The boulder, lodged in her throat, made it difficult.

"We'll know more in the daylight. Sometimes, they skip whole fields. I've seen times when one farm would be wiped out and the next one not touched." Carl nodded and finally looked at her, really looked at her. "We'll know more in the morning."

"Please God, let there be something left," Nora prayed on her knees that night. "I am so confused. I did want to go back to Norway. Now, I want to stay here. How do I explain this to him?" She closed her eyes and let the breeze from the window cool her cheeks. One tear slipped from between her eyelids and trickled down her cheek. "Your will, Father. Amen."

Early the next morning, Nora walked to the edge of her garden. She wrapped her arms around her middle and squeezed against the pain that ripped through her. The sun, shining on what used to be her thriving garden, showed not one blade or leaf of green. The black dirt looked like no one had ever planted there. Gray ashes lay where she had tried to burn the marauders out.

The trees, as if caught in the nakedness of winter, raised empty fingers to the sky. The fields lay bare, like her garden.

As she staggered back to the porch, dead bodies of the winged creatures crunched beneath her feet. She sank down onto the steps, the weight of the destruction too heavy to bear.

By her knee, one tough cane was all that remained of her rosebush. Nora reached down with a shaking finger and stroked the stalk, stripped even of thorns. *I never picked one of your blossoms. The third one had just opened. I was waiting for more. So many buds… now all are gone.* She buried her face in her knees and let loose the sobs that cramped her chest.

By the time Carl returned from the morning milking, her nose still dripped and her eyes were red. She wiped her nose with a handkerchief and tucked it back into her pocket.

"Breakfast will be ready as soon as you are." When she tried to smile, her lower lip quivered.

"Where's Kaaren and Peder?" Carl glanced around the kitchen.

"Still sleeping. Yesterday must have worn them out."

"Me, too." He poured sour cream over his pancakes and added a spoonful of jam on top. After only one bite, he put his fork down. "I rode out to the fields at dawn. There's nothing left." The words dropped into the silent kitchen and spread like ripples on a smooth lake.

Nora closed her eyes. "What will you do?"

"I'll have to buy grain both for feed and for seed next spring."

She waited for him to continue.

Outside on the porch, Brownie scratched at a flea, his leg thumping against the boards.

Carl shook his head. His voice seemed distant, far away like he was talking to someone else. "With no harvest, my savings will go to pay the farm payments. Or, I'll see about another loan." Teeth clenched, he growled. "I hate to borrow money, to be beholding— to anyone."

Silence took over the farm again. One day on a return trip from town, Carl tossed a letter on the table. He shook his head. "Too late."

"What do you mean?" Nora turned from kneading the bread dough.

"A letter from a woman who would like the job of housekeeper. She can even speak English." He poured himself a cup of coffee. "Your reservation is scheduled for the first of October."

Her breath escaped in a hiss, as if someone had punched her in the belly.

Carl tipped back his head and drained the coffee cup. "I heard about a farm that needs hands for the harvest. Can you manage here, if I'm gone a few days?"

"Ja." She took in a deep breath, one that stiffened her backbone. It was now or never.

"Carl, I want to talk to you." Nora formed the dough into a smooth mound and placed it back into the earthenware bowl to rise. As her fingers performed their usual functions, her mind cast around for the right words.

He started to walk out the door.

"Carl! Sit down." She pointed at the chair. Appalled at her tone, she added a gentle, "Please."

He sat. Back straight as a poker, face about as unbending, he turned to face her. A muscle jumped in his cheek.

Nora swallowed. Why had she said anything? She wound her fingers in her apron.

"I told you I don't want to go back to Norway."

Carl waved his fingers, like brushing off a bug. His look branded her a silly female who did not know her own mind.

"We agreed."

"I know. But. . .but things have changed. You don't have money to spare for my ticket. Peder and Kaaren...they...they need me." Her heart wanted to cry, *and I care about you*, but, instead, she sat straighter and forced her errant heart to remain still.

"You want me to go back on my word?" Blue eyes drilled ice chips into hers.

"No, no." She shook her head. "You wouldn't be if it is me that changed my mind."

Carl shook his head. "You are so young. How can you know your mind? What is best for you?" He pushed himself to his feet, the matter closed. "I may be gone for as long as a week. You'll have the team in case you need them."

Nora stood at the doorway to watch him swing himself up onto the bare back of the bay gelding. He picked up his sack that he had rested on a fence post, touched a finger to the black hat brim, and turned the horse to trot down the lane.

Tears, pooling in her eyes, made him shimmer and fade in the bright sunlight.

"Where is Pa?" Kaaren asked at the table before eating her mush.

"Gone." Uttering the one word took much of Nora's strength.

Kaaren raised her gaze from her meal to Nora's face. Her bottom lip quivered and tears flooded her eyes. 'Pa gone like my ma?" The question ended on a whimper.

"Oh, no, Kaaren. Your pa just went to help another farmer with a harvest. He'll come back soon, very soon."

Every morning, every noon, and again at bedtime, Kaaren posed the question. "Pa's coming now?"

"Soon, little one, soon." Nora hugged and petted both children, tickling Kaaren to make her giggle and tossing Peder in the air to hear his belly laugh. With no garden to care for, she concentrated all her care on the children and the livestock.

She sewed Kaaren two new dresses out of some material she had found tucked away in a drawer. She altered a cotton dress of Anna's that hung in a closet so she would have something cooler to wear. The blue print fabric was on the table, waiting for her to begin cutting.

"You're going to need clothes, too, one of these days," she told Peder one afternoon. He waved chubby fists like he knew exactly what she was saying and agreed wholeheartedly. *They must have saved Kaaren's baby things,* she thought, while holding the bottle for Peder. *But where?*

She searched the house over and finally looked up the stairs. She had only been up there to change the sheets on Carl's bed. With one hand on the rail, she mounted the stairs. Heat, like when she opened her oven door, met her when she opened the door to his room. It was as orderly as his barn. Clothes hung on hooks, good boots were polished and lined up under the black wool suit he had worn the day of the funeral.

She heard Kaaren calling from outside. Leaning over the table in front of the window, she pushed up the sash and stuck her head out.

"I'm up here. Upstairs. What is it?"

Kaaren came running around the corner of the house. "Hi, Ma." She stopped, legs spread apart, and, leaning back to get a good view, waved. Her giggle floated on the still air. "Read now?"

Nora shook her head. "Soon." She drew back in, careful not to bang her head. A piece of paper drifted off the table, so she leaned over to pick it up.

Carl's careful lettering, so familiar to her after the long English lessons, caught her eye. She read, the words leaping off the page and branding her heart.

Dear Adolph,

 I am writing to ask if you and Viola would take care of my children for me. If you could come for them after harvest since I have no one here to feed my animals if I leave. The grasshoppers ate...

The words blurred. How could he?

Baby clothes forgotten, Nora put the paper back onto the table and staggered down the stairs. He really meant to send her back to

Norway. What she wanted did not matter. All that counted was his word.

She slumped into the rocker. He did not care for her then, not at all. To him, she was just the housekeeper he had had to marry to save their reputations. "Dear God, what do I do now? I thought he was coming to care for me. But, I was wrong." The heaviness sat on her both inside and out.

The days and nights were so hot their clothes stuck to their bodies. Peder whimpered from a prickly heat rash and even Kaaren drooped like a flower that needed a drink.

The week stretched into ten days. Would Carl never come home?

But when he did ride up on the bay horse, nothing changed. Except now, Nora did not have the animals to care for and, with more time on her hands, she had too many hours to think. She tried to remember the good times with her family, to remind herself that she would be seeing them soon, to think about wading in the stream that rushed and tumbled over the rocks on its way to the Norwegian sea. Cool water. Laughter—and love again.

"Would you please milk the cows in the morning?" Carl asked one evening. "I'm driving over to the creek bed north of here to cut fence posts. I'll be home before dinner so I can take the butter and cream into town."

Nora looked at him, amazement dropping her jaw. He had not strung so many words together at one time since. . .since the grasshoppers.

"Ja, I can do that."

In the morning, Nora went about her chores with a lighter step. Did Carl's request mean that he was drawing out of his silence? Or that they would go back to talking in the evening?

But dinnertime came and Carl did not appear. Nora pushed the pan of fried chicken off to the side of the stove, along with the gravy and the last of the tiny potatoes she had dug up after the hoppers ate the plants.

She walked around the outside of the house and, shading her eyes, searched the northern horizon. Nothing. At the one o'clock vigil, she saw a hawk floating on the rising air currents. At two, a snake of fear slithered around her middle—Carl never broke his word—something had happened.

Nora ran down to the barn and, after grabbing a bridle off the wall and a can of oats from the nearly empty feed bin, slipped through the gate rails and into the pasture. "Here, boy." She shook the can, calling the gelding. The cows mooed in response. At the sound of rattling oats, the dark bay horse raised his head and trotted toward her.

"Good boy, good." Nora fed him the grain from her palm and slipped the reins around his neck. Holding the reins securely with one hand, she slid the bit between his teeth and the headstall over his ears. "What a good horse." She murmured soothing words, all the while buckling the straps in place and leading him up to the fence.

At the house, she tied his reins to the fence and dashed inside. "Kaaren, bring me Peder's shawl. We're going to find your pa."

How would she mount? By herself it was not a problem. She had learned early how to leap on a horse. But, what about with Peder and Kaaren. "Father, help me." She took a deep breath and exhaled, letting her shoulders drop and the tension leave. The porch. Surely, the rail was high enough for her to slide onto this animal's back and grab Kaaren the same way.

She led the horse up to the porch, grateful for his docile manner. Someone had trained him well. With Peder's sling locked over one shoulder, she mounted the railing and slung her leg over the horse's back. Her skirts bunched up around her knees, but she and Peder were secure.

"Kaaren, climb up on the rail just like I did." Kaaren stuck a finger in her mouth and hung back.

Nora gritted her teeth. "We'll go find Pa. Good horse." She

patted the bay's neck. "See? Climb up now."

Kaaren did like she was told.

Nora leaned over and, with one arm, grabbed the little girl around her waist. With the other, she settled Kaaren's legs across the horse and firmly against her chest.

"Thank You, God. Thank You." Nora dropped a kiss on Kaaren's hair. "Such a good girl. Now, hang on tight to this." She made Kaaren's hands grab onto the horse's mane. "Now, let's go find Pa."

Nora reined the horse around and out of the yard. Once on the prairie, she nudged him to a trot. With the hand that held the reins and guided the horse also anchoring Kaaren, Nora tried with the other hand to keep Peder from bouncing out of his sling. To her surprise, the rough ride did not bother the baby at all.

"Faster, Ma." Kaaren giggled and swung her legs, her hands gripping the coarse black mane.

Nora wanted to kick the animal into a lope, but the thought of all of them being dumped onto the ground made her more cautious. As they settled into the pace, the horse's heavy feet thudded across the soil stripped bare by the grasshoppers. New blades of green promised the return of life.

Ahead, Nora could see the tops of denuded willow trees that lined the creek. What should be a spot of green on the horizon stood naked as the rest of the earth.

Where could he be? The creek curved and rambled for many miles. Her questions kept time with her prayers.

"Carl!" The bouncing gait of the horse kept her voice from carrying like it should. She reined him to a stop and, with both hands bracketing her mouth, called again.

A horse whinnied off to their left.

Nora nudged the bay to a trot again. Ears pricked, he lifted his head and whinnied back at a sound he alone could hear.

Looking ahead, Nora spotted the wagon tracks she had been

searching for all along. They led over a hump and down into the flat area bordering the creek.

The horse whinnied again, much closer this time. Nora gave her horse his head and he saw the team before she did. His whinny sounded even louder than back up on the plain.

The team stood patiently, still harnessed to the wagon. The larger gray horse snorted and tossed his head. A few fence posts were in the wagon bed.

But where was Carl?

"Hush." Nora placed her fingers over Kaaren's mouth and strained to hear any noise. Harnesses jingled; horses snorted; a crow cawed his announcement that someone new had entered his territory.

"Carl!" Her voice cracked as she gave his name two syllables. "Ca-rl."

"Yes."

Had she really heard a sound? The horses pricked their ears in the same direction. She called again.

This time the response came stronger.

She nudged her horse forward, skirting the wagon and angling up the creek bed.

"Carl!" This time she knew she was on the right track. She pushed through the willow thicket, protecting their faces with her bent arms.

He lay on the ground, next to a fallen tree. Even from this distance, she could see his blood-soaked leg.

Chapter 13

Go get the wagon!" he cried. Nora struggled between the desire to leap down and make sure he was not bleeding to death and the knowledge that what he ordered was imperative—she had to get the wagon. She turned her horse around and headed back the way they had come.

The patient team pricked their ears and whinnied as soon as they saw the bay.

"Kaaren, I'm going to let you down into the wagon, so be ready." Nora nudged the horse right next to the rear of the wagon. "Here we go. Now, slide your leg over his neck, that's right." She spoke in a gentle voice, calm and patient but inside she was screaming—*hurry! Hurry!* "Good. Now hang onto my hand and just slide down."

Kaaren landed on the board floor with a thump. "See, Ma." She grinned up at Nora.

"Ja, good." Nora clutched Peder in his sling with one hand while she leaned forward and swung one leg behind her. Together, they slid to the ground, as if they had been dismounting like this all their lives. She quickly tied the bay's reins to the rear of the wagon and ran to untie the team. Still bearing her heavy burden, she climbed up onto the seat and released the brake.

"Kaaren, come up here and sit down." She pointed to a spot right behind her, still in the wagon bed. As Kaaren, eyes big, stumbled over the posts, Nora settled Peder in her lap.

He squirmed and let out a yowl, clearly unhappy with such rough treatment.

"Good girl." Nora threw a smile over her shoulder and slapped the reins. "Hup now, boys." The team jerked the wagon to a start.

Nora eyed the thicket ahead. No time to find a way around it. "Hang on, Kaaren." She sheltered Peder with her body and forced the team into and through the slapping, tearing branches. She stopped the wagon within inches of Carl.

He lay on the ground, eyes closed, his face chalky white as if all the blood had drained from his body.

"Oh, God, dear God." Her words ran into a litany, Nora not even aware that she was talking out loud. She lifted Peder in his sling over her head and twisted around to lay him beside Kaaren.

"Take care of baby now." She nodded and smiled at the little girl like this was some new game. "I'll get your pa for you." Nora jumped to the ground and knelt by Carl's inert body.

"You came," he said. "I prayed you'd come."

She could hardly hear his voice, weak as it was. "Ja, my love, we are here. Now you must help me."

"Don't…worry about…bandage."

She bent closer to hear him.

"Used belt…for tourniquet…stop bleeding."

"Yes, Carl. Now, I'm going to pull you up to a sitting position." She wrapped one arm around his back and grasped his closer arm with her hand. "Now!" She pulled, he pushed.

He bit his lip against the groan.

"Now, put your arm over my shoulders and, together, we lift."

This time, he could not suppress the groan.

Nora clamped her teeth together. Sweat popped out on her brow from the strain. But, they were standing.

"Lean on me." This time it was she who groaned as his weight shifted onto her.

Together they took the two steps needed for him to collapse into the bed of the wagon. He pulled himself forward with his arms until his legs were in the wagon, too.

"Pa!" Kaaren had watched all the goings-on with huge eyes. Now, the tears poured out and she threw herself against his chest.

Nora climbed up into the wagon bed. After making sure Carl was secure, she hefted the squalling Peder in his sling and hauled it back over her head and shoulder. Then, she climbed over the back of the seat, sat down, and slapped the team into motion.

The ride to town lasted an eternity of dust, crying children, jouncing, tears, and Carl's fading in and out. When she finally drove down the main street of Soldahl, she had no idea how to find Dr. Harmon. For what seemed like the past 400 miles, she had been praying he would just be there.

"Can you tell me where Dr. Harmon lives?" she yelled to the first person she saw.

The man trotted up to the wagon and peered in. "Oh, heavens. Here, I'll show you." He leaped onto the seat. "Turn right, there, by the blacksmith." He pointed ahead of them. "What happened to him?" He spoke softly so Carl would not hear.

Nora was not sure if Carl was conscious or not. He had not said anything for the last—forever. "He was out at the creek, cutting fence posts. The ax slipped."

"Turn left, here. That's Doc's house and office with the light in the window. I'll help carry your man in." He leaped to the ground before the team came to a full halt. "Harmon!" His yell could be heard clear to Fargo.

A graying man in his shirtsleeves threw open the door. "What'd ya need?"

"Something to carry this man in on. Leg's cut bad."

While the doctor pulled his head back in, Nora climbed back over the seat and laid Peder on the wagon floor. "You care for Peder." She took Kaaren by the hand and sat her beside the baby.

She knelt by Carl's head and put her hand on his chest. Yes, he was still breathing. *Oh, dear Lord. If we've ever needed You, we need You now.*

"All right, ma'am, we'll take him now." Doctor Harmon slid the poles of a stretcher in beside his patient. "Carl!" He turned to look at Nora. "What did he do?"

All the while he was talking, he and the other man lifted Carl onto the stretcher, slid it to the rear of the wagon, and, with one man at each end, lifted the heavy burden. Together, they carried their load up the steps and into the doctor's office.

Nora climbed down and, grabbing Kaaren and Peder, followed the stretcher carriers. She stood in the doorway as they lifted Carl onto a flat, well-padded wooden table.

"Pa, Pa." Kaaren sniffled and cried, hiding her face in Nora's filthy skirt. Peder, worn-out from all the crying, only whimpered now and then.

"Will he…can you— ?" The words stuck in Nora's throat. She wanted to throw herself across Carl's chest and howl out her terror, her love, her prayers. She lifted Peder higher in her arms and buried her face in his sling.

"He's alive." Doctor Harmon looked up only long enough to make eye contact with her. "That's all I can say right now."

"Now, dear." A woman's voice came from behind her. "I'm Mrs. Harmon. Why don't you come with me for now? There's nothing you can do here. The doctor will do the best he can."

Nora turned. Lifting her feet to follow the roundly padded woman with the kind voice took all her strength.

"Let me get you a cup of coffee and maybe your little girl would like a glass of milk and a cookie?"

Nora pulled herself back to the moment. "Please, show me the way to Reverend Moen's. Ingeborg will care for my…for Kaaren and Peder. Then I will come back."

"If that is what you want. But you are welcome to stay here."

"Thank you."

Mrs. Harmon gave instructions while she walked Nora back out to the wagon. She handed Kaaren to her after Nora had climbed up to the seat. "I'll see you in awhile then?"

Nora nodded. "Thank you." She flicked the reins and the horses broke into a trot.

With a small town like Soldahl, the directions were not too complex and she found the parsonage without any trouble. Light beamed from the windows on the ground floor, welcoming her back.

Nora slumped against die board that formed the seat back. Now that Carl was someone else's responsibility, she felt limp, drained of every thread of strength and will. She could feel tears rolling down her cheeks. When had she begun to cry? When had she not been crying?

She stared at the walk from the fence and up the steps to the front door. Could she make it? Would her knees support her?

"God, please." She leaned forward and wrapped the reins around the pole. "You can climb down by yourself, Kaaren. Mary lives here." She pulled herself to her feet. With Peder in one arm, she used the other to brace herself and swung her leg over the wagon side. She stumbled as she landed and the jerk made Peder cry again.

The door opened. Light poured down the walk. "Is anyone— oh no," Reverend Moen's voice deepened. "Nora, what has happened to you? Ingeborg, come quick." As he spoke, he leaped from the steps and wrapped his arm around Nora's shoulders. Ingeborg appeared before her and lifted the whimpering Peder in his sling over Nora's head.

Nora swayed from the lightness of releasing one of her burdens, but John steadied her. They led her inside and sat her in the rocking chair.

"Now, tell me. What has happened?" Ingeborg placed a cup of coffee in Nora's hands and closed the trembling fingers around the warmth. "Drink first."

"Peder. He hasn't been fed for hours."

"Mary, please fix a bottle. John, could you please take the mite in and change him?"

Nora could feel Kaaren attached to her knee.

"Pa's hurt. His leg is bleeding bad."

"He cut himself with an ax cutting down fence posts in the creek bottom. We brought him to Dr. Harmon's." Nora raised her gaze to encounter the sympathy flowing from the face of her friend. "Oh, Ingeborg, he might die. So much blood lost."

"Drink your coffee. John will take you back over there as soon as you have the strength. The children will be just fine here with us."

Her soothing voice and loving hands brought a measure of peace back to Nora. And with it, the strength to pull herself to her feet.

"Mange takk." Nora then went back to the doctor's house and Reverend Moen went with her.

"The doctor is still working with him," Mrs. Harmon said when she met Reverend Moen and Nora at the door. "Why don't you come right in here and have a seat?"

Nora followed her into the parlor and sat down on the chair nearest the door.

"I'll get you each a cup of coffee." Mrs. Harmon bustled out.

"If you don't mind," Reverend Moen leaned over her. "I pray best on my feet and pacing. Will that bother you?"

Nora shook her head. "We need all the prayers we can get."

Several cups of coffee later, Dr. Harmon entered the room. "I've done what I can and I'm sorry to tell you, it don't look good. He's lost a lotta blood. All's I can say is he's in the good Lord's hands now."

"Can I see him?" asked Nora.

"If'n ya want. He's unconscious. Won't know you're there."

"No matter. I want to be with him."

"Just remember, he looks bad." He looked her over. " 'Pears to me you don't look so good yerself. I have an idea. You spend some time with that man of yours and Mrs. Harmon'll heat some water so's you can get cleaned up." He opened the door to a room with a bed. "Here he is."

Nora looked at the white face on the pillow. She stumbled, clamping her teeth against the whirling in her head.

"Grab her." She heard the voice from a great distance.

Arms helped her into a chair and a hand forced her head between her knees. "Easy, now. Just stay that way until the spell passes."

Nora took a deep breath. Her head cleared. Her stomach retreated back to its rightful position.

When she raised her head, she picked up Carl's hand that lay on top of the blankets. She studied his face, every dear line, all the while stroking his hand.

"If we can keep the infection from setting in, every hour he makes it is for the best."

"I'm not leaving him."

"Didn't think you would."

Nora followed Mrs. Harmon's instructions. Get cleaned up, eat, drink, go back to Carl. There was never any change but she felt needed there.

"We have to keep him drinking, so spoon water into his mouth every fifteen minutes or so." The doctor showed her how. With panic trapped in her throat, she watched until she saw Carl swallow. "That's good." Doctor Harmon left her with a spoon and pitcher of water.

Grateful for something to do, Nora followed orders. Sometime in the wee hours, loving hands covered her with a light blanket. Every time she nodded off, she would wake on the minute to administer the water. With every spoonful, she reminded Carl that she loved him, her words soft and gentle.

People came and went through the next day. At one point, Dr. Harmon sent Nora off to bed, where she slept for several hours before appearing at the door again to resume her post.

In the early morning, Nora had heard the clock strike three o'clock. She jerked fully awake. What was different? Carl? She clasped his hand. Ears straining, she listened to his breathing. Was it slower? Did it hesitate?

"Carl!"

She listened again. A breath. . .a pause. . .a breath. Each slower and fainter.

"Carl! You hear me? Listen to me! You can't die. We need you here. I love you, Carl Detschman!" She gripped his hand. "Don't you die on me!"

She held her breath. *Carl, breathe. God, please, make him breathe.*

She waited. The moment stretched to eternity—and back.

Carl took a breath and let it out. And another. And another.

Nora wept.

An hour later, when the doctor came to relieve her, he nodded as she told her story. "Right about this time, the body is at its lowest. Lose patients mostly right about now." He clasped Carl's wrist between his thumb and forefinger. "Pulse is stronger." He applied the stethoscope to the man's chest. "Breathing better, too. I'd say he's past the crisis." He stood straight again. "Will you go to bed now?"

Nora shook her head.

"Thought not. I don't want to be doctoring you, too."

About noon, Carl regained consciousness. Nora watched his eyelids flutter. She placed the back of her fingers against his cheek. His eyelids fluttered again and this time he looked at her.

"Ah, Nora, love." A whisper so faint that if she had not been bending close, she might have missed it. His eyes closed again. One corner of his mouth tipped up ever so slightly.

After that, each time he woke he was stronger. Each time he called her "love."

The next day, he raised a hand to stroke her cheek, to brush away an errant tear. "Crying?"

"Tears of joy." She turned her face and kissed the palm of his hand.

That afternoon, Carl drank the good beef broth that Nora spooned into his mouth. When they were finished, he smiled at her. "I have something to tell you."

"Ja?" She leaned on her elbows beside him on the bed.

"When I was so sick?"

She nodded.

"One time, there was a long black tunnel." He paused. "I was going through it to reach a light at the other end. I couldn't wait to get to the light. It kept calling me, but then I heard your voice. I finally reached the light, so…so peaceful." He paused again.

Nora watched his face. It glowed like candles were lit inside.

"I wanted to keep on going…the love there. Perfect love."

The wonder in his voice, the joy on his face. Nora could feel tears running down her cheeks again.

"But you called to me. You said not to die. You said you loved me."

The touch of his hand on hers, the touch of angel wings.

He smiled. "So I came back." His eyes fluttered closed and he slept.

"Nora?"

She sat up, sleep falling away like the dropping of a stone. Night still darkened the window. 'Ja?"

"Will you marry me?"

"We *are* married. Don't you remember?" She smoothed that stubborn lock of hair off his forehead.

"No, I mean a real wedding—in the church. When I was lying there by the creek, I kept praying you would come. I begged God to let me live. A man comes face-to-face with what he's done wrong at a time like that. And you came."

"You said you'd be back for dinner. You always keep your word." She grinned, a teasing grin that made him smile back. "So, I went to see what kept you from your word."

"So, will you?"

"Will I what?"

"Marry me—again?"

"Can we wait until my sister Clara arrives? She should be here any day now."

"We can wait. I want to stand before Reverend Moen on my own two feet."

"And in the church."

"In the church." He wrinkled his brow. "How is Clara coming?"

"Someone sent her a ticket."

"Who?"

Nora shrugged. "I don't know. We'll ask her when she gets here."

Silence reigned in the sick room. Carl raised her hand and brought it to his lips. "I broke my word."

"Oh?"

"You won't be going back to Norway."

Nora chuckled. "I tried to tell you that, but you are so stubborn." She laid her head on his chest. "Will our children be bullheaded, like their pa?"

He chuckled into her hair. "Look, my Nora. Out the window."

Feather clouds glowed pink and silver as the returning sun promised a new Dakota dawn for Carl and Nora.

Dakota Dream

To call Jude Weinlander a scoundrel was painting him with the brush of kindness. Bully and cheat were equal approbation. Blond, curly hair, blue eyes, the face of an angel, but within his broad-shouldered physique lodged the soul of Lucifer himself. As with all of his ilk, his degree of impunity increased in direct proportion to the weakness of those he harassed.

He'd been hounding his brother Dag since Jude's first squall while in the cradle.

One night in 1910, when fall first nipped the Red River Valley of North Dakota, Jude and his bunch were slapping cards and slugging whiskey in their favorite haunt, Ole's Saloon.

"An' I'll raise ya two." Jude shoved his money toward the growing pile in the center of the green felt-covered table. He rocked back until his chair teetered on two legs, tapping the top of his cards with one finger. "Come on, Shorty. Make up your mind; we don't got all night."

"Na-a-a, too high for m' blood." Shorty threw down his cards and leaned forward so his shoulder blades stuck out of his shirt like wings, bird wings, definitely not those of angel type.

"Henry?" Jude tossed back the brown liquid in his glass and swiveled around to look for the bartender. He raised his glass.

" 'Nother one, Ole. Whyn't ya just leave the bottle?"

"I'll play the next hand." Henry dumped his cards and reached for the bottle the bartender had left. His hand shook, sloshing the liquid over the edges of his glass. His high-pitched giggle belied the broad chest and ample girth.

"Ah-h, you're drunk." Jude fanned his cards again and squinted through the cigar smoke. His chair squalled in protest at the angle it was forced to maintain.

"I'll take that and call you." The dealer laid his cards facedown on the table and pushed his money into the center. He turned his cards. "A flush."

"Hah!" Jude thumped his chair upright and spread his cards on the table. "Full house. Aces high." He reached out and pulled the pile of bills and change over. "Thank you, boys. Sure can use this extra cash. Ya done me a good turn, ya did."

He sucked in on his cigar and blew the smoke toward the ceiling. " 'Nother hand, just to see if'n ya can bet some back?" He stared around at the five men gathered within the circle shed by the hanging gaslight.

"No?" He poured a shot into the glass at his elbow. "Don't say I didn't give ya all a chance." He set the bottle in the middle of the table where his stack of winnings had presided. "Have a little to warm ya on y'r way."

While the others poured and passed the bottle, Jude chuckled to himself. " 'Member I tol ya I had an ide-e?" At their nods he continued. "This'un's a real winner. Dag's gonna be so flummoxed he'll never show his face in Soldahl again."

"What'er ya thinkin'?" Shorty leaned forward, his pencil-sharp elbows digging grooves in the green felt.

"We're gonna get him a woman, that's what." Jude waited for their responses. At the men's quizzical looks, he snorted. "What woman would look once at him, let alone twice? See, this here's how we'll do it." They all leaned close, shoulder to shoulder. "We'll send a ticket to a woman in Norway."

"Hey, how you gonna get'er name?"

"Easy, stupid. I jist happened to read the name and address offa that Detschman woman's letter to her baby sister."

"Oh." The men nodded in admiration. Trust Jude to think of something like that.

"Along with that ticket, we'll send a picture of me and a letter from Dag."

"He can't write no letter. He can't even read." Henry thumped a limp fist on the tabletop.

"I know that. But I can write—and read. The letter'll tell her about what a successful man he is—"

"He is that. Dag's the best blacksmith in six counties."

"Don't remind me! An it'll say how handsome—"

The men guffawed and slapped their knees.

"An' she'll expect to fall in love and marry him—" The laughter raised a decibel or two. One chair screeched in protest when its occupant shoved it backwards, laughing fit to split his britches.

"An' Dag'll 'bout die of embarrassment." Jude raised his refilled glass; the others followed suit. "To the end of Dag."

"The end of Dag."

Chapter 1

The way lay long between Norway and America. Clara Johanson tapped the edge of her sister's letter against her teeth as she strode up the last hill before the home farm. While she glanced up at the newly snow-dusted peaks that rose in ever steeper ridges to the east, she failed to appreciate their grandeur this time. All she could think about was America. How would she get to America?

She leaned against a pine tree to catch her breath from the steep climb. Her sister, Nora, had written about how flat North Dakota stretched, about a plague of grasshoppers, two small motherless children, and a silent, German farmer who was stealing her heart away. But she had no money to send a ticket yet.

Clara removed her wool scarf from her head and smoothed her deep honey hair back into its combs. She shook her head and the waves of gold rippled like wheat across her shoulders. Even in the brisk wind off the fjords, moisture dotted her forehead from the climb.

A squirrel chattered in the branches above her.

"Ja, I know, I'm bothering you. But what would you do in my place?" She stared up through the soughing branches to locate her scolding audience.

"Most of my friends are already married but me...for me there's no one." Pieces of pinecone dropped around her. She tightened her dark skirts around her knees and sank to the ground softened with pine needles.

"Maybe I should volunteer to the government to be an immigrant bride. You know the Norwegian government is sending marriageable women out to different parts of the world to the men who want families." More cone pieces dropped, one landing on her shoulder. "You don't think I'd make a good wife?"

The squirrel chattered. One answered it from another tree.

Clara caught a flash of red as her comrade leaped from a branch above her to the tree across the track. "Well, I hope you do. See, God, even the squirrels have mates." She shifted her conversation partner without missing a beat. "But I don't. You know I am well-trained to be a wife and mother. Just ask Mor. She started teaching me when I was but a babe."

She thought again of the letter from Nora. Her words spoke of such love between her and Carl Detschman. It hadn't been easy, in fact, Carl had nearly died; but the love shone now from her sister's pen. Oh, to love and be loved like that.

With one fingertip Clara traced a cross in the duff. "I know you have a plan for me...for my life. Please let it be in America." She dug the lines deeper. "I'm trying to be patient, really I am." Her sigh lifted and tickled the bows above her. Her prayer rode the sigh to the treetop, begged a ride on the wind, and wafted upward to her Father's ears.

"Uff da!" Dag Weinlander grunted from the force of the kick. "Enough!" He slapped the horse's gray rump with a heavy gloved hand, then wiped the sweat dripping from his brow. He leaned over, grasped the horse's rear off fetlock, and dragged the bent leg between his knees to rest on the platform created by his gripping knees.

"Dag?"

He ignored the familiar voice, instead checking the symmetry of the iron shoe. A knee-length, split-leather divided apron protected his legs from the hot iron shoe that raised a tendril of burned-hoof smoke when he set the iron against the wall of the horse's hoof. With iron nails clenched between his lips blackened by the forge smoke and his muscles bulging, he raised the hammer and tapped each nail into position. Dag set the shoe and cramped the nails puncturing the outside of the hoof. With the easy strokes of long practice, he rasped each head down and formed the hoof even with the shoe.

With a grunt, he dropped the horses rear leg and straightened up, one hand pressed against the small of his back. Only one more to go.

"Dag!" A hint of a whine laced the demanding tone.

"Ja?" Dag peered out from the locks straggling over his brow.

"You won't forget?" Dag's younger brother, Jude, leaned against the post.

"Said I'd meet her." Dag picked up the iron flat tongs and shoved the final shoe back into the glowing forge. After a couple of cranks on the blower, the iron glowed red, then white-hot. He set the shoe on edge on the anvil and, with the hammer, pounded more of a curve into the heels. Sparks flew, bright red and orange, against the dimness of the cavernous shop. He dunked the shoe into the water bucket.

"And you'll drive her out to the Detschman farm." This time it was more an order than a question.

"Ja." Dag brushed an intrusive lock of hair from his eyes, using the back of his wrist. Sweat muddied with soot streaked across his cheek.

"Her name's Clara, Clara Johanson." Jude continued propping the center post.

Dag leaned into the ritual with the remaining hoof. The horse snorted and twitched his tail. "Hold 'im."

"Ja. Easy feller." Will, the young helper, gripped the halter more tightly and stroked the horse's arched neck.

The coarse tail hairs snagged on Dag's head and one caught him in the eye. He brushed it away and clamped the hoof more tightly between his knees. The tearing of the injured eye blurred the hoof for a moment or two.

"I'll be goin' on then," said Jude. "You'll take care of Ma?" Dag nodded, mouth too full of nails to answer. Of course he'd take care of Ma. When hadn't he? Or rather, when had Jude? Surprised at the unaccustomed thoughts, Dag concentrated on finishing off the hoof. The pungent odors of horse manure, cut hooves, horsehide, and smoldering coal all welded together, redolent of blacksmithing. He breathed it in like bellows himself, part and parcel of his life and livelihood.

He rechecked each hoof and, when he straightened his back and looked around, only he and Will remained.

"He left 'bout the time you last answered." Will slipped loose the rope tying the horse to the post. "Seemed in a powerful hurry." He led the horse out the door and toward the livery barn. "You gonna do the other?"

"Ja." Dag heard the two horses whicker to each other, the timeless greeting of friendly horses. Will's voice joined in.

Dag removed his glove and rubbed the back of his neck with fingers so deeply grimed they looked like walnut bark. They matched his neck. He hawked and spit, then kneaded his protesting back muscles with hamlike hands. Outside he could see the daylight dimming.

Will trotted up with the remaining horse and tied it to the hitching post located in the arched doorway of the shingled building.

The train would be in anytime now. Dag stared from the horse to the tree outside. Not enough time. He shook his head. Why'd Jude make such a fuss over his picking up that woman? She could wait till he finished. Johnson's team came first.

He bent to the job at hand.

"You gonna eat first?" Will asked later after stabling the freshly shod horse.

"Nah. You go on."

"I can help you get the buggy ready." Will shifted from one foot to the other.

Dag shook his head. "Go eat."

The train whistle had come and gone long enough for the gaslight above the hotel entrance to be lit before Dag hung his apron on a nail. He shrugged into a black wool jacket, then brushed down his own bay mare. When her coat shone to perfection, he gently laid the harness across her back, careful to smooth every hair under the leather and adjust each snap and buckle. When he backed her into the shafts, it was a contest to see which shown brighter, the horse or the buggy.

He kicked his boots against a post to knock off any clinging mud or manure and stepped into the leather-roofed buggy. Jude had said to take the buggy. Dag shook his head. If that woman had many trunks and such, the wagon would be better.

He picked up the reins and clucked to the mare. The sooner he got this chore done, the better. His stomach rumbled. By the time he drove the nearly one hour out to the Detschman farm and another hour back, his belly'd do more than rumble. He rubbed a hand over a wall of solid flesh. In the dim light he picked a clump of dirt—or manure?—off his pant leg and flicked the matter out of the buggy.

His stomach grumbled again—louder.

He turned the mare in along the weathered train station and stopped beside the raised platform between the hunching building and the ribbon tracks. Two trunks squatted side by side.

With a sound of disgust, Dag levered himself from the buggy. He should have brought the wagon. Now hed have to make another trip tomorrow.

"Uff da," he muttered as he knotted the mare's lead shank around the hitching post. *Let Detschman come in and get 'em. She was his sister-in-law anyway, wasn't she? Why didn't he meet the train? That Jude—what'd he have to do with this whole mess anyway?*

Dag stomped across the wide beaten planks and jerked open the door. It wasn't as if he had nothing else to do. And while Jude said he'd pay for the trip, getting the cash in hand was about as likely as a snowstorm in July.

"Froken Johanson." The words died aborning. Dag tried to swallow, but his mouth suddenly felt like a Dakota dust storm. That same storm left grit in his eyes. Was this what being struck by lightning felt like? Lightning didn't usually accompany dust storms.

He stared at the vision that stood before him. Tendrils of deep honey blond hair peeped out from the sides of a feathered black hat. Eyes the blue-green of a hummingbird's back peeked out from the black veil pinned in a swoop across an alabaster forehead. Turned up nose, lips ruby like the hummingbird's throat and smiling as if they'd been friends for years. When she stood, she barely came up to the middle button on his faded and tattered shirt.

Dag tried again to talk. Breathing alone took an effort. Both failed.

"I'm Clara Johanson." Her voice tickled his ears, which responded in a rush of heat.

Dag wet his lips, or tried to.

"And you're... ?"

When had the Norwegian language been set to melody? He ordered his gaze to leave her face. To look up at the rafters or down at the floor. Instead, rebellious gaze. It traveled her length, from tip of crushable hat to toe of shiny boots—and back up. Now his ears burned like the forge he'd left behind.

Dag leaned forward and picked up the bag set beside her. He waved his hand toward the door and strode out in silence. He who rarely chose to speak, now couldn't.

He slung her gray-and-black bag into the small space behind the seat and climbed into the buggy.

"What about my trunks?" Clara paused at the edge of the station platform.

"Tomorrow." Dag croaked out the word.

Clara climbed into the buggy and settled her skirts. What a strange man. Maybe he was a bit on the deaf side? She sniffed, her nostrils pinching against the odor. Did he never bathe? Or wash that rat's nest of hair? She tried to ignore the fumes. Thank the good Lord above this wasn't the man in her picture.

She clasped her purse in her lap, wishing the buggy were even a few inches wider. She shifted as far to the side as possible.

"Nice evening, isn't it?" Maybe if she breathed through her mouth it would be easier.

Silence from the man beside her. The harness jingled with the trotting horse.

Clara peered ahead, Ja, like Nora had written, the land certainly was flat. A little bounce of excitement slipped past her mother's orders to act like the woman she now was...or would be. The time sequence wasn't exactly clear as to when a person left the exuberance of childhood and entered staid adulthood. She sneaked a glance at the man driving the buggy.

He stared straight ahead. Good. Mayhap he hadn't noticed. If only he hadn't taken so long to come for her. Now it was too dark to see the fields and farms. Off to the right a light from someone's house pinpointed in the darkness.

The mare trotted onward, her puffs of breath a counterpoint to the tattoo of her hooves.

"What did you say your name is?" Her willful stubbornness kicked in. She *would* get him to talk. How could anyone be so rude?

"Have you lived here a long time?" She waited for an answer that didn't come. "Do you know my sister, Nora?" Waiting was getting harder. She wanted to ask him about the handsome man with curly blond hair, the one whose face she'd fallen in love with. The man who sent her a ticket and would be looking forward to claiming her as his wife. But she didn't.

"How far from town do Nora and Carl live?" Pause again. Clara felt like grabbing the man by the ears and turning his face to look at her so he would be forced to answer. "I know you speak Norwegian, I heard you. So I must take it that you are a cruel person at heart who is enjoying my discomfort. Newcomers to America like me must be most entertaining to ignore."

Was that a snort she heard? From the horse? No. Clara ran her tongue over her teeth and tipped her chin a bit higher. "Maybe you just want to hear me prattle away so you can tell all your friends what a simpering fool that new arrival is?"

"*Uff da.*"

Clara nearly clapped her hands in delight. "I agree. No one should be forced to carry on as I have just to get two syllables from her driver."

"Dag. I am Dag Weinlander." How he had fought to ignore her jabs. Dag bit his lip to keep from laughing aloud. What a feisty little thing she was.

"I'm pleased to meet you, Dag Weinlander." Clara settled back against the leather seat. She'd won—the first round. Her forehead wrinkled. What a curious thought. Why should she think there would be other rounds?

Dag focused on the spot up the road between his mare's ears so that his errant gaze wouldn't turn to hers. The tips of his ears still burned or burned again, he couldn't say which.

What did she want from him? He'd been hired to drive her out to her sister's, not entertain her on the way. Once his ears stopped burning, they'd probably drop off from sheer overexertion. No one but Will had talked to him this much since...since...well, maybe they never had.

The clop of hooves, the jangling of the harness, and the creak of the ironclad wheels sang through the dark.

Clara nibbled her lip. As long as she turned her face slightly to the side, she could breathe the crisp night air, unimpeded by the odor of the man next to her. Her nose told her there would be frost before morning.

Ahead, a brass disk peeped its edge above the rim of the earth. As the moon rose, it seemed to fill the eastern horizon with gold.

"Oh-h-h." Her wonder escaped on a sigh. With no mountains or trees to break its symmetry, the moon took possession of the land, rising to float against the black vault of the heavens, bathing the earth in liquid light. Clara forgot the man beside her, her sister in the home awaiting her, and the family she'd left behind. She lost herself in the glory of the harvest moon, the brisk air that kissed her opened lips, and the hush that blanketed all the simple sounds around her. *"Mange takk,* dear God." She whispered, sensing that anything louder might shatter the glory.

A crystal tear slipped down her cheek, testimony to God's nighttime handiwork.

Dag watched the girl beside him. He'd seen a harvest moon before and he'd felt its power and majesty. He'd never seen a woman bathed in moon glow and transfixed by its beauty.

Clara shivered and took a deep breath. She looked around, as if surprised at her reaction. Her glance caught the movement of Dag's head from the corner of her eye. Had he been watching her?

Dag pulled gently on the left rein and turned his mare into the lane leading to the Detschman farm. "We're here."

Clara perched on the edge of the seat, straining to catch the first glimpse of welcoming windows.

Ahead, lighted windows dimmed in the brightness of the moon. While leafless trees shielded the house, the moon reflected off the roof of a large barn, windmill, and various other buildings, all snuggled against the earth's breast.

A dog barked. A horse whinnied from the pasture. The mare lifted her nose and answered.

A door opened, spilling light across the porch and down the steps.

Clara felt the tears gather and clog in her throat. She'd finally reached her sister's new home. Nora's American home. Now they'd be together again.

Before the buggy stopped rocking, Clara leaped from her seat and scrambled down the step to land lighdy on the ground. She darted through the gate, up the walk, bounded the two steps while pulling up her long skirt, and threw herself into her older sister's arms.

"Clara, you're here already." Nora hugged her little sister close. "We didn't expect you until tomorrow or the next day."

"I wanted to surprise you." Clara leaned her head against her sister's shoulder. "I have so much to tell you." She wiped away an escaping tear. "I can't believe I'm here, in America, in North Dakota, with you."

Nora hugged her sister once more and then stepped back. "Clara, this is Carl." She took the hand of the man who waited patiently behind her and brought him forward.

"I am pleased to meet you." Carl extended his right hand, the left still clasped by Nora.

Clara nodded, her speech temporarily drowned by the tears she kept swallowing.

"And this is Kaaren." Nora reached behind her to grasp the little girl's hand, hiding in her mother's skirts. "Kaaren, your Auntie Clara from Norway."

Kaaren, finger in her mouth, buried her face in Nora's white apron.

Clara squatted down and looked the little one in the eye. "Oh, my. Now I'm an auntie. And you're my first niece. We're going to have such fun." She stood again.

"And where is that baby boy I've read so much about?"

"Sound asleep and we want him to stay that way. You can cuddle him tomorrow. Come in now."

"Oh, my bags."

"I'll get them." Carl stepped off the porch and headed for the buggy where Dag waited, patiently leaning against the high wheel.

As the sisters turned toward the warmth of the open door, Clara spun back around. "I haven't thanked Dag for bringing me all the way out here."

"Don't worry, Carl will take care of that for you. Have you had anything to eat? I'll make fresh coffee." They passed into the house.

Dag turned down Carl's offer of coffee and food and, after shaking hands, stepped back into the buggy. He touched a finger to his hat brim, turned the mare in a circle to head back out over the land, and clucked her into a trot.

He listened for the familiar night sounds. How faint they seemed after the chatter that had filled his ears. He'd never realized before how quiet the night could be. And how far away his hovel stood. He ignored the temptation to look back at the lighted windows.

Chapter 2

Ｈow then did you get the ticket to come?" Nora asked. Carl had put Kaaren to bed and gone upstairs himself after wishing the visitor a good night's rest. Nora and Clara were enjoying a second cup of coffee in the now-quiet and peaceful kitchen.

"I'll tell you. Let me get the letter." Clara slipped from her chair at the kitchen table and crossed the room to rummage in her suitcase. When she returned she held a water-stained envelope in her hand. "Here." She laid it on the table in front of her sister.

Nora studied the front of the envelope. She pulled the kerosene lamp closer so she could read the faded handwriting. After carefully studying it, she looked up. "How did this get so stained?"

"I don't know. It happened before—"

"Before you got it?" Nora's voice squeaked in amazement. She didn't pay attention to the fact that they'd fallen back into their old pattern of finishing one another's thoughts.

Clara nodded.

"Then how—"

"Did I get it?"

Nora nodded this time. Silence but for the clunk of a piece of coal falling in the stove waited while she studied the barely discernible script again. She looked up.

"I know. God must have His hand in this—or else He just gave the postman extra good eyesight."

"Uff da." Nora shook her head again.

"Open it." Clara gave a little bounce on her chair. "Read the letter."

Nora grasped the fragile paper and pulled it from the envelope. After unfolding it, she choked back a laugh. "Was it really this bad?" She scanned the lines and loops of script; most of the ink had run together or faded entirely. She peered closely where the signature should be. "Impossible. All I can read for sure is 'Dear Miss Johanson.' At least I assume that's what the heading says."

"Me, too. But the ticket was plain enough to use—barely— and then there was this." She handed Nora a picture, faded in places, but still clear enough to see. "Isn't he handsome? Just think—that's the man who sent me a ticket. Do you know him?"

Nora studied the picture. She glanced up at her sister and then went back to studying the photograph. "If he's as nice as he is good-looking—"

"I know. I think I'm half in love with him already." Clara plucked the picture from her sister's hand and sighed when she gazed at the face of her mystery man. "Such hair, curly like that. And look, I think if he smiled, he would have a dimple." She touched the paper cheek with her fingertip. "You didn't say. Do you know who he is? I wonder why he didn't meet the train?"

"No, I don't. I mean I've never seen him before, but then there are many people in Soldahl that I've never seen. If they don't go to church. . ."

"Surely he must go to church." Clara could feel her heart begin an erratic thump in her chest. "You really don't know him?"

Nora shook her head. She reached for her sister's hands. "No, but mayhap Carl does. Or Ingeborg." She covered both of Clara's hands with her own. "This is surely a mystery, isn't it?" She picked up her coffee cup and sipped.

"Ugh." The face she made accompanied the words. "Cold coffee. Let me warm yours up, too." She started to push back her chair.

"No, not for me." Clara stared at the picture, worrying her bottom lip between her teeth. Should she tell Nora about the little knot of fear that seemed to be cutting off her air? She sucked in a deep breath. A yawn caught it and creaked her jawbone.

"*Uff da.* Here we sit yakking when you just got off the train. I can see you need your bed. We can figure all this out in the morning." Nora tucked a strand of hair behind Clara's ear and caught her own yawn. "You made me yawn, too."

The clock chimed…and chimed.

"There, it is ten o'clock already and we've been sitting here for hours. Come. Carl brought Kaaren into my bed so you can have her bedroom. That way you can sleep as long as you want in the morning." Nora rose to her feet and laid a hand on her sister's shoulder. "Not to worry, little sister of my heart. Your man will show up one day and then you can decide if you like him as much as you think."

"Ja, that is the way of it." Clara stood, slipping the letter and picture back in the envelope at the same time. "I just thought you would know him and this would all be cleared up at once." She tapped the edge of the envelope with her finger.

"And tomorrow you can tell me all the news of home—"

"And give you the presents Mor sent and the letters, too. Everyone wrote when they knew I was to come." Clara lifted her chair so it wouldn't creak on the floor and snugged it up against the table.

Nora picked up the carpetbag with one hand and lamp in the other and led the way through the parlor to the back bedroom. She set the lamp on the oak chest of drawers and the bag in front. A rag doll flopped against the pillow covered by a patchwork quilt on the bed.

Clara sank down on the edge of the bed. "It seems like weeks since I've slept in a real bed." She picked up the doll and studied the black button eyes and smiling mouth embroidered in red. "This looks like your handiwork. Remember the one you made for me?"

Nora nodded. "That was my first. And you pulled the eyes off in the first hour. After the second time I had to resew them, I embroidered the eyes, too, in green to match yours."

Clara laughed and gave the doll a squeeze. "You are very good with a needle. All the hardanger lace for your bride's chest. I had a hard time learning to sit still for so long. Mor did her best. Such patience she has." Nora sat beside her sister. "And your bride's chest? Did you fill it?"

Clara nodded. "But just don't look too close at the stitches. Oh, I forgot. My trunks are still at the station. Mr. Weinlander said Carl would have to come get them since he had only the buggy."

"How did he know to meet you?"

Clara blinked. She looked at her sister. "Why, I don't know. I never thought of it. The stationmaster told me the man from the livery would come for me. I waited quite a time and when he finally came—*uff da.*" She wrinkled her nose. "I don't think he's ever heard of a bath, let alone taken one. And rude." She planted her fists on her hips. "Getting him to speak was—"

Nora chuckled. "And did you? Get him to talk?"

"But, naturally." Clara flopped back on the bed, looking at her sister as if she'd doubted the sun would rise.

Nora shook her head. "Dag just doesn't talk to anyone. He says the fewest words possible to complete his business. And that's all."

"Oh." The little word carried a wealth of understanding. Clara chewed the inside of her lower lip. She felt the chuckle dance around the corridors of her mind before bursting forth full-blown; its merry music skipped from bed to window and around the room.

Nora shook her head. "What are you up to now, sister mine. I know that laugh."

Clara smothered her face with the rag doll. "Nora, dear, the man needs help."

"You just think about your mystery man. When you find him, you won't have time to be fixing Mr. Weinlander." She rose to her feet.

166

"Now you sleep as long as you'd like in the morning. I know you're tired from the long journey and the bed will feel good." She reached out a hand to pull her sister to her feet. "Mayhap Carl can drive to town tomorrow for your trunks. And to tell Reverend Moen we can have the wedding Sunday. We were waiting for you, you know."

"But you're already married."

"I know. But that one seems a sham, so we decided to have a real wedding, in the church and with me wearing my *bunad* and *sølje*. And with you to stand up for me once we heard you were coming."

"I am happy for you." Clara patted a hand over her mouth to disguise the yawn. "I'll see you in the morning then."

Nora folded back the covers. "I'll leave this lamp with you." She stopped again in the door frame. "You'll never know how glad I am you are here. Sleep well, God bless."

Clara stifled a yawn again. *"Mange takk,* dear sister." Her eyelids seemed weighted with stones as she removed her clothing and pulled her nightgown over her head. *"Mange takk."* was all she finished of her prayers before sleep winged her away to dream of a curly haired man with broad shoulders and the promise of a dimple in his right cheek when he smiled.

Clara awoke to silence. Where had everyone gone? She lay in the soft feather bed, reviewing the hours spent on the train, back to the ship, and ended up at her parent's home in Norway. Such a distant place. Would she ever see the rest of her family again?

She bit the inside of her lip against the pain of missing them all. "Not all, silly. Nora's around here somewhere. Think how much you've wanted to see her and now you can." She threw back the hand-stitched quilt and sat up cross-legged in the bed. With her elbows propped on her knees, she rested her chin in her hands.

A song trickled through her mind, one learned in the choir

at home. She hummed the tune while studying the white fabric stretched across her knees. The words came to her mind: *Oh God, our help in ages past.* "Good thing." She left the tune and turned to prayer, clenching her eyes shut so she wouldn't be distracted by the sun's painting squares on the polished floorboards. "Father God, I know You've always been with me and this journey proved Your faithfulness again. But what about the man who sent for me? Where is he? Who is he? How can I marry him if. . .if. . ." She waited for her thoughts to settle down. "I do so want to be married. I know I make jokes about it but, Father, I need someone to love...someone who loves me. I want a home and a family." She paused again. A far off moooo blessed her silence. "Is that wrong of me?" No answer floated down from the heavens. None arose from her heart either.

A sigh rose from deep in her heart. It was hard to wait for an answer. She quieted her mind again. The song returned, the pace faster, the notes livelier. Unable to resist the joy she felt rising from somewhere deep inside, she whispered a final "amen" and flung herself back on the pillows.

She stared up at the high ceiling, then wrapped both hands around her shoulders and squeezed. "I, Clara Johanson, am now in America!" She jumped from the bed, danced on the rug, and then got dressed. While the sun was shining in so warmly, the room felt like a cold fall day after a frosty fall night.

The clock bonged nine times as she opened her bedroom door and walked through the parlor toward the kitchen. While the house was empty, the coffeepot steamed gently on the back of the stove.

"Bless you, sister mine." She poured herself a cup and, wrapping both hands around the warmth, basked in the heat of the stove. As her gaze wandered around the kitchen, admiring her sister's handiwork, she stopped at the loaf of bread resting on the counter beside the jam jar and the molded butter on a plate.

She left her place at the stove and stuck a finger in the jam and then into her mouth. "Ummm." She licked all the sticky sweet berry taste off her finger and, after setting down the coffee cup, sliced herself a piece of bread. After burying it in butter and jam, she took the bread and coffee and eased herself down into the smaller of the two rockers in front of the stove.

"Ahhh." Alternately drinking and chewing, she continued her study of the kitchen. The stove had been recently cleaned and its silver trim gleamed in the beam of sun from the window. The ruffled curtains that framed the picture-perfect fall tree in the window above the sink sparked in the same sun. Clara nodded. Yes, her sister was the spotless homemaker their mother had trained her to be...always the one to be perfect at what she did.

Clara set the chair to rocking with the tip of her toe. Well, at least her hardanger stitching always outdid her sisters. She sighed and leaned her head against the back of the rocker. It was always hard to measure herself against perfection, yet she loved her older sister as only a younger one could.

"I've missed you so," she whispered to the tune of the clock chiming the hour. She plunked her feet on the floor and pushed herself to her feet. "And I've had enough of this lazing around. Nora, dear one, where are you? And those precious children of yours." She set her cup in the sink, covered the bread, and pushed the coffeepot to the side of the stove.

She lifted her coat from the hook on the rack and stepped outside to a glorious day of sun that warmed her cheeks. A fall-nipped breeze lifted the golden tendrils curling about her face. *Maybe today will be the day,* she thought, *the day my curly haired man will come riding up the lane.* She stared up the empty lane with two lines of hard-packed soil the width of wagon wheels. A line of grass grew in the middle.

"Clara, down here." Nora waved from the low building to the side of the barn.

Shrugging off the dream, Clara waved back and, leaping from the porch, trotted down the path. The windmill creaked its song and, when she looked up, she saw a *V* of geese heading south, adding their wild cries to the plaintive notes of the windmill.

"You can carry the eggs," Nora said, her smile wide and eyes dancing, "or Peder." She motioned to the baby slung in a scarf and riding on her hip.

Kaaren, finger in her mouth, peeked from behind Nora's dark wool skirt. Her coffee-colored hat had tilted slightly to the side, nearly hiding one blue eye.

Clara squatted down, eye level with the shy little girl, and crossed her arms on her knees. "I'm your Auntie Clara, remember?"

Kaaren nodded, her finger stuck firmly in place.

Clara itched to reach out and straighten the hat, but she could remember being the shy one. "Maybe you could show me the cows and horses."

"Pa's cows." The finger left her mouth and pointed off to the barn. "Horses gone."

"Shall we go see?" Clara raised back to her feet and extended a hand.

Kaaren studied the hand and then looked up at Nora, as if asking approval. Nora nodded.

Kaaren reached out and slipped her hand in Clara's. When they started off, she hung back. "Ma come, too?"

Nora shook her head, her smile a benediction. She adjusted the baby's sling and picked up the basket of eggs. "You two go on. We'll have coffee when you come up to the house."

"I'll take those." Clara nodded at the egg basket. "After we see the cows."

Nora shook her head and started up the path.

Hand in hand, Clara and Kaaren meandered from the watering trough where the cows stood head to swishing tail, to the pen where the big black-and-white sow came to beg for bits of grass, to the corral where the work team dozed in the sun.

"Your pa is a good farmer," Clara said, admiring the tight fences and healthy-looking livestock.

"Pa's gone to town." The finger went back into the little girl's mouth. Kaaren switched from English to German to Norwegian, depending on whatever word she wanted.

"Let's run." Clara tugged on her hand. Together, the two of them dashed up the path, through the gate, and bounded up the porch steps, Clara lifting her by-now-giggling-charge up the three stairs. She swung the little girl up in her arms and whirled her around before hugging her close and kissing her rosy cheek. "You're good enough to eat." Clara nibbled on the squirming little girl's neck.

Laughing and giggling they entered the house and removed their coats. When Clara picked Kaaren up so she could hang up her wrap, the little girl wrapped one arm around her aunt's neck after placing her coat on the hook.

"I see you've made friends." Nora set a plate of cookies on the table. "Wash your hands while I pour the coffee." She shifted the baby in her arm to the other side. He grinned and waved a chubby hand when Clara chucked him under his double chin.

With each holding a child on her lap, the two sisters dunked their cookies in their coffee and smiled at each other across the checkered red-and-white oilcloth table cover.

"I wasn't sure this would ever happen." Nora's look encompassed the entire scene.

"I know." Clara held her coffee cup steady while Kaaren dunked her cookie, too. "If it hadn't been for that letter, who knows how long it would've been?"

"Surely Carl will know who it is when he comes back. He went in to talk with Reverend Moen about having our wedding on Sunday right after services."

"How will you get ready?"

"There's not so much." A pink tinge brightened her cheeks. "Oh, Clara, he—my Carl—he is such a good man. God is surely good to me."

"And to him. Look how you have cared for his children and—"

171

"But he had much sadness."

A silence fell and Clara reached out to cover her sister's hand with her own. "But now there will be much happiness. And I am here to make sure this marriage is done right. This time you will wear your *bunad* and sit for a portrait so we can send one home to Mor and Far."

"And maybe soon we will celebrate a wedding for you."

Clara shook her head. "When we find my mystery man. You don't suppose something has happened to him—"

"Like with my Hans, you mean?"

Clara nodded. "To come so far like you did and your man had just died." She shuddered, as if a goose had just walked across her grave. "I don't know how you—" She shuddered again.

"As Mor says, 'We will give God the glory,' ja?"

"Ja, that we will." She rested her chin on the head of the little one against her breast. *And maybe one day, I'll have lambs like these.* Clara kept the thought in her heart. She had to find her man first.

When Carl returned from town, he shook his head over the picture. "No, I don't know this man, but maybe Reverend Moen will. He knows everyone for six townships."

"Or perhaps Ingeborg will?" Nora finished putting the last of the supper on the table. "Let's eat and you can tell all about your trip at the same time."

After bowing their heads for grace, Nora dished up the plates, set them in front of her family and then she sat down.

Carl turned to her, a twinkle in his eyes. "Reverend Moen said he'd be delighted to remarry us on Sunday since the first one didn't seem to take."

"Carl." Nora blushed and pushed at his arm. "You know that's not the reason."

He covered her hand with his. "So you say. And Ingeborg invited us all for dinner afterward."

"Did you ask her what we could bring?"

Carl nodded. "And she said, 'Just yourselves.' This is to be her wedding gift to us." He took a bite of the pork chop smothered in applesauce on his plate. "Oh." He waved his fork for emphasis. "She said you are not to worry about a thing. New brides have too much on their minds already."

Clara watched the byplay between Carl and Nora. The tint creeping up her sister's neck was most becoming. How pleasant it was to watch someone with the love light shining so brightly in their own eyes, they needn't light the lamps. She felt a lump lodge in her throat.

"Auntie Clara."

"Ja, what is it?" She bent over to listen more closely to the whisper.

"Are you going to stay forever?" Kaaren stared up with eyes dark in the lamplight.

Clara felt the lump melt and begin to burn behind her eyelids. This little girl had already lost more than any child should when her mother died. "I don't know how long forever is, but I plan on being around a long, long time." Her whisper seemed to be just what Kaaren needed to hear as the smile that brightened her face more than matched those exchanged by the two other adults at the table

Kaaren's pigtails bobbed, she nodded so emphatically. "Good."

How long is long, Lord? Clara prayed that night after helping tuck Kaaren into bed and cleaning up the kitchen. Nora had set cooked cornmeal into loaf pans to fry for breakfast and started yeast rising for bread baking. How different it was watching her sister do the things their mother had always done. *Am I ready, Father?* Her prayer continued. *I know Your hand has been leading me, but now ...what has happened?* She shoved the niggling worries down and slammed a door on them. God wouldn't have brought her all the way to America without a purpose in mind. Would He?

But doubting was a sin. . .wasn't it? He did bring her. . . didn't He?

The thought of the man with curly hair flashed across her mind. Along with her mother's admonition, "Handsome is as handsome does." Clara had never understood what that meant.

The man was certainly handsome—wherever he was. Whoever he was. What should she do with the doubts? "Father, forgive me. Help me believe…and trust."

Chapter 3

In the name of the Father, and of the Son, and of the Holy Spirit, I now pronounce you man and wife." Reverend Moen closed his prayer book and nodded at the two standing before him. "Carl, you may kiss your bride." In an undertone, only for the ears of those four closest, he added, "Again."

Clara bit back a giggle. She could tell Carl and Nora had some ribbing in store for them since they had asked to be married a second time. But the teasing was such fun with the Moens.

The organ struck up the recessional. Clara handed her sister the white leather Bible with a small spray of gold and rust chrysanthemums on the top. Nora, clad in her black *skyjørt,* red vest, and white *forkle,* looked the perfect Norwegian bride even if she wasn't wearing the formal bridal headdress.

Clara reached up to kiss her sister's cheek. "God bless." She needed to wipe her eyes, but her handkerchief lay in her bag, wherever that was. How come she always cried at weddings? It wasn't as if this were a sad occasion. She turned and followed Carl and Nora down the aisle.

Some members of the congregation had elected to remain to help wish the newlyweds God's blessing. Clara found herself searching the faces for a certain curly haired man, but she hadn't found him by the time they all exited the sanctuary.

She hugged her sister again. "Oh, if only Mor and Far could

have been here." Clara felt herself choke up again on the words. She wiped a tear from the corner of her eye.

"I know," Nora whispered back, "but at least you were here."

The pastor's wife, Ingeborg Moen, a baby in each arm and the other children clustered about her like chicks with a hen, herded her brood to the door.

"Here, let me take Peder." Clara reached out for the sleeping baby. She took the quilt-wrapped bundle carefully in her arms and, at the babe's whimper, slipped into the swaying motion common to women everywhere. She watched as Carl and Nora greeted the people around them.

"Such a wonderful story and with a happy ending," Ingeborg sighed at Clara's elbow. "Your sister is a fine woman. She has made Carl to laugh again."

"She never told us much about those early months." Clara patted Peder's back when he began squirming. "We had to read between the lines, more what she didn't say than what she did."

"It wasn't easy. Peder was colicky, Carl wanted her to speak only English, and who was there to teach her and Kaaren, poor mite, who missed her mother so bad. I tell you, those two earned their happiness."

Peder ignored the comforting sway and added his opinion to the discussion. As with all babies, his idea of communication after the first subtle whimpers that had been ignored was a full-throated howl.

"Shush, shush." Clara jiggled harder.

The baby yelled—louder.

Clara looked around the room for the baby's mother. "They've gone into the office to sign the marriage certificate. Come." Ingeborg nodded to the outer door. "Let's take these two young ones home and feed them. And I have a marvelous idea." She picked up the conversation again after they'd corralled the older children running around outside and started down the street.

"Why don't you and the children stay with John and me tonight? Carl and Nora deserve to have a night alone, don't you think?"

"Why...why, I'm sure that is a fine idea, but do you have room?"

"Oh, there's always room for one more."

"Ja, but this is three and one of us isn't always the best company." She glanced at the baby whimpering in her arms.

"Did Nora tell you that I helped nurse Peder there for a few days?" Clara shook her head. "So that baby and I were pretty close for a time. We'd love to have him back, and you can see how much Kaaren loves to be with Mary. You can have the same bed Nora used when she first came."

"If Carl and Nora agree, who am I to argue?" Clara now knew what it must be like to be pushed along like a leaf on a spring freshet. How could you turn down a person who made everything look as if you were doing her a favor? And besides, who wouldn't want to be alone the first night? She felt a warmth creep up her neck. At least that's what folks said about newlyweds.

Clara didn't have time to think about the picture she had tucked away in her bag until after she and Ingeborg had kissed the children good night and listened to their prayers.

"What a wonderful day." She sank into one of the rocking chairs in front of the gleaming black-and-silver cookstove.

"Ja, I know those two will be truly happy. And did you see the blush on your sister's neck when we told her about you and the children staying here?" Ingeborg set the chair on its creaking song with the toe of her foot. "Oh, to be so young again and beginning a life together."

Clara felt a tug in the region of her heart. She'd already pinpointed those twinges she'd identified as jealousy. Where was the man who had sent for her?

"I have something to show you." She leaned over and picked up her bag from the floor by the chair. She'd brought it back into the kitchen with her after kissing Kaaren one last time. Surely Ingeborg would know who this curly haired dream man was.

With trembling fingers she opened the mouth of the black leather bag and pulled out the picture. "Here." She extended her hand across the space and handed the picture to Ingeborg. Why did her breath catch in her throat and her stomach feel like cream being tossed in a churn?

Ingeborg smiled her comforting smile and glanced down at the picture. "Ja, he is a fine looking man." She looked over at Clara with a question in her eyes. "Who is he?"

The churning in her midsection clumped together and fell to her toes. "I thought maybe you would know. This is the man who bought my ticket to America. He thinks he is getting a Norwegian wife, but I've been waiting. He never appears."

"Oh, my." Ingeborg patted Clara's hand where it strangled the wooden arm of the rocker. She studied the portrait again, all the while shaking her head. "Oh, my dear, I wish I had good news for you." She paused. "But maybe John knows this man. I'll go ask him."

Clara leaned her head against the back of the rocker and let her eyes close after Ingeborg left the room. The memory of her mother's voice calmed her rampaging thoughts. Prayer was Mors answer to anything and everything. *But Mor,* she wanted to plead, *it's been four days and I haven't heard from him.* Like the kiss of butterfly wings, her mother's voice reminded, *Pray for him.*

"That's not so easy," Clara muttered. "I don't know his name or anything about him." She could feel a smile tickle the sides of her mouth. But oh, he was beautiful.

She opened her eyes when she heard Ingeborg in the doorway. What was the look she caught on the woman's face? It had been so fleeting. Was it—no—she didn't get a chance to think about it again.

"John thinks the man looks familiar but...ahh...he isn't...he can't say he knows him either." She stuttered in an uncharacteristic fashion.

Doubts crowded into Clara's mind again. "Is there something wrong? Something you're not telling me?" She leaned forward in the chair, her hands clamped together in her lap. "Ingeborg, what is it?"

"Nothing, nothing at all. We. . .uh, John and I, we'll ask around." She turned to move the coffeepot over the hotter part of the stove. "John said he'll be in for a cup of coffee in a minute and then you can tell him the entire story." She crossed to the cupboard and took down the coffee cups.

Clara commanded that her hands unclench themselves while she took in a deep breath and let it out slowly. There was something they weren't telling her. There was. She could sense it.

But later when the three of them had taken their places at the table and munched crisp molasses cookies with their coffee, the feeling left. She told the entire story from the moment she first saw the water-stained and smudged envelope until the present.

"And you haven't seen anyone that looks like this man since you arrived?" Reverend Moen leaned forward in his chair.

"No. And not heard one word. It's as if he fell off the face of the earth." Clara took a sip of now-cool coffee to quell the dryness in her throat. "Each day I think now this will be the time he comes forward but—" She raised her hands, palms up in a gesture of resignation. She looked from the pastor to his wife. "He doesn't come."

Reverend Moen rubbed the bridge of his nose with one long finger. He nodded and looked up at her. "We shall see. We shall see.

That night in bed, Clara listened to the sounds of the house creaking and settling for the night. So far the only men she'd met in this new country had been Carl, Reverend Moen, and that blacksmith who carted her out to the Detschman farm. And none of them looked anything like the man in her picture.

A week later, when the weather dropped below freezing and hovered there even during the day, Carl announced they would begin butchering the next morning. All the young hogs were fattened and ready.

"Dag will be bringing out his scalding tank and helping me dip and scrape. I thought we'd give a side to the Moens." He glanced at Clara sitting at the other end of the table. "You ever raised pigs and butchered them?"

"Of course. Far and the boys did most of the work, but I can grind sausage with the best of them. And headcheese." She nodded her head. "Mor taught us how to season it just right." She looked at Nora for confirmation.

"And the hams." Nora joined her sister in the memory. "But where will we get the hickory for flavor?"

"Don't you worry." Carl patted his wife's shoulder as he rose to go back outside. "We know how to smoke the bacon here in North Dakota, too. You just get all the knives sharpened and the pans ready."

"Selling the meat will surely help buy feed for the winter." Nora cleared the table after he left. "Those grasshoppers ate nearly everything. Clara, I've never seen anything like it. So many they blotted out the sun. Only the root crops lived through it. Thank the good Lord the rains came and the grass grew again so the cows could pasture. And the hay was already in the barn."

Clara shuddered. Insects had never been her favorite friends. "Does that happen often?"

"I hope not."

Clara was still brushing her hair the next morning by lamplight when she heard the dog barking and horse harnesses jingling. She could see her breath in the room, the night had turned so cold. As Carl had said, perfect butchering weather. A twinge of sorrow for the animals about to lose their lives crossed her mind. But at least here she hadn't cared for them for months and played with the babies when they were tiny.

She braided her hair in back and coiled it in a bun at the nape of her neck. Wearing her worst dress covered with a huge apron, she felt ready for the day.

"You remember Dag Weinlander," Carl said when he brought the men in for coffee before beginning. "And this is Will, his helper." Carl introduced two other men. Clara nodded to each, secretly studying each face in case it matched her picture. She didn't bother to look too carefully at the blacksmith. It was obvious he hadn't washed since their first meeting. She wrinkled her nose and tended to pull away when she refilled his coffee cup.

"Mange takk." Dag's deep voice surprised her.

"Ja." She responded automatically. The man could speak. She flinched inwardly. She could just hear her mother scolding her for thinking unkind thoughts about another of God's children. As she passed around the table with the coffeepot, she glanced up to catch him watching her. He ducked his head when he caught her eye.

The same thing happened at dinner. This time Clara could feel the heat rise on her neck. She shrugged off the feeling and headed back to the stove for another bowl of chicken and dumplings. She must be imagining things. But his voice stayed with her, even if the only exchange had been the polite "Thank you" and "You're welcome."

By the time she'd served the fresh fried liver for supper, Clara didn't care if she never saw a pig again. Or smelled the odors of blood and fresh meat. She and Nora had washed all the intestines to ready them for sausage casings and set both the shoulder and hindquarters to soak in brine before they could be smoked. They would have to grind the fat and begin rendering it out for lard the next day. And steam the krub, sausage made of ground potatoes and the fresh blood. They'd serve that for dinner as a special treat.

"Come, little one," Clara lifted Kaaren onto her lap when she and Nora collapsed into the twin rocking chairs. Nora held the bottle for the nearly sleeping baby Peder. "You've been such a good girl today," Clara said as she snuggled the nightgown-clad child close.

"Pa made me a ball."

"Ja. That old pig bladder has a new use now." Clara looked to her sister, glad she didn't have to remind Nora of all the fun they'd had with pig bladders after butchering time. Her return smile said it all.

Kaaren leaned her head against Clara's shoulder. A yawn started with Kaaren and traveled from mouth to mouth to mouth. The little girl giggled as she yawned again. "Mr. Weinlander is a nice man."

Clara stopped rocking and stared down at the little one in her lap with eyes drooping shut. Where had that come from?

"He threw my ball." The words spaced out as sleep overcame her.

What kind of a man is he? Clara thought as she snuggled down in the flannel sheets in her bed a few minutes later. She didn't have time to dwell on it or even say brief prayers before sleep closed her eyes like it had Kaaren's.

"Clara, I can't tell you how grateful I am for all your help," Nora murmured two nights later after they'd collapsed into the rockers again. The children were already in bed and the two sisters were enjoying a last cup of coffee and the quiet of a sleeping house.

"Ja, it's been good." Clara lifted the cup to her lips and inhaled the rich aroma. "How come it was easier at home?"

"More of us and we had Mor to run things." Nora shrugged her shoulders up to her ears and rotated her neck from side to side. "And there were no little ones to help us the last few years."

"That is true." Clara pushed herself to her feet and went to open the oven door. She pulled a pan of browning ground lard forward and, with a large spoon, began skimming the melted fat off and pouring it into the bread pans. When she'd dipped all she could, she picked off a piece of the crispy remainder and popped it into her mouth. "We should make cornbread with some of these cracklings tomorrow."

"That sounds good." The yawn nearly cracked Nora's jaw. "Thank you, again." She pushed herself to her feet. "When all this is over, we'll have to start on English lessons for you." She patted a hand over the next yawn. "Good night. Sweet dreams."

Clara was too tired to even picture the curly haired man, let alone dream.

Nora had just pulled the pan of cornbread from the oven the next afternoon when they heard the dog barking.

Clara parted the starched white curtains to see out the window better. "It's Reverend Moen."

"And Ingeborg?"

"No, by himself." Nora opened the door. "Come in, come in. You're just in time for hot cornbread and coffee."

"Thank you." He turned and shook hands with Carl, who had come from the springhouse. "And thank you for the side of pork." The two men shook hands. "We are truly grateful."

After the flurries of greetings, everyone gathered around the table. Clara cut the cornbread and, after placing the golden squares in bowls, drizzled maple syrup over the tops and passed the treat around the table.

By the time they'd poured the second cups of coffee, most of the news had been shared. Reverend Moen cleared his throat. "While

I appreciate the coffee and the visit, I really had a special purpose in coming out here today." He stopped and looked directly at Clara across the table. "We have an older woman in our congregation who is in need of help...Mrs. Gudrun Norgaard. Her husband died last winter and lately she hasn't been very well herself. She really needs someone to live with her all the time." He paused.

Clara could hear the kettle hissing on the stove.

"I thought of you, Clara. Would you be willing to move into town and help take care of Mrs. Norgaard?"

Chapter 4

Does she speak Norwegian?" Clara's voice squeaked on the last word. Reverend Moen smiled and nodded. "Yes, and English and even some German. Her husband used to be the banker in town and, besides having an abundance of guests, they traveled."

"What will Clara be doing?" Nora asked. When she looked up from studying her coffee cup, the sheen of tears hovered in her eyes.

"She'll be companion, maid, and sometimes help the cook, who is also the housekeeper. Mrs. Norgaard has spent much of her time in bed lately, but the doctor feels someone young and lively will help her regain her strength." Reverend Moen smiled again at Clara. "I think our God provided the perfect person in you."

"But...but—" Clara clamped her lips together. *God, why?* she pleaded within her heart and mind. *This isn't what I thought You planned for me. I'm supposed to be getting married and...and.* She sent pleading looks to Nora, then Carl, and finally to Reverend Moen.

"How soon do you need to know her decision?" Nora sat up straight in her chair.

"Mrs. Norgaard needs someone immediately since Mrs. Hanson, the cook, has to go home to care for her mother for a time. That was one reason I thought of Clara. I . . .we. . . were hoping you could return to town with me. I'm sure Carl would bring the remainder of your things when they come to church on Sunday."

"Yes, of course." Carl nodded as he spoke. "Nora, you would help her to get ready?"

Just a minute, Clara wanted to pound her fist on the table and make the dishes rattle. *You're deciding my life. I want to make my own decisions.* She bit off the thoughts before they could become full-blown words.

Reverend Moen leaned his elbows on the table and tented his fingertips. The silence in the room was broken only by the mewing of the cat at the door to go out.

Clara knew what an animal in the circus must feel like with everyone staring at it. She scrubbed the front of her teeth with the tip of her tongue.

"I don't want Auntie Clara to leave. I needs her here with me." Kaaren slipped from her mother's lap and ran around the table to cling to Clara's skirt.

Clara bent over and laid her cheek on the little girl's head. "I won't be very far away and I'm sure Mrs. Norgaard would love to have you come visit." Clara felt her stomach drop down around her knees. The decision was made. She'd just said so. She gave Kaaren an extra hug and, planting her hands on the table, pushed herself to her feet. "I'll be ready whenever you need me to be."

"It's not like you'll be across the ocean or some such," Nora reminded them both as she helped Clara gather her things and pack them in the well-worn carpetbag.

"I know." Clara removed her gray Sunday dress from the nail on the wall.

"And maybe by living in town, your young man will find you more easily."

And maybe not, Clara thought as she looked around the room for anything she'd forgotten.

"Just think, you'll be closer to Ingeborg. Why, you could run over to see her anytime you'd like."

Clara hefted the bag and marched out the door. Why did she feel like the red caboose being towed along by the steaming engine whether it wanted to or not? She shook her head at the thought. She had made the final decision——hadn't she?

After one more neck-wrenching hug from Kaaren, Clara allowed Reverend Moen to assist her into his buggy. She waved good-bye as he guided the horse in a circle to turn the buggy around and trot out the lane. When her heart wanted to send a plea heavenward, she stopped it. Right now she didn't want to talk with Him. Miffed was the word that came to mind. Could one be miffed at God? She resolutely closed her ears to the sound of her mother's admonishing voice.

Clara could feel Reverend Moen watching her in between guiding the trotting horse. She let herself relax against the back of the seat as he began whistling. When she recognized the tune, she sneaked a peak at the man beside her. Yes, the courage of "Onward Christian Soldiers" was what she needed right now.

"Why are you worried?" His voice was gentle, like the sun warming her shoulders.

"I...I've never cared for someone who is sick before. Or who lives in a grand house." She took in a deep breath and let it out in a sigh.

"You'll do just fine or I wouldn't have asked."

Clara fingered the corner of her picture through the fabric of her bag. Did she dare ask him if he'd remembered who the picture reminded him of? If he'd remembered, wouldn't he have told her? And anyway, if the man hadn't come forward by now, did she really want to know him?

Clara rubbed the spot between her eyebrows where frown lines showed. Her mother said lines like that showed one didn't trust God with everything. But it's hard to trust when things aren't going the way you thought they should. Clara continued listening to the arguing and questioning in her mind.

The raucous call of a crow from a willow by the creek caught her attention. He didn't sound too happy with his life right now, either. He flew off, black wings glistening in the sun.

Up ahead, Clara could see the outskirts of Soldahl. The lonely whistle from the westbound train floated back on the breeze. Smoke from the engine smudged the faded blue sky. Clara shivered as the late afternoon breeze warned them of the coming frost. Would she be lonely and cold like the crow and the train?

Reverend Moen turned his horse into the lane of a two-story square house surrounded by pillared porches. A leaf from one of the two sentinel elm trees floated down as he pulled the animal to a halt amid a rustling of leaves already hiding the ground.

Clara stared at the windows, all curtained or draped. The place was big, like a palace, and beautiful with its white paint and dark shutters. But it certainly needed a bit of life; everything seemed so quiet.

"You ready?" Reverend Moen broke her concentration. "You know, if you really are unhappy here after trying it for a time, we'll find someone else."

Clara nodded. She took in a deep breath and let it out, while stretching her mouth into a smile. She clamped her teeth to stop the quiver in her chin. She squared her shoulders after Reverend Moen helped her alight. Maybe that way she'd feel more like one of those soldiers he'd been whistling about.

The woman who met them at the door must have been born smiling. "Come in, come in." She held open the dark oak door set with fancy cut glass. "I'm Mrs. Hanson and I know you're Clara. Reverend Moen, she's all you said she would be. You just come right on in here and..."

Clara felt like she'd been swamped by a wave of words and was being washed out to sea. At the same time, she caught her breath at the richness of the dark woods on the floor and walls, the carved stairs curving off to the left, and the fire crackling and snapping in the fireplace. A real fire, with wood, not the glow of coal.

"I thought a fire would make all of us feel better, so now you just sit down and make yourselves comfortable. Mrs. Norgaard, bless her heart, is taking a nap, she sleeps so poorly at night you know, and she told me to make you feel right to home. Now I have the coffee almost ready and after Reverend Moen brings the rest of your things in, we'll just have a bite."

Clara nodded and did just what she was told. She didn't have to worry about what to say because the woman never took a breath. She felt a bubble of laughter rising like warm yeast down about her middle. All her worry and fears of the housekeeper's not liking her, all gone to waste.

And after she met Mrs. Norgaard, Clara's remaining fears took off like the crow they'd seen on the drive in. Even propped by pillows, the frail woman lay dwarfed by the carved, four-poster bed. A lace-trimmed cap covered yellowed gray hair and her eyes mirrored the sorrow she'd lived. The smile that nearly appeared flitted away before it could dimple the sunken cheeks.

"Thank you for coming so quickly."

Clara had to bend close to hear the words. "You are welcome. I hope that I can be of help to you."

"Mrs. Hanson has to leave in the morning, so she'll show you where everything is."

Clara nodded.

Reverend Moen stepped up to the side of the bed. "I must be going now. I'll stop by tomorrow or Ingeborg will."

"Thank you." She sank back against her pillows as if the brief exchange had been too much.

Clara followed the reverend out the door. "Is she really so sick?"

"At heart. And when the heart is heavy, the body gets too tired to continue. She feels she has nothing left to live for and that she'd rather join her husband in heaven."

"But...but, how can I help her?"

"Ask our heavenly Father, He'll tell you." Reverend Moen settled his hat back on his head. "Bless you." And with that he shut the door behind himself and went whistling down the walk.

The tune stayed in her mind. But who said she wanted to be a soldier anyway?

Clara trailed her fingers up the splendidly polished banister as she climbed the stairs. Her room was just across the hall from Mrs. Norgaard's, and she paused at the door before turning back to check on her new charge. She tapped lightly and entered the dim room.

The first thing I'd like to do, she thought, *is open those draperies and let the sun shine in. And get her sitting up in the chair in front of the window so she can watch the glorious leaves drifting down.* Did they have squirrels in North Dakota? Surely they must.

"Is there anything I can get for you?" she asked gently.

"No, no thank you."

Clara waited by the bed. The silence matched the dimness of hue.

"You can go settle into your room. I'd like to sleep again."

Clara struggled with the faint order. She'd been hired to care for this poor sick woman. *God, what do You want me to do? How can I help her the best?* She waited, hoping against hope that God wouldn't mess this one up like He had her marrying the young man in the picture.

Instead of God's voice, she heard her mother's. "A merry heart doeth good like a medicine." Clara knew it was a quote from somewhere in the Scriptures, probably Proverbs. How was that supposed to help her?

"I will lift up mine eyes unto the hills, from whence cometh my help." Well, so much for that one, Psalm 121. The last hills she'd seen were just out of New York. Her mind's eye flitted to the mountains of Norway, the glistening peaks, and the granite faces. The wind singing through the pine trees. Now, those were hills worthy of lifting up one's eyes.

"Are you still here?" The faint voice was painted in querulous tones now.

"Yes, ma'am."

"What are you doing?"

"Praying, I think."

"Well, pray then that I may go home soon."

Clara thought of the hills and the strength they always gave her. "No, I think not." She turned around and strode to the tall windows, draped in a dusky rose velvet. With determined hands she pushed back the heavy lengths of fabric and then the sheer cream panels, tying both back with the cords at the sides. After checking the latches, she bent over and pulled up the sash.

"What are you doing? Young woman, ah..."

"The name is Clara, Clara Johanson, and I'm letting in what little is left of today's sun and fresh air."

"I...I'll freeze. It's November, you know." The voice sounded stronger already.

"Now, why don't I help you over here so you can see out? And while you sit in the chair here, I'll straighten your bed and—"

"No, this is the height of foolishness. I'm ringing for Mrs. Hanson and she'll tell you what I can and cannot do." Mrs. Norgaard leaned over and pulled on a cord beside her bed.

"Good, then she'll help me help you." Clara closed the window again and strode back to the bed. "Why don't we have her bring a tray with coffee and cookies on it at the same time. How do we go about telling her what we want?"

Mrs. Norgaard flopped back against her pillows, her hand pressed to her chest. "We want?" The words ended on a squeak.

"Mrs. Norgaard!" Mrs. Hanson stopped in the doorway. She stared from the windows to Clara and then to the woman in the bed. A smile started, immediately hidden by the clenching of her lips. Her eyes refused to match her mouth and, instead, danced with delight.

"We'd like coffee and maybe something sweet, if you have it." Clara clamped her hands together. Was she understanding Mrs. Hanson right? "But if you could help me move Mrs. Norgaard to the chair first?" She nodded at the dainty upholstered chair by the low table. "We'll turn the chairs so we can watch the trees and the sunset." Clara suited her actions to her words.

"That sounds wonderful." Mrs. Hanson bent over the bed. "Up we go, my dear."

"But, but, I...I—" Mrs. Norgaard found herself ensconced in the chair with a blanket over her knees and a shawl around her shoulders before she could so much as fluster.

"A tray will be right up." Mrs. Hanson left the room with a wink to Clara.

"I am so grateful you speak Norwegian," Clara said as she straightened the blanket and tucked it around Mrs. Norgaard's feet. "Now, is there anything I can get for you before I make up the bed?"

The little woman shook her head, her chin set at a pugnacious angle. The lace on her cap fluttered in the motion.

Lord, I sure hope I'm doing the right thing, Clara thought as she pulled off the covers and stripped off the sheets. Only the sounds of her actions rustled the silence of the room. The thought of Reverend Moen's whistling made her smile. What would happen if she began whistling? She knew how. Even though well-brought-up young ladies did not whistle. She sighed. Whistling was out for now.

But the tune wasn't. Her mind fit the words with the melody. "Onward Christian soldiers, marching as to war..." Was this really a war going on here? She shook her head. No, only a skirmish—and she knew who the winner would be.

"Where do you keep the clean sheets?"

"In the linen closet. You'll find it on your left in the hall." Mrs. Norgaard shifted in her chair. "Before you do that, could you please bring me that footstool? If it would be no trouble."

Clara did as asked and tucked in the blanket again. "I'll be quick."

"No hurry, I. . .ah, see the sun through the reds and golds of the tree leaves." She snapped her mouth shut as if afraid she'd said too much.

Clara put a clamp on her grin and hurried to finish her chore.

While the coffee time passed quickly, it wasn't because of the inspiring conversation. Mrs. Hanson joined them and, unlike her voluble self of the earlier hours, said very little. Her bright eyes missed nothing however, and her nod clearly expressed approval.

Mrs. Norgaard sipped her coffee and, after taking two bites of cake, crumbled the sliver of pound cake into her napkin. When she leaned her head against the back of her chair and let her eyes droop closed, Clara took pity on her.

"Here, ma'am, let's put you back to bed." She set the cup and saucer on the tray and clasped the older woman's delicate hands. Together, she and Mrs. Hanson helped Mrs. Norgaard back to bed.

She sighed as the covers were smoothed over her. "That did feel good. Thank you."

"I'll let you rest now. Dinner won't be for another hour or so." Mrs. Hanson paused at the doorway. "Would you like yours up here on a tray, too, or would you come down?"

Clara shrugged in consternation. "What is best?"

"We have much to go over."

"Ja, that is right."

A deep sigh came from the vicinity of the bed.

The two women looked at each other, over at the bed, and then, covering their mouths with their hands, tiptoed out.

"Come down as soon as you've settled yourself in your room." Mrs. Hanson patted Clara's arm. "You'll do real well with her."

Clara opened the door to her room and immediately crossed to the windows to open the draperies. Why did everyone like it so dark in this house? She stood at the window, gazing at the long yard fronted by the street. Two young girls walked by, swinging empty lard pails that had contained their lunch. The sun was slipping downward as if in a hurry to get to bed.

Clara turned from the window and surveyed her new home. A canopied bed piled high with lace pillows and a crocheted spread took her breath away. Never had she slept in anything so grand. A lace-skirted dressing table with a triple mirror reflected the fading sunlight, and, on the opposite wall, a tall armoire stood open to receive her few clothes. Clara sank down on the edge of the bed. All this for her?

She traced the intricate pattern in the spread with one finger. The rose-colored coverlet underneath set the design off to perfection. She glanced up to catch her reflection in the mirror. Was that really Clara Johanson she saw and not some young woman born to all this wealth and beauty? She felt like pinching herself to make sure she wasn't dreaming.

"Speaking of dreaming, girl, you need to go downstairs and learn all you can before tomorrow, when this house and that woman in there all become your responsibility." She spoke sternly, but the girl in the mirror couldn't resist a wink.

By the time she returned to the haven of her room, she'd followed Mrs. Hanson through the entire house, learned where all the food was stored, how to stoke the cellar furnace with coal, the location of all the cleaning supplies, and tried to memorize a list of all Mrs. Norgaard's likes and dislikes. The recipe books were all in English, as were the books in the library. She needn't worry about the laundry or the deep cleaning because Mrs. Hanson expected to be back in a week or two at the most.

"Just keep doing what you started," Mrs. Hanson said as she puffed her way back up the stairs. "I've settled her for the night and she has a bell by her bed to call you with since the bell pull only rings downstairs. If you need anything fixed, we always ask Dag, the blacksmith, and anything else, Reverend Moen will help." She put a finger to her bottom lip. "I can't think of anything else—oh, the doctor is two streets over and one back. We have an account at Lars Mercantile for groceries and what else."

Clara felt like her head was spinning. What in the world had she gotten herself into—correction—what had she been gotten into?

"I'll be leaving right after breakfast, so you get a good night's sleep now." Mrs. Hanson opened the door to Clara's room and, after lighting the lamp by the door, stepped back. "Good night, my dear, and God bless."

"And you." Clara staggered across the room and collapsed on her bed. No wonder people with grand big houses hired others to work for them. The thought of all the dusting to be done made her shudder. She hefted her carpetbag onto the bed and removed her few garments, hanging some in the armoire and laying others in the drawers. She placed her Bible on the stand by her bed next to the lamp and her brushes on the dressing table. By the time she changed into a flannel nightgown and brushed her hair one hundred strokes, she could feel her eyelids drooping. She sank to her knees and leaned her elbows on the spread.

"Father in heaven," she paused, waiting for the right words to come. "Thank You for this day.' She paused again. "I guess." She shook her head, her thumbs rubbing into her eyes. "Mor says to thank You for everything and while that doesn't seem to make much sense to me, I know Your word says that also. So thank You for Mrs. Norgaard and my new home and position in this beautiful house." She huffed out her breath. "And thank You that we haven't found my young man yet." She shook her head again. "Forgive me for not being very thankful. Amen." She started to rise and sank back down. "Amen—again."

She blew out the lamp and climbed under the covers. Hands crossed on her chest, she stared at the canopy over her head. She thought back to the way she'd taken over in Mrs. Norgaard's room, ordering her around like that. *Clara, I can't believe that was you,* she told herself. Maybe God had a hand in it after all. She fell asleep with that thought in her mind.

A jangling snatched her back from the deep well of sleep.

Chapter 5

Where was she? The jangling came again. Clara sat up in bed and threw back the covers. Mrs. Norgaard—the bell—was something wrong? She fumbled for the flint to light the candle then slid her feet into waiting slippers. Light in hand, she crossed the room and opened her door. The bell came again.

"Mrs. Norgaard, are you all right?" She knocked and opened the door almost in the same motion. Moonlight streamed in the windows, painting branch shadows on the floor.

"Please, I have to use the chamber pot. I'm afraid I might fall."

"Yes, of course." Clara set the candle and holder down on the table beside the bed, along with the weight of fear she'd shouldered with the bell jangle. Such a simple task and yet so important.

After she had Mrs. Norgaard tucked back in bed, Clara clasped the hand that lay on top of the coverlet. Gently she stroked the papery skin that stretched over bones so light as to be air-filled. "Is there anything else I can do for you?"

"You might sing again. You have a lovely voice—so long since there's been any singing in this house." The words came slowly as if with great effort.

Clara closed her eyes and began to sing, "Beautiful Savior, King of creation, Son of God and Son of man…" When she finished the second verse, she picked up her candle and, leaving the door open a crack, made her way back to her own room. With both doors open, she would hear the summons more quickly.

This time when she crawled back into the bed, she, too, felt blessed by the music. She thought of all the years her Mor had sung her children to sleep just like this. Who'd have thought these songs of her childhood would play an important part in her life now?

By the time Mrs. Hanson left for her train in the morning, Clara was feeling like the train had run over her, or at least dragged her down the track. Mrs. Norgaard showed her restlessness by ringing her bell or pulling the cord every few minutes with something she either needed or wanted to tell Mrs. Hanson. The stairs were looking higher and higher with each trip.

"This is a good thing." Mrs. Hanson nodded up the stairs just before she left the house. "Herself is at least taking an interest in life again." She patted Clara's cheek. "I knew the minute I saw you, you'd be just what she needed. Now remember, I'll be back for the laundry and such. You spend as much time with Mrs. Norgaard as she allows." Her eyes twinkled. "Rather as much as you can talk her into."

Clara nodded. "I hope your mother will be well soon." She waved and then leaned her back against the door after closing it. "Because I wish you were back here already."

The bell tinkled from the second door on the right—upstairs.

"Coming." Clara checked her appearance in the long mirror over a carved walnut table in the hall. She smoothed one side back and reset the comb that held her wavy golden hair up and off her face. After fluffing the tendrils of hair that insisted on curling over her forehead and wrinkling her nose at the image in the mirror, she trotted up the stairs.

"Ma'am." Clara stepped to the side of the bed.

Mrs. Norgaard opened her eyes as if the effort were beyond her strength. "Is Mrs. Hanson on her way?"

"Ja and none too soon. It is a good thing we are not too far from the station."

"Could you help me sit up against my pillows?"

"I can do better than that." Clara crossed the room and picked up the oval-backed chair to bring it back by the bed. "Let's get you up in this while I freshen your bed. You must have a wrapper around here somewhere." She checked all the usual places—foot of the bed, coat tree, under the covers—and finally stepped to the carved walnut armoire and opened the doors.

The scent of lavender wafted out. Clara sniffed appreciatively and studied the garments hanging in front of her. Morning dresses, shirtwaists, bombazine skirts, all in rich fabrics and jewel colors. She reached out to stroke the sleeve of a sable fur jacket. Such luxury. Resisting the urge to lay her cheek against the sleek garment, she turned instead to the hooks on the door. Both shawl and wool robe hung there, plain hens among peacocks.

"Here, now." She carried the robe to the bed and smiled down at her charge. "Once you are sitting up, I could brush your hair for you. That was always a treat for me, when my older sister would brush my hair."

Mrs. Norgaard nodded and eased over to the side of the bed. Clara helped her sit upright and snuggled the robe around the thin shoulders. Once situated in the chair, the woman sat up straight, obeying the dictates of a lifetime.

Clara picked up the hairbrush from the dressing table and, after removing the cap and pins, began drawing it through the limp strands. She smiled when she heard a sigh of appreciation. "That does feel good, doesn't it?" She continued the long, even strokes. "Perhaps tomorrow I could wash it for you. Mrs. Hanson said you were about due for a bath. Think how wonderful soaking in the tub would feel." She leaned forward to peek around the woman's shoulder. Mrs. Norgaard's eyes were closed but a slight smile hovered at the corners of her mouth.

Clara felt like she'd just been given a gift. *In for a penny, in for a pound,* she thought, quoting one of her mother's often-used maxims. "I know you've had a great sorrow in your life. Tell me about your husband, Mr. Norgaard. What was he like? How did you meet?"

Clara waited. Maybe she should have kept her mouth shut? *God, please keep me from saying or doing the wrong things. I so want to help.*

"He was such a handsome young man, my Einer. I lived in Minneapolis with my parents and this young man came to work at the bank there. My father owned a store and he frequently sent me to the bank for him since I helped him with the accounts and behind the counter when he needed me."

Clara kept up the soothing motions. "So you met him at the bank?"

"No, I saw him at the bank. But we weren't introduced until church one Sunday." She chuckled softly. "Back then one didn't have the freedom of young folks now. We had to be properly introduced by an outside party. I think he bribed the pastor to introduce us." Only the risp of the brush and gentle breathing disturbed the silence.

"Such a smile he had." She shook her head. "And he was trying to be so proper, to impress my mother and father, you know. They stayed right on either side of me." She tipped her head back so Clara could reach the brow more easily. "Penny novels talked of love at first sight, but I thought they were making that up—until Einer spoke to me." Silence fell again.

Clara peeked around to catch the sight of fat tears rolling down her charge's sunken cheeks. She fashioned the gray strands into a bun and pinned it high on the back of Mrs. Norgaard's head. Then, after placing the brush on the dressing table, she knelt in front of the older woman and covered the trembling thin hands with the warmth of her own.

The tears flowed unchecked. Mrs. Norgaard sat upright, as if her back touching the chair were a mortal sin. Her body remained perfectly still, except for the quivering hands and the coursing tears.

Clara felt like her heart was being torn from her chest. Tears burned at the back of her throat and behind her eyes. *Lord God, have mercy on her. Bring healing for her grief.* She reached into her pocket for a clean handkerchief and gently wiped the tears away.

The clock on the tall dresser struck the hour, eleven chimes. Clara found herself counting them, as if at the end there might be some incident of great import. The last bong faded away.

"I believe I'd like to return to my bed now." Mrs. Norgaard pushed herself upright using the arms of the chair, placed her hand on Clara's arm, and crossed to the bed. Once under the covers, she patted the sides of her hair. "Thank you, child. You were right; that did indeed feel good."

After Clara left the room she wasn't sure if Mrs. Norgaard meant the hair brushing felt good or maybe the talking—and the tears? She hummed the refrain of "Onward Christian Soldiers" all the way down the stairs and into the spotless kitchen. Soon, the whistling teakettle accompanied her.

"What we need in this house is some music," she told the pink geranium hanging in the kitchen window. A black-capped chickadee landed on the tray attached outside the window where Mrs. Hanson left crumbs for the birds. "That's it." Clara spun in place. "A bird to sing. One of those golden canaries like my aunt had. I wonder where you would find one clear out here on the prairie?"

She thought about it as she sliced the bread to toast for dinner. Mrs. Hanson had made a pot of chicken soup before she left, and now it was warming on the monstrous iron stove.

"I'll just have to ask Ingeborg when I can go see her. Nora said Ingeborg knows everything and everyone in Soldahl." She cocked her head at the flower in the window. "I think you better learn to talk or, better yet, sing, because if someone comes they will think I am surely losing my mind." The geranium wisely kept silent.

The peal of the doorbell brought Clara rushing downstairs

again; she had just taken Mrs. Norgaard her dinner. By the time she reached the door, the thing clanged again.

"Uff da," she muttered. "I'm coming." She reached to open the door. A man, face showing florid around a mustache more salt than pepper, all topped by a mashed down fedora, touted a black bag that gave away his identity without a word. "Doctor?"

"Yes, I'm Dr. Harmon." He took off his hat as he stepped across the threshold. "Mrs. Norgaard asleep?"

"No, I just took her dinner up to her." Clara moved back to give the portly man room to enter the hall. "May I take your coat?" She shut the door and, after helping him remove his black wool coat, hung it on the brass tree next to the hall table.

"Good, then I can talk with you first." He walked into the parlor like he'd been here many times before.

"Ah, would you like some coffee?" At his nod, she added, "And have you eaten? I could bring you some chicken soup."

"That sounds wonderful." Instead of sitting in the parlor, he followed her into the kitchen. "Why don't I join you in here? Make it easier for all." Just then the bell pull sounded. "Ah, herself is callin' you. She wants to know who's here, no doubt. You run up and I'll just pour myself a cup of coffee and make myself to home." He suited his actions to his words and pulled out a chair at the round oak table in the corner.

Clara darted a look over her shoulder to make sure he was all right and climbed the stairs. She made a point of not counting how many times she'd been up and down them already today.

"You've hardly touched your soup," Clara said before her patient could respond. "And here it was nice and hot. Mayhap I should bring you another bowl."

Mrs. Norgaard shook her head. "No, I had a bit. Now, who is it that came? I thought I heard Dr. Harmon's voice."

"That's right. He's going to eat downstairs first, then he'll be up. Or—" Eyes narrowed, Clara studied her patient. "Or, he can eat up here with you." She spun out the door. "I'll be right back" She descended the stairs in a swirl of skirts and indecision. Should she take charge here or not? Would the company make Mrs. Norgaard eat better, maybe smile? Let's see, they could move that table from over by the window and put it up against the bed. Then chairs for her and the doctor.

She smacked one fist into the palm of the other hand. She would turn this into a party yet.

Doc Harmon beamed at her, all the while nodding his head while she shared her plan. Together they set two trays with soup in a rose-sprigged tureen, coffee in a silver server, and buttered toast nestled by a pot of jam. Clara included a plate of sour cream sugar cookies for dessert. Like two conspirators in a crime, they set out.

"Good day, Mrs. Norgaard. We've come to share our dinner with you." He set his tray on the dressing table and crossed the room to bring the round table to the bed. "Now, would you rather have a chair or dangle your feet over the edge of the bed. Clara says you've already been up for a while this morning."

Mrs. Norgaard could hardly get a squeak in edgewise.

Just as they had the furniture all rearranged and Mrs. Norgaard moved to her chair, the doorbell pealed again. Clara dashed down the stairs and pulled up at the door, feeling like she was flying apart.

"Reverend Moen." She stepped back and motioned him inside.

"Good day, Clara. How is Mrs. Norgaard today?"

"Would you like to come up and join us for coffee? Or soup? Dr. Harmon and I were just about to eat."

"Coffee, yeh, soup, *nei takk,*" he said as he hung up his coat.

"You go on up. I'll get another cup." Clara dashed off to the kitchen. Talk about having a party.

When she got upstairs, Dr. Harmon had settled his patient in her chair, pulled up two more, and dished up the soup. Clara finished pouring the coffee and asked Reverend Moen to say grace. As the familiar words flowed forth, Clara could feel herself back home in

Norway with her family gathered around the dinner table.

At the "Amen," she looked up to see Mrs. Norgaard reach up with a tentative hand to smooth her already sleek hair.

I'm glad I did her hair this morning, Clara thought. *No woman likes to have company when she feels a sight.*

It was quickly obvious that the two men were good friends who liked to give each other a bad time. And as Clara suspected, her patient forgot her lack of hunger and downed both soup and toast.

By the end of the meal, Clara knew all the latest news of Soldahl. A young boy had fallen out of a tree at recess over at the school and sprained his wrist. His mother threatened to break his arm if he didn't stay out of trees. Doc had agreed with her.

"That young whippersnapper is an accident waiting to happen, not waiting as the case may be." The doctor snorted after telling his story. "He can get into more mischief."

"Isn't he the one who put a mouse in the new teacher's desk drawer?" Reverend Moen asked.

The doctor nodded. "And the frog in the water pail."

Clara squeezed her lips together. It sounded like they were describing her younger brother. Mor had been afraid Lars wouldn't make it to manhood.

"Well, I must be on my way," Dr. Harmon finally said after pulling out his pocket watch and checking the time. "This has been most enjoyable, Mrs. Norgaard. Thank you for your hospitality. How about if I check you over before I leave?"

"And I, too, must be going. Good day, Mrs. Norgaard." Reverend Moen patted her hand. "This has been a real pleasure."

"Thank you for coming." Mrs. Norgaard let the men assist her to her feet and back to the edge of the bed. "Perhaps next time you come, you could bring your daughter, Mary."

"I'll do that. Clara, here, let me help you take these things downstairs." He picked up the larger of the trays and waited while Clara added the bowls and cups to it. Together, they took the trays back to the kitchen.

"Do you need anything?" the reverend asked as he placed his tray on the kitchen table.

Clara shook her head. "No, wait, I mean yes. Do you know anyone who has a canary?"

"A canary?"

"Yes, for sale." Clara set her tray down. "You see, it is so quiet here, not a sound, so I thought the bird would sing and make Mrs. Norgaard feel happier."

"True." Reverend Moen rubbed the bridge of his nose in the gesture that Clara already knew meant he was thinking. "I'll ask Ingeborg." He walked down the front stairs still chuckling about her wanting a yellow bird to sing.

"I think that's a good idea," Dr. Harmon said when Clara asked him about the canary. "Might be just what the doctor ordered—if he'd thought of it." He shrugged into the coat Clara held for him. "Now don't you worry so much about the house and spend your time with her. I'll see you again in a day or so."

Clara leaned against the door after they'd left. She could feel the silence settling back down on the house. The bell tinkled from upstairs.

The next morning she talked Mrs. Norgaard into a bath and hair washing. Each time Clara helped her charge, she asked about Mr. Norgaard and each time Mrs. Norgaard shared a bit more. And each time the tears flowed.

One night after shed helped Mrs. Norgaard to bed, Clara sat on the edge of the mattress to say good night.

"Don't go." The old woman clutched the hand of the younger. The silence settled around them, close and comforting this time, as if in benediction.

"This is the hardest time," Mrs. Norgaard spoke from the dimness. "When the lights are out and all my memories crowd in, piling on top of each other, pushing and shoving until I can't sleep, can't rest." The silence reigned again. "And when I feel so guilty."

"Guilty?"

"Yes, I should have been able to help him more. If only I'd made him stay home and go to bed when he first felt ill." Clara waited. "And if I'd thrown out those awful, smelly cigars, maybe he wouldn't have had a cough to start with." Her voice floated on the stillness, like a leaf kissing the surface of a pond.

Clara stroked the papery hand that lay in hers. *Father,* she prayed while she waited for the voice to come again, *please bring healing to Mrs. Norgaard. Help her to give up the bad feelings. Help her to want to live.* The thoughts seemed to drift heavenward, like smoke rising from a chimney on a still, winter day.

"Einer insisted on going out to that farm with Dr. Harmon. So many people were sick that the well ones did what they could, chores and such. I was helping Mrs. Moen. She collected extra children and housed them until their parents could care for them again. Ah, me. Maybe I was the one who brought the sickness home." Silence again. "We'll never know."

Clara could hear the tears begin to drown out the woman's voice.

"But he was so sick. I was right here beside him. He'd been tossing and turning and finally settled down. I...I thought he was finally resting, so I dozed off myself. When I woke up..."

Clara squeezed her eyes closed, but the tears refused to be swallowed.

"When I woke...he was gone." Deep sobs, the kind that come after being forced back too long, shuddered through her frame, shaking the bed.

Clara gathered the straining body into her arms and held her. What could she say, even if she could talk around the tears that rained down her own cheeks?

Mrs. Norgaard reached for the edge of the sheet to wipe her eyes. "I never—" she choked on the words, "I never said good-bye.

He was gone and I never said good-bye. Did he know how much I loved him?"

Sobs interrupted her words, making them difficult to understand, but Clara murmured soothing noises, whispering the litany of love she'd learned at her mother's knee.

Eventually, hiccups punctuated the silence, and Clara placed a handkerchief in Mrs. Norgaard's hand. After blowing her nose, the now-spent woman lay back on her pillows. She put her hand back in Clara's. "I'm sorry to get you so wet."

"I'll dry."

"Do you think God will forgive me?"

"For what?"

"For being so angry at Him for taking my Einer." She paused. "For wanting to die."

"All you have to do is ask. Mor says He forgives even before we ask, that's what sending His Son to die for us meant. Forgiveness and love that never dies."

"Your mother is a wise woman." Mrs. Norgaard blew her nose again. Her sigh snagged on a leftover sob.

Clara could feel the yawn that caught Mrs. Norgaard and then sneaked up on Clara. She covered her mouth with her hand but still felt the hinges in her jaw creak with the strain.

"Thank you, my dear." Mrs. Norgaard breathed deeply and patted Clara's hand. "You go on to bed now; I'll be just fine." She yawned again. "In fact, I'm almost asleep already."

"I can sit here for a while. There's no hurry."

Clara was about to rise from the bed, thinking her charge almost asleep, when Mrs. Norgaard said with a catch in her voice, "Would you . . . do you know the Twenty-third Psalm?"

"Ja, I do. We memorized that in Sunday school when we were small."

"Would you say it for me?"

Clara closed her eyes and thought of the shepherd with his flock.

"The Lord is my shepherd; I shall not want. He maketh me to lie down in green pastures; he leadeth me beside the still waters..." Her voice caught in the part about the valley but grew stronger again as she came to, "And I will dwell in the house of the Lord for ever."

"Amen."

"Ja, Amen." Clara nodded. When she rose a few minutes later, Mrs. Norgaard was breathing the soft and even rhythm of healing sleep.

"Thank You, thank You, thank You." Gratitude poured forth as Clara blew out the lamps and undressed for bed. Even while her mind sang the praises, her body felt like a garment with all the starch washed out. She was asleep almost before her head touched the pillow.

When Clara walked into Mrs. Norgaard's room with the coffee tray in the morning, Mrs. Norgaard was sitting up against her pillows.

"I want you to go over to Reverend Moen's this morning and ask him to come here." Even her voice was stronger. "Tell him I'm ready now."

Whatever for? Clara wondered, but she only nodded, a smile tickling the corners of her mouth.

Chapter 6

She had a feeling this was more like the real Mrs. Norgaard. The doorbell rang before Clara could finish her duties and get out the door. She answered the chimes, still wiping her hands on her apron.

"Good morning, Clara." Doc Harmon tipped his hat with one hand, the other carrying his black leather bag. "How is our patient this morning?"

"Better, I think." Clara stepped back and motioned him in. "She wants me to go for Reverend Moen."

"Whatever for?" Doc laid his hat on the hall table and brushed a hand over his steel gray hair.

Clara shrugged. "Maybe if you ask her, she'll tell you."

"And maybe she won't. The won't is much more likely." Doc started up the stairs. "Do you by any chance have the coffee hot? I've been out delivering a baby north of town and I could use a pick-me-up."

"Ja, I do. There's bread and some cheese if you'd like." She waited with her hand on the carved ball of the walnut newel post.

"Fine. And after you've brought it up, you can run over to the reverend's. I'll stay and visit that few minutes."

Clara did as asked and, within a few minutes, darted out the front door. It was the first time she'd been out since Reverend Moen brought her here. She drew in a deep breath of air redolent of burning leaves and crisp fall weather. As she kicked her way through the leaves blanketing the ground she looked up through the naked tree branches stretching to the lemony sun in the watery blue sky. If the weather patterns were the same here as in Norway, it felt like a storm hovering on the horizon.

She turned to the left and walked briskly down the packed dirt street. She passed the houses, playing the *I wonder who lives there* game that she and Nora used to play on their way to school. But in Norway it was *I wonder what they're doing there,* since they knew all the inhabitants of their small village.

It was different here. Clara refused to allow the worm of homesickness to dig its way into her beautiful day. She thought back to the night before instead. "The Lord is my shepherd...," she sang the song, the ancient words set to a tune they'd learned in Sunday school. Why was it she always felt better when she began singing? How much easier it was to remember Bible verses when they'd been set to music.

She sang her way up a cross street and down the main street until she saw the white picket fence of the Moen home. When she knocked on the door, the reverend himself answered it, his shirt sleeves rolled up to his elbows.

"Clara, how wonderful to see you. Come in, come in." He stepped back, opening the door wide in welcome.

"What brings you to our house? Ingeborg, we've company."

Clara stopped inside the door. "I can't stay but a minute. Dr. Harmon is with Mrs. Norgaard so I could do what she asked."

"And what is that?"

"She said for you to come now, she was...is ready." Clara recited the words, hoping the man in front of her would understand the meaning.

"That's all?" He rubbed the bridge of his nose with one finger, his right hand tucked under his left elbow.

Clara nodded.

"Oh, I'm so glad you are here. Sit down, sit down. John, you haven't taken her coat yet. What is this world coming to?" Ingeborg whirled down the last of the stairs and enveloped Clara in a hug that left no doubt as to her joy. She leaned back and studied the younger woman's face. "You look like caring for Mrs. Norgaard is agreeing with you."

"Ja, it is. Such a beautiful place." Clara patted Grace on the head and squatted down to say hello to little James. "But I must get back."

"The coffee will be ready in a minute."

"Another time, *mange takk*. Reverend, you will be coming?"

Ingeborg looked from one to the other, her eyes bright and dimples ready to leap into view with the least encouragement. "Is Mrs. Norgaard feeling up to visitors?"

"She asked for Reverend Moen."

"She isn't worse, is she?" The dimples dove into hiding.

"Nei, nei. I think she's better."

Reverend Moen rolled down his sleeves preparatory to putting on his coat even as they talked. "I shouldn't be long." He removed his hat from the hall stand and, putting it on, went out the door, only to return. "Would you rather stay a few minutes to visit or walk with me?"

"Oh, stay," Ingeborg pleaded.

Clara felt like a length of cloth being pulled at both ends. Duty won over and she smiled her apology. "Another time. Perhaps you and the children could come to call soon. That house is so silent. It needs the sound of children laughing."

"We will." Ingeborg patted Clara's arm. "I'm happy that you like it there. I'm sure Mrs. Hanson is grateful she needn't worry about her charge."

"Farvel," Clara said as she waved good-bye from the steps. She trotted after Reverend Moen, who waited for her at the gate. Halfway down the walk, Clara spun around and darted back to the porch. "Do you know anyone who might have a canary for sale? I think the bird s song would cheer Mrs. Norgaard up. And it would make some music

in that still house."

Ingeborg shook her head, her brow wrinkling in thought. "Not now, but I'll ask around. That's a wonderful idea. *Farvel.*" She stood in the doorway, waving until they were up the street.

Reverend Moen set a brisk pace and Clara found herself trotting to keep up with his long strides. When they arrived back at the Norgaard place, they met Dr. Harmon just coming down the stairs.

"I don't know what you've done, my dear, but keep it up, whatever it is." He shrugged into his coat and picked up his hat. I'll check back in a couple of days. Now, Reverend, don't go messing with my patient."

Clara could tell he was playing by the twinkle in his eye.

"She's on the mend so you can't have her yet," the doctor teased.

"And I'm sure you think your medicine did the trick?" Reverend Moen tried to look serious and failed utterly.

"What else?" The doctor chuckled as he strode out the door, waving, one hand behind him.

"You go on up," Reverend Moen said. Clara took his coat at the same time she heard the summoning bell from upstairs.

"I'll be right back." He grabbed his coat and slipped out the door, hitting the ground running. He turned and jogged backwards. "Don't worry," he called back. "It's good news."

Clara shook her head as she climbed the stairs. What a strange day this was turning out to be.

"Just put the tray over there." Mrs. Norgaard pointed to the table in front of the windows. "We'll wait for Reverend Moen and serve then. Do you think you could brush my hair before he gets back?"

Clara set the tray down and turned to find Mrs. Norgaard sitting on the edge of her bed, slipping her arms into the sleeves of her robe. Clara paused to see what her patient would do next. Mrs. Norgaard belted and tied the sash then looked up.

"Could you please help me to the chair? I know it's easier for you when I'm there." She took Clara's arm and raised herself to her feet. Clara waited while Mrs. Norgaard swayed a bit and then steadied herself. "I'm weak as a kitten." The tone was colored in exasperation.

Clara felt like singing as she brushed the long, gray tresses. What could have brought on the change? Their talk last night? The tears? Her prayers? Probably a combination of all three but whatever— Clara gave God all the glory. Her whispers of "Thank You, thank You" played counterpoint to the melody.

When Reverend Moen returned a few minutes later, he carried a small leather case along with his Bible. Reverently, he removed an embroidered stole and placed it around his neck. Then he set out his communion supplies.

So that's what she was ready for. Clara tucked the last pin in the coil of hair on the back of Mrs. Norgaard's head.

"I'd like the chairs over by the window, if you please." Mrs. Norgaard looked up at Clara. "Thank you, my dear. That felt wonderful. I believe you have the gift of healing in those hands of yours."

Clara held her hands out in front of her, turning them over and back. Could that be? They looked just like her hands had all her life. No different. She shook her head.

"Here, let me help you while Reverend Moen moves the chairs." After seating Mrs. Norgaard, Clara turned to leave the room.

"No, please stay. I'll feel more like we're in church if it isn't just me." Mrs. Norgaard clutched Clara's hand.

Clara nodded.

But I'm not prepared, she thought. *I haven't time to review my sins. When was the last time I received communion? So long ago.* Clara took one of the chairs and folded her hands in her lap. She breathed deeply, letting all the air out till her shoulders slumped. She closed her eyes.

Reverend Moen began reading. "From chapter one of First John. "That which was from the beginning . . . God is light and in him is no darkness. . .But if we walk in the light, as he is in the light. . .If we say that we have no sin, we deceive ourselves. . .If we confess our sin, he is faithful and just to forgive us our sins and to cleanse us from all unrighteousness.' Let us be quiet now and confess those sins that stand between us and Him."

Clara thought back over the last weeks. *I confess that I doubted You,* she thought. *I know I have not always come to You first but tried to do things on my own. I doubted that You have a plan for my life and I resented not meeting the man in my picture.* She continued thinking about the things she had done wrong. *Father, forgive me,* she prayed. *I don't want anything to stand between us.*

Reverend Moen flipped to Matthew, chapter twenty-six, in his Bible and began again, this time with the Last Supper.

At Jesus' words, Clara could feel the tears clogging the back of her throat. "This is my body. . .this is my blood of the new testament, which is shed for many for the remission of sins." When she had finished the communion, she wiped the flowing tears away with the corner of her apron.

Mrs. Norgaard reached over and borrowed the other corner. She sniffed and wiped her tears again with the backs of her fingers. The sigh seemed to come from the depths of a soul released from bondage and now ready to walk in the fullness of God's light and freedom.

"Now remember those words, He not only forgives but cleanses us." Reverend Moen closed his Bible and made the sign of the cross. "The Lord bless you and keep you. The Lord lift up His countenance upon you and give you His peace. Amen."

"Amen." The two women chimed together.

A chorus of angel choirs could not have been richer than the quiet that filled the room and made its home in her heart. Clara recognized peace when she felt it.

Time passed but no one disturbed it until Mrs. Norgaard sighed deeply and raised her head. "Thank you, Reverend Moen. I believe I can go on now. I know that Einer is with our Father and I will be, too, one day, but I guess that day hasn't come yet. Not for me anyway."

She reached over and took Clara's hand. "So we'll just have to get me well again. Right?"

Clara nodded. She covered Mrs. Norgaard's hand with her own. "God willing."

"Oh, I think *He's* been willing all along. It's this stubborn old woman who wanted to go the other way."

After Clara rewarmed the coffee and served, she settled Mrs. Norgaard down for a nap and walked Reverend Moen to the door. "Thank you for a beautiful service."

"All I did was read God's Word. We forget how wonderful and powerful it is, especially when read aloud. As told in Matthew, chapter eighteen, He meant it when He said, 'For where two or three are gathered together in my name, there am I in the midst of them.' "

Clara leaned her cheek against the edge of the open door. "I felt it. . . His presence. . .I mean. I feel like laughing and crying, both at the same time." She wiped away a tear with her fingertip. "Thank you so much."

"You're most welcome. I felt and feel the same. These moments make all my days worthwhile." He placed his brown felt hat squarely on his head. "God bless."

Clara felt the "God bless" for the rest of the day and through the evening. She felt it when she gave Mrs. Norgaard a back rub.

"Tell me how you came to this country," Mrs. Norgaard asked when she was settled against her pillows again.

Clara leaned back against the chair. As she related the story of the stained letter and the picture of the curly haired man, she could feel a difference. She didn't resent God for "messing things up" as she'd thought before.

"I had to confess being angry today because I thought God wasn't playing fair. I thought I understood He was bringing me to America to be a wife—right away. Even though I didn't know the man, I thought God would make it all right."

"And He didn't?"

"I don't know. No one seems to recognize the picture. No one has come forward to say, 'Where's my wife, the one I bought a ticket for and who never showed up.'" Clara leaned her head back against the frame. "But after today, it isn't so important."

"Well, I shall always be grateful He brought you here, however He did it." Mrs. Norgaard folded her hands across her chest. "I know most of the people around here. Why don't you bring the picture here and show it to me?"

Clara thought about the suggestion. "Would you mind if we waited until morning when the light is better?"

"That would be fine." The quiet settled back. "Would you recite the Twenty-third Psalm again? That is such a comfort." The words fell into the quiet of the room and the peace of their hearts, spreading like ripples on a pond.

When Clara fell into bed, she could only whisper, "Thank You, *mange takk.*"

She woke to a day filled with the brightness of sun glinting off frost. It glittered on the trees and the frost fronds painted on the edges of the windows.

After breakfast she took her picture in to Mrs. Norgaard. Clara studied the older woman's face as she studied the picture. Clara saw the jaw clench and the cords stand out in Mrs. Norgaard's birdlike neck.

"Clara, please go over to the blacksmith's and bring Dag back with you. I want to talk with him."

"Now?"

"Now!"

Chapter 7

Whatever could she want Dag for? Mrs. Norgaard peered at Clara over the spectacles perched on her nose. "Well?"

"Yes, ma'am." Clara turned and hustled out of the room. She stripped off her apron and hung it on the hook, at the same time reaching for her gray wool shawl. While her hands went about their chores, her mind worried at the question like a dog with a bone. What would Dag have to do with her picture? She thought again of the taciturn blacksmith. Hopefully he talked to others more than he did her.

She flew down the stairs and out the door, catching her breath at the bit of the breeze. Her nose tingled and began to run as quickly as her feet. While the sun was gorgeous, winter not only nipped her nose but bayed hard on the heels of fall.

Clara paused a moment at the wrought iron gate and raised her face to the sun. Eyes closed, she savored the hint of warmth and freshness of the world outside the silent house. She would have to get outside more, that's all there was to it.

She felt like skipping down the street and, after checking to see no one was watching her, did just that. Back in Norway, she might have been racing Lars over the hills or riding their pony up to the summer hut where they took the cows to pasture in the warm season. Thoughts of home killed all desires for skipping.

What would Mor and Far be doing now? She scrunched up her

eyes to think better. What part of the day was it in Norway now? She shook her head, letting the shawl fall back on her shoulders. Home was so far away, like another life. She rolled her lips together and looked up to the sky above. Her prayer winged upward like the steam rising from the rooftops. *Keep them safe,* she prayed, *and let us be together sometime again. Mange takk for this wonderful day and the new friends I am making.*

The picture of Else, her best friend since beginning school, took over her mind. But Else was already married and expecting her first baby.

Clara sighed and turned the corner to the blacksmith's shop. She'd just have to make a new best friend along with the new life in this new country. She glanced up the street to the fields beyond. This new, extremely flat, and amazingly huge country.

She had her smile back in place when she stopped in front of the weathered building, open to the street, with BLACKSMITH in black iron letters across the face. She wrinkled her nose at the distinctive aroma of trimmed horse hoof. A gray horse stood on three legs, its rear fourth clamped between Dag's knees.

"Hello, *froken* Johanson," called Will from his place holding the horse's head.

"Hello, Will." Clara smiled at the lanky lad and waited, expecting Dag to join in the greeting.

The man bending over the shoe, tapped home another nail, set down his hammer, and picked up the crimper.

Clara waited.

"Fine day, isn't it?" Will shifted to the near side of the horse.

"Ja, that it is." Clara looked back to Dag. He finished crimping the nails over, set aside the crimper, and picked up the rasp.

"Can we do something for you?" Will looked from Dag to Clara. He caught her gaze, glanced back at the man bending over the hoof, and shrugged.

Clara felt a little fume begin about her heart region and make its way to her mouth. She clicked her tongue against her teeth. *Had the man no manners at all? After all, it wasn't as if they were strangers.*

Dag eyed the final balance of the hoof and straightened. With a gloved hand he stroked the horse's haunches and made his way around to the other side.

He could feel a burn rising from his chest and up his neck. *What could she possibly want? Was this a social call? Who made social calls to the blacksmith? Mercy, but she was beautiful. The sun setting her hair afire above eyes the green of a newly risen field of wheat.* He clamped a lid on his thoughts with the same strength he pounded iron.

He also forbade himself to peek around the horse's rear to see if she were still there. Why couldn't he just say "Hello" like Will did? Such an easy thing—for most people. If he dusted off his shirt and walked over to her, would she smile at him, like she had the boy?

The horse snorted, breaking a silence that stretched like a spider web between two blades of grass.

Clara cleared her throat. Why this urge to yell at him?

Dag rubbed his chin with the back of his pigskin gloves. Just a simple "Hello."

"Tell your master that Mrs. Norgaard would like to see him, if he can find the time." *Or the words,* she wanted to add but nearly drew blood biting her tongue.

"Yes ma'am." Will ducked his head.

Clara spun around, her skirts swirling about her legs. Her steps jarred her knees. Insufferable—rude—crude. Each word matched each stomp.

"Tell Mrs. Norgaard I'll be there as soon as I finish shoeing this horse." The deep voice echoed up the dirt street after her.

Clara straightened her spine and her shawl. "Tell her yourself." Her mutter carried no farther than her shoulder.

Even though she'd smiled at a woman on her way to the store and nodded at a man in a wagon who raised his hat in greeting,

Clara smacked her hand against the latch on the gate. The gate flew open, clanging against the fence. The sound jerked her back from casting dire consequences upon the head of the man who couldn't be bothered to be civil.

She carefully closed the gate behind her and switched her stomping to a normal gait while at the same time forcing herself to search the two naked elm trees for squirrels. A crow chastised her from the peak of the second-story dormer.

Clara inhaled a deep breath of the sparkly air, mounted the steps, and, by the time she entered the house, had herself totally under control. After trotting up the stairs, she hung up her shawl, retied her apron, and peeked in on Mrs. Norgaard.

The bed stood empty. Clara opened the door all the way and discovered her employer sitting in a rocker in front of the window. Clara swallowed her amazement.

"Could you please fix my hair before he comes?"

Clara nodded and picked up the brush and pins from the dressing table. As she brushed the long hair, she tried to think of something to say. Should she tell Mrs. Norgaard that Dag had been, well, less than helpful? But then he had said he'd come. She heaved a sigh and continued her ministrations.

"Wouldn't you rather tell me about it?" Mrs. Norgaard leaned into the rhythmic strokes of the brush.

"About what?"

"Whatever upset you. I watched you come through the gate—and up the walk."

"Oh." Clara tucked several hairpins in her mouth—to keep from answering or to be more efficient? She braided the long strands, looped the braid into a figure eight and inserted the pins. That left her with an empty mouth and, after thinking about her trip to the blacksmith's, with an empty smile.

"I—" The bell pealed from the front door.

"Show him up and bring us a coffee tray in about fifteen minutes." Mrs. Norgaard patted Clara's arm. "We'll talk later."

On the way down the stairs, Clara considered. Had that last comment been a threat or a promise? Either way—why did that man have to be so infuriating? Her heels clicked on the stairs, each step reminding her that now it was her place to be polite—or not.

She opened the door, her normal welcoming smile tucked safely away.

Dag stood there, porkpie hat clutched between his hands.

Clara motioned him in and led the way up the stairs. She could feel his eyes burning holes into her back. She held herself rigidly straight, her chin at an angle that brooked no appeal. Only the slight trembling of her fingers as they trailed up the banister revealed the effort it took. If he could be silent, so could she.

Dag knew the way. He'd been to the house often, repairing the stove and installing the pump and piped-in water. The iron fence surrounding the property had been hand-formed in his own shop. He sniffed appreciatively. A fragrance of lavender drifted back from the starchy figure ascending the stairs before him. The rustle of her skirts made him conscious of the trim anatomy, rounded where it should be and slender, especially in the ankles.

He jerked his attention to the hand trailing the banister. That, too, slender, with long fingers, dainty but very capable. How gentle those hands had been with the children on the Detschman farm.

Enough! He focused his gaze on his boots. Dusty, bits of mud, and probably—oh, if only he could go outside, clean them off, and start all over again. If only he could fly back to the smithy and answer the blond angel that had said "Hello" in a way that set his heart to hammering. Hammering louder than the sledge upon steel to sharpen a plowshare.

She pushed open the door and motioned him through. "Mr. Weinlander." He heard the sheet of ice tinkle and crackle around him as he walked through.

"Good morning, Dag." Mrs. Norgaard called from her window

seat. "Please, come sit with me while Clara brings us some coffee. And make sure you bring three cups, my dear."

Dag sat, dwarfing the chair with his broad shoulders and tall body. He glanced back in time to see Clara glare daggers at him one more time before she turned and, after closing the door with a definite snap, tap away down the hall. If she'd called him a vile name, he wouldn't have felt it more.

He sighed and turned his attention to his hostess, who gave away her awareness of his turmoil by a gentle smile.

Her words however were, as always, politely correct. After asking about his health, the weather, and the state of the smithy, Mrs. Norgaard leaned forward and picked up a picture from the table. "Please look at this and tell me who you think it is." She handed the stained and faded likeness to him.

Dag studied the curly haired man in the photograph. He looked up, puzzlement wrinkling a brow barely peeping from behind the wild hair. "It is Jude, my brother, as you well know."

Mrs. Norgaard nodded. "Yes, I thought as much."

"But where—" Dag studied the picture again. "Where did you get this?"

"That I'll tell you another time. But for now... where is he?"

Dag shook his head, the matted and twisted hair swinging in the force of it. "I don't know. He stopped one day—" Dag wrinkled his brow remembering, "to tell me to take care of Ma. He was going to be gone for a while."

Silence but for the ticking clock filled the room. Mrs. Norgaard waited.

Dag nodded. "He told me to pick up a woman, *froken* Johanson, at the station and take her to the Detschman farm. That is all."

"And you haven't seen him since?"

Dag shook his head again. "Is something wrong?"

Mrs. Norgaard reached for the picture and laid it face down on the table. "No, I think not." She clasped her hands loosely in her lap. The silence returned. "Did he marry that woman over in Hammerston?"

Dag started. Did she know *everything* that went on? "Maybe that's where he went, but he'd have invited Ma to the wedding at least—I think." He twisted the hat in his hands. What was going on here?

Mrs. Norgaard sighed and nodded at the same time, as if she'd come to a decision.

Dag waited, expecting her to either continue the discussion or tell him what to do next. He'd learned long ago that one didn't rush Mrs. Norgaard and that no one in town or the surrounding counties treated him with more care and civility.

Clara entered the room, carrying a tray laden with coffeepot, cups, and a plate of apple cake.

Dag nearly tipped the armless, needlepoint chair as he leaped to his feet to take the tray from her. She relinquished the ebony handles, losing her hands in his for just a moment. She resisted the urge to dust them off on her apron. Funny, a tingle like a spark had gone up her arms. She moved the picture of her man off the table so Dag could set the tray down. What was her picture doing here? Had Mrs. Norgaard shown it to Dag?

Her thoughts chased each other like squirrels in an oak tree. All the while, her hands poured the coffee, and passed it and the cake around with the napkins, before she took her own chair. She glanced up in time to see a look of pleasure cross Dag's face as he chewed and swallowed her cake, then sipped the coffee from a cup nearly hidden in his hand.

"More, Mr. Weinlander?" She offered the cake plate again. And again. Until there were only crumbs. Goodness, had the man never had apple cake?

When the coffeepot, too, was empty, Dag set his plate and cup on the tray and, picking up his hat again, stood to go. *"Mange takk."* He nodded both to the old woman sitting so straight in her chair and the young one rising to escort him out. "Is there anything else, ma'am?"

"No, I think not. Thank you for humoring an old woman and coming so quickly."

When it appeared her attention had turned to the window, Dag bobbed his head and turned toward the door.

Clara, trying to determine what the undercurrents in the room meant, let him get ahead of her. Well, of all the—again her mind found something to blame him for. Didn't he know it was *her* place to show him out? Her shoes tapped out her displeasure on the hardwood floor. How could she go around him? The hall wasn't wide enough. She glared at the back of the man. She'd have to find some new names to call him, the ones she'd used so far were wearing out!

Dag stopped at the head of the stairs. Clara did, too, with her nose in his back. Would he *never* do what she expected?

"Excuse me," she muttered, her head down to hide the blush she could feel flaming up into her face. She passed in front of him and preceded him down the stairs. Right now she could do with one of those fans she'd seen in a lady's book.

When she opened the door for him, she looked not higher than the missing button on his shirt. Wool underwear that might have once been white but had forgotten the experience long before showed through the gap of the shirt. Neither had had a recent acquaintance with a washtub.

Dag paused, as if to say something, then mashed his hat on his head, strode out the door, and down the walk

Clara watched him stride away. For such a big man, he walked with the grace of...she couldn't think of a word. The picture of her father, head and shoulders above most of the Norwegian giants of home, whirling Mor around the dance floor in a spirited polka came to her mind. Ya, Dag moved with that same grace. She corrected the thought—Mr. Weinlander. The bell summoned her from upstairs. She gently closed the door and made her way back up the staircase.

Thoughts of the curious bear of a man wriggled in and out of her mind as she continued with her tasks of the day. What would he look like without that matted rat's nest of a beard? Why wouldn't he talk with her, even to say just the polite formalities? Why had her picture been on the table? Why didn't she just ask Mrs. Norgaard and get her questions answered?

That night as she prepared her charge for bed, Clara could feel the questions welling up and pleading for voice. After blowing out the lamp on the stand, she cleared her throat. Only the light from the hall disturbed the darkness.

"Would you repeat our psalm again?" Mrs. Norgaard derailed Clara's train of thought.

"Ja, that I will." Clara sat down on the edge of the bed and closed her eyes. Her voice gentle, she began. "The Lord is my shepherd, I shall not want. . ."As she continued, the words sank into her heart and mind, reminding her of the promises God wrote for everyone. When she finished, she bowed her head. *Peace and quiet have the same sound,* she thought. *Why is it that words written so long ago have such power to bring peace?*

"Our Father which art in heaven. . ." Mrs. Norgaard's voice with these other ancient words only added to the blanket of comfort. Clara joined her and together they whispered "Amen."

When Clara began to rise, Mrs. Norgaard laid a hand on the younger woman's arm. "Stay with me awhile, if you will. I have a story I want to tell you." The words came softly out of the shadowed bed.

Clara settled herself with her back against the carved walnut foot. She waited.

"It all began a long time ago. A man here in town lost his wife one winter and left him with a small son. He had a hard time of it but eventually found another woman to marry. There has never been a surplus of marriageable females here in the Dakotas, so he felt blessed. The family was fine until the new wife had a baby. All she could think of was her son, and the older boy was pushed aside.

"Now as the lads grew, the younger son was quick to learn. None could resist his laughing eyes and curly hair, least of all his mother. And so he grew to take advantage of his older brother, who was not so quick to learn or glib of tongue.

"When the older was ten, the father died, making his elder son promise to care for his stepmother and half brother. They both treated him cruelly, but he finally left school that, although he was slow, he loved, and he then took an apprenticeship under the local blacksmith.

When the blacksmith died, he willed his business to the young man, who had proven to have an amazing aptitude.

"And the younger son? Since his mother spoiled him so terribly, he felt that others should treat him like she did and drifted in with the wrong element of town."

"And of the older brother?" Clara forced the words past the lump clogging her throat.

"He continued to withdraw, caught, I believe, in a web of agonizing shyness, convinced he was not worth more than his family had repeatedly told him. And that was nothing.

"It reminds me of Esau and Jacob." Mrs. Norgaard sighed and a pause deepened. "I don't know, God worked a miracle for those two brothers of so long ago and I pray the same can happen today."

"You've prayed for them?"

"Oh, for years. The elder and I struck up a friendship back when he was a lad and was helping me in my garden. My Einer was much too busy in the bank to dig up the garden and help prune the trees. We never had children. Sometimes I wonder if God didn't trust us enough to take good care of them."

"Oh, no." Clara bit back any more of a response, afraid she would halt the flow of gentle and dreamy words.

"So I made it a habit to acquaint myself with the village children and help where I could. One of my girls attended teachers' school in Fargo and one young man has finished medical school. Dr. Harmon keeps hoping this young man will return to North Dakota where we need doctors so desperately." Silence again.

"I receive letters from others who have married and moved away. They all were so special to me, not that I spoiled them, you know. I just made sure that if they wanted to do more with their lives, they could."

Clara drew a bit of flannel from her pocket and blew her nose. "And the younger brother?"

"I haven't seen him in a long time. Good riddance to bad rubbish, I say, but then I have to remember my Lord's commands and pray forgiveness both for my bad thoughts and his bad actions."

The clock chimed from the top of the six-drawer chest.

"You must go to bed now, my dear. Thank you for listening to an old woman's ramblings."

Clara bent over and brushed a kiss on Mrs. Norgaard's forehead. *"Mange takk."*

"God bless."

I have to help him. Clara lay in bed and stared upward at the canopy she could barely discern. *How can I? What can I do? He won't even talk to me.*

She waited for heavenly inspiration.

The clock chimed the quarter hour.

An owl hooted out in the backyard.

"How, God, how?"

Chapter 8

Clara woke with the same thought. As she hurried through her morning ablutions, she ignored the gray skies without and the gray cloud within. How could someone have mistreated a young boy so? Especially the woman who agreed to be his mother.

And what could be done now?

No wonderful solutions had come to her during the night. Was she expecting too quick an answer to her prayers? She brushed her hair, frustration lending vigor to her brush strokes. Mrs. Norgaard said she'd been praying for years. . .and nothing. The lilt had left Clara's voice when she answered the summoning bell. Along with the snap in her step.

Shortly after dinner, the doorbell pealed. Clara wiped her hands on her apron and hurried down the paneled hall between the kitchen and the front entry. It was probably the doctor needing a cup of coffee during his daily round.

"Ingeborg!" Clara reached out to draw her guest inside and instead found herself enveloped in a hug that immediately made her think of Mor. "Come in, come right on in."

"I hope I'm not intruding. John agreed to stay home with the little ones while they napped and so here I am." Ingeborg unbuttoned her coat and let Clara remove it from her shoulders and hang the heavy black wool on the coat tree.

"I'm afraid Mrs. Norgaard might be asleep. She had a busy

morning." She led the way into the parlor. "I'll go see and be right back."

"No, I came to talk with you." Ingeborg took a seat on the brown velvet sofa and patted the surface beside her. "'For, you see, I have an absolutely marvelous idea and I need your help."

"Me?"

"Yes, I am thinking of starting a class to teach English to those Norwegians who just immigrated."

"Like me?" Clara put a hand to her chest.

"Yes." Ingeborg gave a bounce on the slippery sofa.

"Wouldn't you love to be able to speak and read the language of your new country?"

"Ja, for sure that I would." A cloud dimmed the rising excitement in her eyes. "But how could I leave Mrs. Norgaard?"

"I think that can be arranged. I just kept thinking what a struggle Nora had had and I know many others feel cut off because they can't talk easily—"

"That's it!" Clara clasped her hands and buried them in her apron between her knees.

"What? Tell me what?"

"You said anyone who needs help with talking?"

Ingeborg nodded.

Clara turned to face her friend. "Even though he—I mean, they, might have lived around here all their lives."

"I hadn't thought to include someone like that, but, of course." Ingeborg's brow wrinkled in concentration.

"Dag Weinlander." Clara leaned against the back of the sofa. "Ingeborg, you are the answer to my prayers."

"I'm glad to hear that since you aren't making a lick of sense."

"What do you know of Dag Weinlander?"

Ingeborg rolled her eyes upward and pursed her lips. "Not a great deal, I must admit. He doesn't come to church or any of the town socials. Besides, I have never found him to be very friendly when

I've met with him anywhere. You know, in a town this size, everyone knows everyone else and all their business, too. But he seems a puzzle." She tilted her head to the side and studied her friend. "I take it you know more?"

Clara told her the story she'd heard from Mrs. Norgaard. At the end of the tale, Ingeborg removed a cambric bit from her bag and dabbed at the corner of her eye. "I had no idea. Oh, the poor, poor man." She paused, staring at the bit of fabric in her fingers. She nodded and looked up at Clara, a smile widening her lips as she spoke. "We'll just have to help him out, won't we?"

That Sunday at church, during the announcements, Reverend Moen invited all those who would like help with their English to meet at the church on Tuesday evening at six-thirty.

Ingeborg looked over the heads of her brood to Clara. Their private smile acknowledged that others would be invited, too.

When Clara returned home, she hung up her coat and tripped lightly up the stairs. The closing hymn kept echoing in her mind so she sang along, "Blest be the tie that binds, our hearts in Christian love ..."

Mrs. Norgaard waited for her in the chair by the window. "I love to hear you sing and that song is one of my favorites. Maybe I'll soon be able to go to church again. I think I miss the music most of all."

"Ja, these folks, they sing good." She took the other chair. "He did it—Reverend Moen said the English class will begin on Tuesday."

"Good. Then our next step is to invite Dag here for me to tell him about the class. His shop is not open for business today, so the livery is where he'll be. After dinner, if you would, walk over there with a message for me. Do we have any more of your apple cake? He seemed to enjoy that."

"No, but I could put one in to bake while I finish the dinner." Clara stood and barely refrained from skipping out the door.

Down at the livery stable a while later, Will came out at her call, rubbing the dust off his hands as he came. "C'n I help you, *froken* Johanson?" His grin displayed a gap between his front teeth, besides showing his delight at her arrival.

"I hope so. Is Mr. Weinlander here?"

"He's at the forge. You need a horse or sumpin' ?"

"No." Clara shook her head, a wistful smile betraying her desire as she looked to the stalls. "Perhaps someday I'll ride again, but for now, Mrs. Norgaard is asking for Da—Mr. Weinlander to come see her."

"Right away." Will touched a finger to his forehead and trotted back through the barn to the separate building facing the other street. Ringing sounds of hammer on steel announced that Dag was hard at work. The lad returned in a matter of seconds. "Said he'll be right over, soon's he finishes the piece he's working on."

"Thank you." Clara refused to recognize the letdown feeling the answer gave. Had she expected him to walk back with her? She paused a moment. "You know, there's fresh apple cake if you would like to come, too."

Will rubbed his mouth with grimy fingers. "That'd be right fine, Miss, but one of us has to stay here. There's a team comin back."

"Maybe another time?"

"I'd like that."

Clara quelled the urge to walk slowly in case Dag might overtake her and instead hurried to prepare the tray and make fresh coffee.

Dag was more taciturn than ever, if that were possible, when Clara showed him upstairs. He answered each of her carefully thought-out questions with a grunt or nothing at all. She shook her head as she left the room. Getting him to talk was perhaps going to be more of a challenge than she'd thought.

When Clara reentered the room carrying the coffee tray, it was obvious Dag didn't agree with Mrs. Norgaard. He sat with arms crossed over his chest, his jaw set like a snapping turtle.

"Just think about it, please," Mrs. Norgaard pleaded. "You would find it easier to deal with your customers if you spoke more fluent English."

"I have plenty of business." Hoarfrost shimmered on each word.

"Well." The old woman straightened her shoulders and shot him a look that would have melted steel. "Do what you must. All I ask is you give it some thought. Set that down here." She pointed to the table by her side.

Clara hazarded a glance at Dag after carefully positioning the tray so Mrs. Norgaard could pour. He didn't appear to be melting.

Dag watched her hands as she set down the tray. Each movement flowed with the grace of a half-grown wheat field dancing in the wind. Why should he go to an English class? Resentment chased good sense around in his mind. They talked about speaking, but would the class include reading? He thought wistfully of newspapers and the books that graced the shelf at his mothers house. He could barely decipher Norwegian, let alone English.

Why had he been so slow in school? Maybe he was a dumb dolt like Jude said. Stupid and slow—and ugly as a troll. Yeh, the trolls were big and strong, like him, and ugly.

He heard a voice as from a great distance.

"Mr. Weinlander, your coffee. And would you have some apple cake?" Her voice sang like the birds at courting time.

Two of his favorite aromas, coffee and cinnamon. He sniffed appreciatively and accepted the offered food. *"Mange takk." English, speak English, you dolt! Show her you can. But Clara doesn't talk English,* the other side stated. He felt like his brain had become a battlefield.

"Will seems like such a nice young man."

Answer her! Dag choked on his apple cake. He coughed and took a swig of coffee that only made him cough more. When he could breath again, he leaned back in his chair. Sweat beaded on his forehead. He looked up at Clara, expecting to see condemnation, but all her blue eyes radiated was compassion.

A glance at Mrs. Norgaard left him reeling. Dag staggered to his feet. "I must go." He left the house as if a hound of heaven bayed at his heels.

"Wait! Dag, wait!" He was at the gate before her cries penetrated the voices raging in his brain. He strangled the spires on the gate with shaking hands. He could hear her shoes tapping out her hurry.

"Here." She thrust a napkin into his hand. "I wrapped this for Will since he said he couldn't come with you."

Dag nodded without looking above her hands and fled out the gate.

"What are we going to do?" Clara asked that night as she brushed Mrs. Norgaard's hair in preparation for bed.

"First we pray and then we wait."

Clara sighed. "But—"

"No buts, my child. Our Dag has his own devils to work out and only our Father can do that for him. But you and I. . .well, I think we shall invite both Dag and Will for supper. Wednesday would be a good night, don't you think?"

Clara fell into bed, both restless and relieved. Waiting was so hard, but at least she had someone with which to wait. Dag had no one. Her prayers matched her feelings—confused.

Monday there was a letter for Mrs. Norgaard when Clara went to mail hers to Mor and Far. Clara studied the handwriting. If only she could understand English! On her way back to the house, she went by the blacksmiths and handed Will a note to give Dag. It was an invitation to supper.

"Umm. . .ah—" Will stuttered. He looked from the note to Clara, over his shoulder to Dag working at replacing a wagon wheel rim, and back to the note, his gaze darting like sparks flying from the anvil.

"Is there a problem?" Clara could sense his hesitation even if she couldn't have seen it.

"Ah, no." Will shook his head. "He can't stop what he's doing right now or he'll have to start all over, so I'll give him this when he's done."

"Oh." Clara felt a stab of disappointment. More waiting! "Well, all right then." She turned and walked back to the big house, her shoulders hunched against the bite of the north winds. As the postmaster had said, it looked, felt, and smelled like a snowstorm was on the way.

The note, delivered later by Will and crudely lettered as if the writer had missed more school than he had attended, declined the invitation.

Mrs. Norgaard tapped the folded paper against her hand. "I have a question for you, Will, and I want an honest answer."

Will shuffled his feet, hat squashed between his two hands. "Yes'um."

"Who wrote this?"

Will wrinkled up his forehead, clicked his tongue, shuffled his feet again, and rendered his hat totally useless. "I did."

"Did Dag see my invitation?"

Will nodded. He rubbed his chin with one index finger.

This time it was Mrs. Norgaard's turn to nod. "Clara, why don't you take the boy down and give him a sandwich and maybe some of that apple cake if there is any left. Good day, young man. I hope to see you again soon."

"Yes'm. Thank you." Will bobbed his head and followed Clara out the door. By the time he'd eaten his fill, hard pellets of snow were dashing themselves against the window. He mashed his hat on his head and trotted down the walk, turned once to wave again, and then picked up his feet to hurry home before he froze.

Clara thought about the discussion upstairs as she cleaned up the kitchen. What was going on? And the letter that came. Would Mrs. Norgaard share that with her as she had the others? And on top of all that, what would be their next sally in the war on Dag Weinlander?

"Tomorrow I think I shall want to go downstairs for dinner."

Clara immediately thought of all the steps. How would they ever manage? While Mrs. Norgaard could now walk around her room, she hadn't left it in…in…Clara had no idea how long.

"I want you to go to the smithy in the morning, if the weather cooperates, and ask Dag to. come to carry me down. If he refused to join us for dinner, why then he can return to carry me back up."

Clara felt a chuckle bubbling up from her midsection. She tried to contain it but failed miserably. "Gladly," she answered when they could both talk again.

"Oh, Clara," Mrs. Norgaard said, as the younger woman was leaving the room for the night. "That letter, it was from Mrs. Hanson. She'll be returning next week."

Clara felt like she'd been struck by a widow maker.

The feeling of doom persisted as she crawled into her bed. If Mrs. Hanson was returning, she could go back to the farm with Carl and Nora. Why didn't the thought please her? Since the move to town, she'd only seen her sister once and that was at church.

But what would she do for a job? And how could she help Dag when she would be so far out in the country? And what about the English classes? *God, are You sure You know what is going on here? How can I thank You when I am so confused? Every time I think I have things under control or at least figured out, something changes. Please help me.*

"Why the long face?" Mrs. Norgaard asked when Clara brought in the breakfast tray. "The sun is shining; we can proceed with our plan."

Clara nodded and poured the coffee. She probably wouldn't be doing this for much longer. She walked over to the windows and drew back the heavy draperies. Sun refracted from the diamonds bedded in the inch of pristine snow covering the yard. How clean and pure everything looked. Snow frosted the black branches of the elm tree and bonneted the wrought iron fence posts. An unconscious sigh lifted her shoulders.

"All right. Out with it. This is a side of Clara I've never seen and I'm not sure I like it." Mrs. Norgaard set her coffee cup down with a snap.

Clara sighed again, this time fully aware of what she was doing. But sighing seemed all she was capable of at the moment. She turned to face her employer. "I just want to say how much I've appreciated working for you and—"

"Clara, what are you saying? Are you going to leave me?" Mrs. Norgaard pushed away the bed tray and made as if to rise.

"Well, the letter from Mrs. Hanson. If she's to come back..."

Mrs. Norgaard flopped back against her pillows and patted her chest with one hand. "Oh, my dear, is that all? Why, you silly goose. Did you think I would let you go just because Mrs. Hanson—oh, no, no, no. You have given me life again. I want you as long as you'll stay. Please, come here to me." She held out both hands.

When Clara took them, Mrs. Norgaard drew her young helper down on the bed. "Now, promise me if you are unhappy here, you will tell me."

"But I'm not. I just thought—"

"And that when you have concerns that trouble you, you'll bring them to me so we can work them out."

Clara nodded. The lump in her throat made an answer impossible.

"Good. Now that we have that all taken care of, what shall I wear for my first trip down to the dining room? I must look my best if we are to have company."

When the preparations were all complete, Clara threw on her coat, pinned her hat cockily over one eyebrow, and started out for the blacksmith shop. Her breath puffing out like miniature clouds delighted her as did the squirrel scolding her from the oak tree.

"I thought you'd be hibernating by now," she scolded back. "Go wrap yourself in your bushy tail and stay warm." She leaned over and scooped up a handful of snow, packed it, and fired it at the trunk of a tree, where it splatted perfectly.

I'm staying, I'm staying, thank You, God. Thank You, thank You. "Praise God from whom all blessings flow. . ." Her clear soprano voice rose on the puffs of air and joined the crunch of her boots in an aria of praise.

"To carry her downstairs?" Dag looked at her like she was missing a spoke somewhere.

Clara nodded, determined to keep a straight face. "She can't manage the stairs yet, but she so wants to be free from her bedroom for a change." She carefully injected a note of pleading into the last words. It was the truth.

"And then back up."

"After we eat."

"Tell her I will come to carry her down and back up." He slapped one hand into the other. "But no dinner."

Clara nodded. "At twelve then?" She caught Dag's nod as he walked off into the dimness of his shop. He had talked to her, at least. She allowed herself one skip on the way back home.

While Dag carried Mrs. Norgaard with a gentleness that belied his huge size, he refused to answer any of Clara's questions or comments. And he didn't stay to eat. The reverse process was no different.

"And tomorrow, Dag?" Mrs. Norgaard settled herself on the edge of the bed.

He nodded.

"Then I thank you. You have no idea what a treat this was. I think Clara's determination to make me live again is paying off, don't you?"

Dag nodded and set off as if that hound were on his heels again.

"I'm off now," Clara said from the bedroom doorway that evening. "You sure you'll be all right alone?"

"Perfectly. You just go and learn as much as you can." Mrs. Norgaard settled her spectacles more firmly on her nose. "I'm just grateful I can enjoy reading again." She waved her hand as if shooing away a fly. "Go on, go on."

Clara danced up the stairs a couple of hours later. She was learning to talk English! She and about fifteen other people. And Ingeborg, what a teacher. Everyone had had such a good time, why the hours passed like…like a party. She wrapped her hands around her shoulders and squeezed, at the same time spinning in a circle.

"I take it you had a good time." Mrs. Norgaard laid down her book and removed her gold-rimmed spectacles.

"Ja…*nei*…yes. Good evening."The English words came haltingly but they came. "And we are to meet on Thursday, also." Clara switched back to Norwegian, having used up her store of new words. "Oh, I am so happy."

Wednesday and Thursday Dag appeared to do the carrying— but not eating.

On Friday, when Clara answered the door, she fought to keep the shock from showing on her face.

Chapter 9

Dag had washed himself—and his clothes. Clara clamped her teeth together and made sure her cheeks spread in a smile. "Good morning." She hesitated over the words but persevered, determined to use her new language.

Dag nodded and started toward the stairs.

"Ahhh." The word for coat totally left her mind. She reverted to Norwegian.

Dag paused, one foot on the bottom stair. He turned to face her. *"Ja. Mange takk."* He shrugged out of his black wool, thigh-length coat and handed it to her.

Clara hung it on the tree and stared up the stairs. Even his boots were polished. What she'd give to see the look on Mrs. Norgaard's face! Clara ran up the stairs and down the hall. She burst into the bedroom just as Dag was leaning over to pick up his charge. His broad back hid the diminutive older woman from Clara's sight, but when he turned around, Mrs. Norgaard just smiled like this was an everyday occurrence.

Clara stepped back and let them precede her down the hall. As they passed, Mrs. Norgaard winked at Clara, then continued her conversation with Dag. He even answered her question.

Clara leaned against the door frame and watched them disappear down the stairs. She clapped both hands to her cheeks and felt a shiver of pure delight course through her. She rolled her lips together, straightened her spine, and made her way downstairs.

Dag and Mrs. Norgaard visited in the sitting room while Clara quickly set another place at the table. After bringing in the bread she'd baked just that morning and the stew that had simmered for hours, she crossed the hall to announce the meal.

"No, I'll walk," Mrs. Norgaard insisted when Dag bent down to pick her up. "It's just the stairs I can't manage. Here, let me have your arm to lean on."

Dinner passed with Clara and Mrs. Norgaard carrying the conversation, but Clara could feel Dag's gaze on her from time to time. He answered when asked a direct question, but other than that, he ate in silence. Clara and Mrs. Norgaard made a point to discuss the English class taught by Ingeborg.

"We'll have our coffee in the sitting room," Mrs. Norgaard said after inserting her napkin back into the silver ring by her plate. Dag surreptitiously followed suit and leaped from his place to help her to her feet.

This became the pattern for the next three days until Saturday, when Mrs. Norgaard suggested Dag help her down the stairs, rather than carrying her.

"You're sure?" He stared intently into her eyes.

"Clara's been making me walk around my room morning, noon, and night. You'd think she took lessons from an army sergeant."

"I'm just following doctor's orders," Clara defended herself.

"I know, my dear." Mrs. Norgaard smiled at her. "But you must admit you take your duties seriously."

Dag watched the byplay between the two women, aware as ever of the way they made him feel. Was this the way people really treated each other? He'd never heard or sensed a cross feeling between the two of them. Just a caring that flowed peaceful and smooth like the Red River on its summer journey. And they extended that warmth to him. *Him.* Dag Weinlander. *Why?* Sure, he had a strong back for carrying Mrs. Norgaard down the stairs, but she had always made him feel welcome. Why?

Soon she wouldn't need him anymore. He thought of the gift he'd been carving for her in the evenings in front of the fireplace of his sod hut. Even that would help her need him less. The thought caused another pang in his chest. He kept his fingers from digging at the collar of his shirt.

Instead, he offered the old woman his arm, just like they did downstairs. She clutched his arm with both hands as she took the first step downward. He could feel her shaking. Another step. And another. When they reached the bottom, she gave a sigh of relief. His matched.

He swallowed and rubbed his mouth through the beard with one hand. Together, they marched directly into the dining room. After seating her, he sat down, refusing his body the privilege of slumping in the chair. Helping her downstairs was worse than shoeing ten cantankerous horses in a row.

She let him carry her back up. "We'll see you tomorrow then. Dinner is at one, after Clara returns from church."

He nodded. "Oh, and Dag, please bring Will with you. I'd like to become better acquainted with that lad."

"Yes, ma'am." Dag turned to leave. "And *mange takk.*"

"Dag, it is I who should be thanking you."

"Umm." Dag departed on that noncommittal reply.

That night he resanded the apple-wood cane he had fashioned from a gnarled branch and applied a last coat of varnish. The twisted wood gleamed in the firelight as Dag set it aside to dry one last time. Each succeeding coat of varnish had deepened the patina, bringing out the highlights of the grain.

"That's beautiful," Will said from his stool by the fire. "When ya gonna give it to her?"

"Tomorrow, when we go there for dinner."

"We?"

"Ja"

"Who's gonna tend the livery?"

"Me. While you heat water and take a bath."

"A bath! It's the middle of the winter."

"Ja, a bath." Dag ignored his assistant's fussing and put away his varnish and rag.

"I'd druther stay with the horses." Will crammed his hands into his pockets.

"You can, after dinner."

"What if someone needs a horse?"

"He can come back."

Will muttered his way to bed.

Dag remained by the fire, lost for a time in his thoughts. When he realized how many of those thoughts centered around a certain golden-haired angel, he abruptly stood and headed for the cornhusk-filled mattress he called bed.

"Dag, this is beautiful." Mrs. Norgaard rubbed her hands down the satiny finish of the cane. "I knew you were a master with metal, but I had no idea you could create in wood, also." She gripped the handle and, standing, leaned her weight on the cane. "And the perfect height." She looked up at him with a smile crinkling the corners of her eyes. "Tired of carrying me around?"

Dag shook his head. "You're sure it fits? I could make it shorter if you want."

"No, this is perfect." She thumped it on the floor. "Now, shall we join the others downstairs?"

Dinner passed swiftly with Will finding time to answer questions in spite of putting away a prodigious amount of roast beef, mashed potatoes, gravy, and green beans.

"I ain't never had such a fine meal." Will leaned back against his chair.

"We have apple pie. I'd be sorry if you were too full to join us." Mrs. Norgaard smiled as she spoke.

"No'm. I'll find room for that."

Clara stood up to clear the table.

"I'll help you, miss." Will leaped to his feet. He grinned a cheeky grin. "That way I'll have more room for pie."

"Have you thought of joining the English class, Will?" Mrs. Norgaard asked when the coffee was poured and pie handed out.

"Nah. I can talk Norwegian, English, and some German. I don't need no class."

"But can you read English?"

"Pretty good. Pa made sure I went to school till I was eleven. Then we started west." He took a last bite of the pie.

"Where are your folks now?" Clara asked.

"Dead." Will scraped up every last bit of apple from his plate.

Clara wished she'd bit her tongue before asking such a question.

"Then Dag found me and asked if'n I wanted to help him as an apprentice." He licked the tines of his fork.

Mrs. Norgaard motioned Clara to get the boy another piece of pie.

"I told Dag he should go—to that class, you know." He grinned at Clara when she set another slab of dessert in front of him. "Winter's a good time, not so busy. He could go."

Dag felt warmth creeping up from his chest and making his collar even tighter. Kicking the boy from under the table was beginning to seem more and more like a good idea. He'd never seen him so loose-mouthed.

Will looked across at his employer. He grinned again. "Could."

"We'd better get back in case someone needs a horse." Dag accompanied his pronouncement with the shoving back of his chair.

"*Mange takk* for my cane," said Mrs. Norgaard. She rose to her feet. "Perhaps just your arm today, helping me with the stairs." As they made their way slowly upward, she added a thought. "See you tomorrow?"

Dag nodded. "Ja." Was that gratitude for another day's reprieve he felt welling up in his heart? How terrible to wish she weren't getting better so quickly. *Just like a dolt like you,* he chastised himself with each upward step.

Mrs. Norgaard stopped three steps from the top. She put her hand to her heart and leaned against Dag's strength while trying to catch her breath again. When Dag made to lift her, she stopped him. "No, I'll make it. Just weaker than I thought." A pant separated each word.

See what you did? His inner tormentor continued. *You were in such a rush to get back to the barn, you...* Dag clenched his teeth. *Won't you ever do things right?*

"Good afternoon," Clara practiced her English as she showed the men out. "See you at class Tuesday." She shut the door before Dag could answer.

Clara scoured the kitchen and polished all the furniture on Monday morning while the bread was rising. Mrs. Hanson would be arriving on the four o'clock train and she didn't want the housekeeper to find one thing not up to snuff. Ham and beans browned in the oven, sending a delicious aroma throughout the house.

Dag sniffed appreciatively when he walked up the newly swept walk While the sun tried to shine, high gray clouds kept drifting across its warmth. A north wind nipped around the corner of the house and caused Dag to shiver. His hands were still cold from the scrubbing he'd given them in the horse trough. This cleaning up for dinner every day took some doing. He tucked a button back into its hole before ringing the bell. He'd have to buy some new clothes—and soon.

Clara answered the door while wiping her hands on her apron. "Good morning." The English was coming easier since she'd been practicing. "Come in."

Dag nodded and stepped inside, removing his coat as he did so and hanging it up himself. While his nose might be more accustomed to perfumes of horse, coke fire, and steel, he could recognize beeswax, lemon oil, and especially freshly baked bread with ham and beans. This, like every meal he'd enjoyed here, would be good—very good.

"See, I'm stronger every day, thanks to you and Clara," Mrs. Norgaard stopped at the bottom of the stairs. She looked back up. "I didn't think I would ever leave that room again, except to greet my Lord in heaven."

Dag covered the small hand that lay on his arm with his large one. "I'm glad you decided to stay with us."

"As I said, thanks to you and Clara." She released his arm and set out with her back rigid but her weight partly supported by the apple-wood cane clasped in her right hand. "See how well this works? Thank you, my friend."

Dinner indeed lived up to what his nose had promised him. He cleaned his plate and nodded when Clara offered to dish him up some more. "You are a good cook."

His comment caught the women by surprise. He never offered anything except *"Mange takk"* unless spoken to first.

"Why, thank you," Clara answered, heat blossoming in her cheeks. "I ... I wanted everything perfect for when Mrs. Hanson comes back."

Dag looked around at the gleaming furniture and his healthier friend and nodded. "It is."

Clara felt like she'd been given a medal by the King of Norway. Her heart pitter-pattered in her throat—her very dry throat. She blinked against the surge of moisture that should have been in her throat but instead wanted to slip from her eyes. "Thank you" seemed such an ineffectual response to so great a gift but what else could she do? *"Mange takk,"* she replied.

"Take this to Will," she said as she thrust a package into his hands on his way out the door. "And," she gave him a saucy grin, "see you at class tomorrow night."

Mrs. Hanson clapped a hand to her chest when she saw Mrs. Norgaard sitting in the parlor, her royal blue bombazine skirt topped with a white, lace-tucked shirtwaist. Her mother's cameo glowed from its position pinned to the high.collar.

"Well, I declare, what has been going on here while I was off caring for my ma?"

Clara giggled behind her. "We wanted to surprise you."

"Lord love you, that you did." She walked over and stood in front of Mrs. Norgaard. "How'd you get down here?"

"I walked." She touched her cane and beamed at Clara. "With help, of course, but I shan't need that much longer. Doctor's prescription here in Clara has done its marvelous work."

Mrs. Hanson sank down in a facing brown velvet chair. "Then you won't be needing the likes of me no more."

"Don't be silly. Now you sound like Clara when I told her you were coming home. I need and want you both. So unless you have another idea, that will be the last time we'll talk about such a matter." She thumped her cane for emphasis.

Clara and Mrs. Hanson swapped grins.

Mrs. Norgaard looked from the cane to their happy faces and chuckled herself. "Never thought of a cane as part of a conversation before."

In class that night, the students were practicing their greetings and farewells when the door opened and a big man walked in.

"Can I help you?" Ingeborg asked, then clapped her hands to her cheeks. "Dag Weinlander, is that really you?"

"Ja," he replied, nodding his freshly barbered head and neatly trimmed beard. The wild mass of stringy hair now lay on the cutting floor. Thick sable hair waved back from a broad forehead and ended just above his collar. A wide mouth with smiling lips split the beard that just covered his chin.

Clara noticed every detail. The way his ears lay close to his head and the richness of the waving hair. But what caught her attention the most were his eyes. No longer shrouded by clumpy hair and shaggy brows, eyes the blue of high mountain lakes on a summer's day stared back into hers.

She swallowed. She'd been attacked by dry throat again. "Hello, Dag," she croaked.

That night while Ingeborg was explaining the alphabet, Clara caught herself watching Dag. He didn't participate, but sat observing. He looked so different. From wild man to handsome. She couldn't wait to tell Mrs. Norgaard.

"I've been thinking," Mrs. Norgaard said over breakfast, and after they'd wondered at the change in Dag, "about ways to help you with your English. Now that Mrs. Hanson is back and I'm so much better, your duties will be of a different sort."

Clara stopped with a spoonful of hot cereal halfway to her mouth. She set the spoon back in the bowl. "What do you mean?"

"I know how hard you are trying with your English lessons, so I have decided we will speak only English in this house. Mrs. Hanson and I agree. We'll help you, prompt you, whatever we can do, but there will be no more Norwegian. What do you think?"

I think I'm going to throw up, Clara thought. She stared from Mrs. Norgaard to Mrs. Hanson and back again. "But, but...I—" She licked her lips. One of her favorite Bible verses floated through her mind. "I can do all things through Christ which strengtheneth me." She sucked in a deep breath. Her smile flickered like a candle in a draft and then steadied. "All right." She let her rigid shoulders slump. What on earth had she agreed to?

Thanksgiving passed in a daze for Clara. The English-only rule applied when Dag and Will joined them for the annual feast. Will thought it was great fun, while Dag and Clara sneaked each other commiserating glances.

But Clara never felt persecuted. While discouragement sometimes dogged her, she knew they were all taking great pains to help her learn the language quickly. And it was working. With the daily repetitions, lessons with Mrs. Norgaard morning, afternoon, and evening, and her classes at the church twice a week, Clara could finally communicate.

She practiced on the shopkeepers, people at church, the postmaster. She talked to the woman in the mirror and dreamed of taking her new skill out to the Detschman farm.

All the while she spent learning English, she also prepared for Christmas. She fashioned a cloth baby doll dressed in a baptismal gown for Kaaren and sanded wooden blocks for baby Peder. While memorizing vocabulary words, she worked the hardanger lace for an apron for Nora. Mittens and a stocking hat for Carl could be knitted while she conversed with Mrs, Norgaard.

Her present for Mrs. Norgaard was the main problem. No one had found her a canary yet.

One night Dag walked her home from the church. "Won't you come in for coffee?" she asked, her English no longer halting on the simple phrases.

"Yes, thank you." While Dag sounded more stilted, he, too, followed the English-only rule.

"Ah, welcome, Dag. Come in, come in." Mrs. Norgaard beckoned from her chair in the sitting room. "You know, I've been thinking—" she began after the coffee was served.

Clara felt her stomach fall down around her knees. Every time she heard "I've been thinking" from Mrs. Norgaard, their world turned upside down.

"I think you should come over every evening when there is no school and join us for extra work on English, both speaking and reading. And you could bring Will. I have a hunch he needs some help and is afraid to ask." She peered over her spectacles. "Or embarrassed. Not everyone is able to finish school, in fact, few are."

Dag stroked his chin. He stared right back at the woman across the room. "Yes."

"That's all?" Clara's voice squeaked on the last word.

"It won't be easy." Mrs. Norgaard continued her observation. "Nothing is."

Clara thought about that bald statement when she lay in bed that night. "Nothing is." Was that the way Dag's entire life had been? She thought to her childhood, to the laughter, the pranks, and even school. For her, learning was easy. Even this learning a whole new language was more time-consuming than hard. But then, look at the people she had helping her.

She snuggled down under the covers. Now Dag would have those same people helping him. Plus her. She'd be glad to help. Would he be able to accept *her* help? She thought of the stubborn look on his face when he read aloud in class. If determination was all it took, Dag had it by the mountainful.

Each night as she said her prayers, she included him. After all, she'd promised to do what she could and if Mrs. Norgaard could pray for Dag all these years, could she do less?

Funny, lately she hadn't been praying for her curly haired husband-to-be. When she thought about it, several weeks had passed with him not even entering her mind. "Please take care of him, wherever he is and whoever he is," she concluded. "Amen."

Several days later when Reverend Moen came to call, Clara stopped him in the hall and, in a low voice, asked him if he'd located a canary yet. At the shake of his head, Clara felt a moment of panic. Christmas was almost here and she'd been so sure she'd have a singing present for her friend.

"I'm sorry," Reverend Moen said.

"Me, too."

That evening Clara asked Dag to come into the kitchen with her while Will was settling down with his books by Mrs. Norgaard in the dining room.

"Do you know anyone who might sell a singing bird?" She paused, trying to remember the word. "A canary. I will give this to Mrs. Norgaard for a Yule present so she has music in her life."

Dag nodded as she finished speaking. "Ja, yes," he caught himself, "I do. My mother raises canaries to keep her company. I will ask her."

Clara stared at him in amazement. "Can you do everything?"

"I will see about this." He reached out with one finger and touched her smiling cheek. When he pulled away as if burned, both he and Clara returned with all speed to the other room.

For the rest of the evening, her cheek felt hot to the touch, as if it had been fire that leaped between them.

The doorbell rang several days later. When Clara opened the door, she saw Will nearly buried under the green needles of a pine tree. "The train brought in a load of Christmas trees and Dag made sure you got the finest." He dragged it inside. "Where do you want it?"

"In the sitting room. We cleared out in front of the window. Mrs. Hanson brought up a bucket of sand from the cellar." Clara felt like a child again, dancing with excitement. She wanted to clap her hands and whirl around the room but instead she helped Will stand the tree up. "Oh, it is just perfect."

"There are more branches for you to decorate with, but I couldn't carry everything at once." Will started to brush the needles off his coat but looked around, guilt flagging his already red cheeks.

"Let me take that for you." Clara helped him shrug out of his coat and took it outside to shake. By the time they had the tree set in the bucket, Mrs. Hanson had brought the decoration box down from the attic.

"I gotta be going." Will stared wistfully at the colorful balls and candle clamps in the box.

"Would you like to help us decorate the tree?" Mrs. Norgaard caught his look and asked.

Will nodded. "But I gotta get back to the stable. Dag needs me."

"That is fine. But both of you be here at six and tonight, instead of class, we'll pop popcorn and decorate the tree."

Joy sparkled in Will's eyes as he darted out of the room, returned to grab his hat and coat, and went plunging out the door. They heard his "Yee-haw" as he leapt off the porch and ran down the walk.

Dag hadn't looked her in the eyes since the night he touched her cheek. Clara frowned at the face in her mirror as she gave her golden hair a final brushing and swooped the sides back and up with her mother-of-pearl combs. What was she to do with him? After all, it was just a *touch*. She caressed the spot with her fingertips. And what was a touch between friends?

Should she mention it tonight while they were decorating the tree? She shook her head. No, better to act as if it never happened.

She nodded and tried on a smile. A fingertip touched the place again. He had been so gentle. Like the kiss of a butterfly's wing. Her eyes flew open—wide open—at the word kiss. She turned and ran from the room as if chased by. . .by the thought of hugs and kisses—and love.

The evening was an unmitigated disaster as far as Clara was concerned. Dag never once spoke to her. He acted as if she were invisible. Clara lifted her chin higher and teased Will like she did her younger brother at home. She kept everyone laughing with her antics—all but the big man with the somber mountain lake eyes.

The tree, however, became the most beautiful she'd ever seen. Because she couldn't resist any more than a child, Mrs. Norgaard broke tradition and let them light the candles, just for a minute.

"Ohhhh." Their breath, expelled all at once, became a sigh of gratitude for something so lovely. The tree shimmered and sparkled, each glass ball and icicle refracting the candlelight and magnifying the glory.

As they pinched out the flames, the memory lingered, a preview of Christmas to come.

Clara and Mrs. Hanson spent the days baking. *Krumkake, fattigmanns*, and frosted sugar cookies. Clara took one day rising and kneading the sweet dough for *julekake*, the Norwegian Christmas bread, studded with currants and candied fruit and flavored with cardamom. The house smelled heavenly. And each evening, there were new goodies to share with her two fellow students.

Dag rapped on the back door early on December twenty-fourth. He put his finger to his lips when Mrs. Hanson started to greet him.

"Is Clara here?" he whispered.

Mrs. Hanson nodded. "Come in and I'll get her. You want some coffee? Breakfast will be ready soon."

"I have the canary for her for Mrs. Norgaard."

Mrs. Hanson pressed her hands together in delight. "I'll get her."

Dag had returned with a quilt-padded bundle and was unwrapping it when the two women tiptoed into the room.

"How did you keep it warm enough?" Clara asked, reaching to help in the dismantling. At the bottom were several stones, still warm from the oven.

"Ma and I packed him real careful. She says he's one of her best singers."

Just then the bellpull from Mrs. Norgaard's room chimed. They started, like kids caught with their hands in the cookie jar. Mrs. Hanson clapped a hand over her mouth to stop the giggles. "I'll go see what herself wants. If I'm talking with 'er up there, she might not hear you." She turned back at the door, her eyes alight with excitement. "Like we talked, Clara, I think the furnace room is the safest place for him. It's warm and dark so maybe he won't sing."

"Ma says that sometimes when you move them like this, they don't sing for a while." Dag removed the last cloth. A bright gold canary cocked his head and looked the two of them over. He cheeped and hopped down from his perch, then up to the sides of the cage, all the while watching his observers. He cheeped once or twice and then attacked the seeds in his dish.

"He's beautiful." Clara clasped her hands together. "Do you think she'll like him?"

"I'm sure she will." He began folding the quilts. "I brought a bag of seed and Ma says you can sprout some for him in the windowsill. He likes greens sometimes and fresh water."

"How much do I owe you?" Clara couldn't take her eyes from the bit of sunshine hopping around the cage.

"Nothing."

"But, Dag—"

He picked up the cage and turned toward the cellar door. "Maybe we should put a lamp down there with him for a time, just to keep him company."

"But Dag, this is my present to give."

"Just include Ma in it. She was pleased to be able to return a favor."

"And you. Without you I wouldn't have found him." Clara looked up into the face of the man towering over her. Why was it that she felt both safe and. . .and. . .she put her hand on Dag's. "Thank you, my dearest friend." Warmth flowed up her arm and curled in the pit of her stomach.

"Ah, good," Mrs. Hanson said as she reentered the room. "I'll check on the bitty thing every hour or so. This is turning into the best Christmas this house has seen in years. Hurry with that and we'll all eat together. Clara, help Mrs. Norgaard get ready, and Dag, you can bring herself down as soon as she rings."

Clara flew up the stairs to help Mrs. Norgaard with her toilet.

"Who is that downstairs?" the old woman asked.

Feeling caught, Clara stuttered. "D—Dag."

"What did he want so early in the morning?"

"Ah-h-h." Even a little fib was outside Claras capabilities. She resorted to the ruse her parents always used. "You shouldn't ask questions. Remember, this is Christmas."

"I'm not about to forget with all the secrecy that's been hatching around here." Mrs. Norgaard tried to look stern but failed miserably.

The weather held fine for Christmas Eve, so Clara hoped her sister and her family would be able to attend the service. Dag promised to bring a sleigh so Mrs. Norgaard could attend also. This would be her first time in church since her illness.

"Are you sure going out won't lay you low again?" Mrs. Hanson asked quietly, but Clara heard the exchange.

"No, I am fine in health and thankful for this my new family, since this will be the first Christmas without my Einer."

Clara started. In all the excitement, she hadn't thought about Mrs. Norgaard's feeling sad. No wonder she had been quieter lately.

"But this huge house needs lots of people like this coming and making Christmas right. We need little children here. We must invite the Moens, they have no family in town either."

They were gathered in the hall when the jingle of harness bells announced the arrival of the sleigh. When they stepped out the door, the cold bit their noses and cheeks, but Dag soon had them all swaddled in robes, right up to the tips of their noses.

Once out on the street, Clara looked up to see the stars hanging low and brilliant in a cobalt sky. "Oh, look." She pointed to the north. Aurora borealis, the northern lights, danced on the horizon, flaring reds, blues, and greens in an unending heavenly display.

"Only God could create something so magnificent," Mrs. Norgaard whispered. "And to think He brought them out tonight just for me to see. Only He knows how much I have always loved the northern lights."

When they entered the church, the heavenly chorus from outside seemed to follow them in. Clara found herself sitting between Dag and Will, right behind Nora and her family. Ingeborg turned from her place in the front pew and wiggled her fingers. The old familiar hymns soared to meet the stars and the reading of the Christmas story settled into every heart.

When Dag shifted on the words, "Peace among men with whom He is pleased," Clara slipped her hand into his. He stilled immediately. Wasn't that what friends were for, to help each other out?

She could feel him looking at her. She stared straight ahead, concentrating on the sermon.

As they stood for the final hymn, their hands touched, holding the hymnbook. When she allowed her glance to travel up to his face, he stared back—and smiled.

Silence fell after Reverend Moen pronounced the benediction. A silence deep and full with the promise of Christmas. As they turned to leave when the organ swelled in triumphant joy, Dr. Harmon made his way to Clara's side.

"Clara, I hate to ask this, but I have a sick family with no one to help. Could you come?"

Chapter 10

But my family."

"I know and this is your first Christmas in this land, but I'm afraid if I don't have help, the Ahmundsons won't see another Christmas."

"I could go," Mrs. Hanson volunteered.

"Thank you, but someone younger and stronger could help me more. Besides, Clara seems to have that healing touch."

"I will go." Dag's strong voice came from beside and above her.

"Thank you, Dag. I can use you both."

"We will save the presents until you come back." Mrs. Norgaard patted Clara's arm.

"And the dinner." Mrs. Hanson nodded her head, setting the rose on her hat to bobbing.

Everyone seemed to be making the decision for her. Clara felt trapped. She looked back at the altar, the golden cross shimmered in the candlelight. He, too, was telling her to go.

Clara turned to the doctor. "I am ready." She reached across the pew and hugged Nora and the children.

Carl shook her hand. "We will come for you when you have finished. Then we will all celebrate our Christmas."

"Go ahead like we had decided," Clara whispered to Mrs. Hanson. "I just won't be there to hear its first song."

They dropped off the other passengers and followed Dr. Harmon and his cutter out of town. Only the jingle of bells and harness and the snorting of the horses broke the stillness of the midnight air.

The stench of illness smote them in the face when they opened the door to the farmhouse. They found the mother collapsed on the floor beside the cradle of her dead infant.

Dag fired up the stove as soon as they had the woman in bed beside her delirious husband and soon had warm water so Clara could bathe the sweating bodies.

"Give them as much water as you can get them to drink and keep sponging their bodies to break the fever." Doc glanced at the cradle. I'll take care of that one later, when we have time. I brought onions to make a poultice, see if we can't help them to breathe easier. Soon's the stuff's cut up and steamed, we can apply it. Mr. Ahmundson needs it the most."

Clara listened with one ear while she moved from bed to bed checking on the five children. Only one was cool to the touch and sleeping normally. "Let's move this one to a bed by himself," she suggested. "He's either had a light case or not sick yet."

Dag tenderly lifted each of the children while Clara changed the filthy beds and bathed the dehydrated bodies. When the littlest girl cried out and thrashed around in her agony, Dag crooned a little song that reached her fevered brain and let her relax. Working together, Dag and Clara were able to accomplish their tasks much more quickly.

The three of them worked through the night and the next day, taking turns sponging hot bodies, forcing water between parched lips, and collapsing on the spare bed when there was a moment. One by one, the children cooled, slept, and awoke. Only the parents suffered on.

Dag took time the next day to check on the livery, while Dr. Harmon looked in on other patients. Clara dragged herself around, caring for the children and keeping the parents as comfortable as possible. At three the next morning, the father passed the crisis and slipped into an easy healing sleep.

"Thank You, Father." Clara dropped down by the bed, resting her head on her hands. "Please" and "Thank You" had been her litanies for the last few days.

Dag returned in the morning with a kettle of soup, another of chicken broth, and clean sheets for the beds. He sent Clara to bed and took over the care again. When Clara awoke in the afternoon, the mother was tossing from side to side, mumbling and calling for her baby. Mr. Ahmundson slept in a chair by the fire, a towheaded three-year-old asleep on his lap.

"Thank you, miss," he muttered, clutching her hand. "You're an angel for sure, come to save my family. Thank God for ye."

Clara patted his hand and headed back to her post beside the mother.

"She seems quieter when you are here with her." Dag stood to let her have the chair. "Doc said he would be back later tonight. He thinks the crisis will come soon."

Clara could hear Dag in the other room, setting out bowls of hot soup for those well enough to come to the table and feeding those who couldn't. Neighbors had come in to do the chores, she heard him tell Mr. Ahmundson. Clara continued dripping spoonfuls of water between the mother's lips and sponging her heat-ravaged body.

"You go get some sleep," the doctor said when he returned late in the evening. "I'll watch with her now."

Clara shook her head. "I can't." She nodded to where the frail woman clutched her hand. "She needs me."

The candle flickered and died and Doc went into the other room to find another. Clara could feel death hovering in the corner. Prickles chased each other up and down the back of her neck, making her afraid to look in case she should see his face.

"No!" She gritted her teeth. "Father, hear us. Her children need her. Please, come with Your Spirit and breathe life into her body."

The woman's breath grew fainter. The exhalations farther apart.

Clara breathed for her, with her. With each intake she whispered, "Live," and with each sigh, she called on the name of the Father.

Mr. Ahmundson stirred from the chair on the other side of the bed where he had drifted off. Tears ran down his sunken cheeks as he took her other hand and pleaded, "Don't leave us, my Inge. Please come back, we need you so."

"Come on, you must fight to live." Clara wanted to jump to her feet and pound her fists on the wall. Instead, she smoothed the cool cloth over Inge's forehead again and down the sides of her face.

"You must let her go," the doctor said softly.

Clara shook her head. She laid her face down on the woman's hand and let the tears bathe the dry skin. "Go with God, Inge." The woman's hand twitched in hers. Clara could hear a breath, a shuddery breath, and a long pause.

Inge breathed again and then again. Her breathing steadied and a slight smile touched the corners of her mouth.

"She's sleeping. Thank the good Lord, He brought her back." Dr. Harmon gripped Mrs. Ahmundson's shoulder. "She's turned the crisis."

Clara sank down on her knees beside the bed. This time tears of joy helped cool the hand she held. "Thank You, Father, thank You," she repeated over and over. When she looked in the corner, all she saw was a dress hanging on a hook.

The first thing Clara heard when she returned home a couple of days later was the trill of a canary. She followed the song to the sitting room, where Mrs. Norgaard sat in the window reading her letters. Mrs. Hanson occupied another chair, her knitting basket at her feet and turning the heel on a gray wool stocking.

"Child, you're back." Mrs. Norgaard rose to her feet so swiftly, her letters scattered across the floor. "Come, sit down. Mrs. Hanson, the coffee. Are you all right?" Her words ran over each other in her haste.

"Oh, isn't he beautiful?" Clara stopped in front of the cage where the small gold bird with a patch of black on his wing eyed her from a beady eye. She continued over to be enveloped in a hug that left no doubt of her welcome. "And yes, I am fine. Just tired."

"Have you eaten?" Mrs. Hanson joined them, alternating between patting Clara's shoulder and removing her coat and hat.

"Thank you, my dear, for my songster. He woke us on Christmas morning with a trill of joy. Our Savior is born and even the birds rejoice." Mrs. Norgaard leaned toward the cage and made chirping noises. The little bird cocked his head and responded in kind. "I think he would talk if he could."

Mrs. Hanson appeared with a coffee tray and set it on the glass-topped coffee table. "The soup's warming and after you get something filling in you, you're going up for a wash and bed. You look like you haven't slept for a month of Sundays." Mrs. Hanson bustled them both over to the couch and had coffee cups in their hands almost by magic.

"Dag told us how you cared for the Ahmundsons. Dr. Harmon says that without you, he'd have lost half the family."

"I saw death hovering in the corner, black and ugly." Clara shuddered in remembrance. "But God's love drove him back. I don't know, I've heard stories like this but—" She paused. "Inge says she heard us calling her, so she came back. It was so hard to tell her the baby had died. You can't imagine how those poor people lived. Your soup made all the difference." She patted Mrs. Hanson's plump hand after accepting a steaming bowlful herself.

"It was them grasshoppers that did it for the farmers. They ate everything showing above the ground. Vile things." Mrs. Hanson shook her head, her tongue clicking in time.

"What can be done for them?"

"You just get some rest and leave that to us," Mrs. Norgaard said firmly.

Clara slept for two days, only rising for the necessary bodily functions. When she made her way downstairs after dressing after a bath in the hip tub, she heard voices in the sitting room. Following the trail of both masculine and feminine voices, she found all the chairs occupied. When she smiled at the folks gathered, she realized all the leaders of the town were gathered.

"Times are hard all over," the postmaster was saying, "but like you said, Mrs. Norgaard, we got to take care of our own. I got me a deer last week, I can put in that. And a sack of flour. Martha says we got extra spuds, too. Some reason those thievin' hoppers missed our place."

Clara felt tears sting behind her eyelids as everyone around the room listed what they could share.

"We'll deliver things on Saturday, then." Dag looked to Reverend Moen for confirmation. "From the church. You and Doc know who needs supplies the worst?"

Reverend Moen nodded. "The ladies'll get together and break the sacks down into smaller pieces so's there's some for everyone."

"We'll take the coal out Friday. You say we have three tons, right?"

"So far." Reverend Moen consulted a list he held in his hand. "We can always use more of everything, so pass the word along. As Christ said, 'Whatever you do for the least of these my brethren, ye do it onto Me.'"

Clara thought to the account at the bank where she had been saving her earnings. It would pay for bags of beans or whatever they needed the most. Were Nora and Carl some of those in need? Wouldn't her sister have said something if they were going hungry?

When she mentioned her concerns later to Mrs. Norgaard, the

older woman shook her head. "No, Carl wasn't wiped out like others of the farmers, even though he was stripped."

"How do you know?"

"I own the bank, remember?"

"Oh." Clara chewed on the tip of her finger. "I guess I knew Mr. Norgaard owned the bank, but when he died, I..."

"Who else could he leave it to? We have no children and his brother died before he did. I have a good manager and now that I am feeling back to par, I will be more involved." Mrs. Norgaard leaned forward on her cane. "But let me tell you, the men of the town aren't too happy about having a woman at the helm of the bank." They chuckled together.

The belated Christmas celebration was more than Clara ever dreamed possible. The Detschmans sleighed into town and the Moens walked over after church. Dag and Will joined the group and Mrs. Norgaard's wish of children laughing in her house came true.

There were presents for everyone. Toys for the children along with dresses for the girls and pants and shirts for the boys.

"How did she get the right sizes?" Ingeborg asked Clara during the middle of the melee.

"I'll never tell." Clara smiled at her friend.

Ingeborg stroked the heather gray, fine wool shawl she'd found in a package with her name. "I've never had anything so grand."

"You had something to do with all this," Nora said, after snagging Peder back from pulling himself up on the Christmas tree.

Clara just smiled. Never had she shopped and spent money like those last few weeks before Christmas. Since Mrs. Norgaard couldn't manage the streets yet, everything not ordered from a catalog had come home under the steam of either Clara or Mrs. Hanson.

"Thank you, Auntie Clara," Kaaren whispered, leaning against her aunt's knees. "You made my doll good. I call her Clara."

The lump that was never far away took up residence in Clara's throat again. She watched Dag's eyes open wide when Mary Moen handed him another package. When he read the tag, he looked over at Clara, his face inscrutable.

She watched him finger the muffler she had knitted out of wool to match his eyes. Those eyes had an uncharacteristic shine when he looked at her again.

There was one red-wrapped package left. Mary brought it over to Clara. Slowly she opened the box. Inside she found a white leather-bound Bible. When she opened it, the words were all in English. The front fly read, "From your friend, Dag." She raised her gaze to meet his. The shine matched in both pairs of eyes.

By the time everyone had devoured the feast the women had prepared and gathered their presents, dusk crept over the land.

"We must be going," Carl said, rounding up his brood. "Thank you for the wonderful party and all the presents. We will never forget your goodness." He shook Mrs. Norgaard's hand and put the other around the shoulder of his wife. "Who could know when we waved good-bye to Clara what wonderful things would come of it."

Nora hugged her sister. Clara felt like she'd had a piece of home as they embraced. "I'll try to come out more often," Clara whispered in Nora's ear. "I have so much to tell you."

"And the man in the picture?"

Clara shrugged. "Who knows?" *And who cares?* she thought.

The winter months passed quickly with evening classes both at church and at the house. Clara was called to help sick families several times and, each time, she prayed for those ill as much as she cared for their physical needs. Each time she was gone, she looked forward to telling Dag about her experiences upon her return.

One night after she returned from a week of caring for a woman with a newborn, she entered the house to find Dag in his usual seat at the dining room table, splitting his concentration between the book he studied and the page of sums he worked over. Mrs. Norgaard, hand on Will's shoulder, was explaining something to him, and he with his usual grin was making her laugh.

Slowly and quietly, so as not to bother anyone, Clara unwound her muffler and removed her coat. Was that a frown on Dag's broad brow? He concentrated so hard, not wanting to waste a moment now that he'd rediscovered the joy of learning. Her fingers itched to smooth the frown away.

Clara stared at her fingertips. What were they thinking of? She shifted her gaze to the man on the far side of the table. Sensing her attention, he raised his head. A smile broke forth that lighted his eyes and showed the gleam of his teeth.

Clara felt her heart clench in her chest. When it started beating again, the warmth spread clear out to the tips of her fingers and toes.

"Clara, you're home." He bounded to his feet and with him came all the others to welcome her back. When he took her hand in his, she felt a jolt clear up to her shoulder.

The memories kept her awake once she finally found her bed. They were friends, good friends, she and Dag. There was no problem with that—was there? But what if what she felt was more than one would feel for a good friend—a male, good friend, a handsome male, good friend?

But what about the man in the picture? a small voice niggled at the back of her mind. Aren't you supposed to marry him—whoever he is? Wherever he is?

Dag strode home that night, his hands locked behind his back, shoulders hunched. He could still feel the jolt like lightning that coursed up his arm. What was he thinking of? No woman, especially not an angel like Clara, would want to love him. Love, there could be no love in his life. Only worthy men found love, and he, Dag, was the most unworthy of all.

You must not see her again, he ordered himself. But the thought of no more lessons, no more sightings of her smiling face, no more Clara beat him downward like a load of steel on his back. He couldn't do it.

You must! The inexorable voice pounded his brain and heart.

Warm chinook winds melted the snow and, with the kiss of the sun, green blades popped up almost overnight. Clara strolled down the street on her way to the post office and then to the general store. Two men on horseback raised their hats in greeting as they passed her.

Clara felt punched in the stomach. One of them, the one mounted on the striking palomino, was the curly haired man in her picture. She spun around to get a second look and saw him glance back over his shoulder at the same time. It was him. Absolutely.

Forgetting the errands, she picked up her skirt and, once out of sight of the main street, raced toward the house. She stopped to unpin her hat that was flopping in a most decidedly unladylike manner and took off again. When she reached the porch, she clung to the white pillar.

Whew! She patted her pounding chest and tried to catch her breath. What she needed was a race or two up the mountains with her brothers.

"Clara, are you all right? What is wrong?" Mrs. Norgaard crossed the porch and stood in front of the panting girl.

"I'm fine. But. . .but—" Clara sucked in a deep breath and forced herself to stand still. "I saw him!"

"Who?"

"The man in my picture. He just came riding into town. He's here! Right here in Soldahl."

"Oh, no." Mrs. Norgaard paled and clutched her cane with both hands.

Chapter 11

He's already married," said Mrs. Norgaard. "But he can't be. He sent me a ticket to come here, and his picture. Why would he do that if he were already married?" Clara found it difficult to breathe around the boulder sitting on her chest.

"I don't know."

"You know him then?"

Mrs. Norgaard nodded.

Clara swallowed. "You knew who it was when I showed you my picture?"

The old woman nodded again.

"And you didn't tell me."

"No, child. I knew he was no good, and since nothing came of it, I hoped he would never return." Mrs. Norgaard turned back toward the door. "Come, let us sit and talk about this thing."

Clara looked up at the sky. Yes, the sun was still shining. Then why did everything seem so dark?

"Nothing has changed, you understand." Mrs. Norgaard continued when they were sitting knee to knee on the couch.

"But it has!"

"No. Now think about this. When you didn't know who he was—"

"I still don't," Clara interrupted.

The older woman ignored her. "When you didn't know who he

was, you went right on building a good life for yourself here."

"But I'm not married. I came to America expecting to be married."

"Yes, but think of your life in the last several months. Would you not have all that's gone on? You have good friends, you speak English well, you can read the language, you have literally helped keep people alive or brought them back from near death."

"No. Yes. I don't know. Does it have to be one or the other?" Clara fought back the tears that threatened to blind her. Here she'd been so excited and now all was ashes. "I thought maybe he was coming for me."

Mrs. Norgaard shook her head, clucking her tongue in sympathy.

"At least tell me his name, if you know it."

Mrs. Norgaard paused. She lowered her gaze to their clasped hands. "His name is Jude."

"Jude. Jude! As in Judas?" Clara threw herself against the back of the couch. "If that isn't poetic justice. Now I really understand what betrayal means." She looked up to catch a look of consternation cross Mrs. Norgaard's seamed face. "I think I'll go up to my room for a while. Don't call me if a certain young cowboy comes calling."

As she fell across her bed, she let the tears come. All of a sudden her life seemed in pieces when but a short while ago she was glorying in the signs of spring. Betrayed! She'd been betrayed. But what was the purpose behind all this? After all, a ticket from Norway to North Dakota cost a great deal of money.

As her brain functioned again, the tears dried up. Now she vacillated between anger at a man who would do such a things—to a person he didn't even know—and curiosity. Why? She got up and, sitting down at the dressing table, began brushing her hair. The soothing action always made her think better.

She took out the picture and the stained letter and tried to read the letter again but to no avail. Even knowing the man's name, the faded script made no sense. She studied the smiling mouth and laughing eyes. How could one who looked so...so...charming, the only word she could come up with, do such a terrible thing?

After washing her face, she made her way back downstairs. She still hadn't finished the errands. Maybe she'd stop by the blacksmith's and talk to Dag for a bit. He always made her feel better.

Clara walked the way to the blacksmith's first. As she drew closer, she heard two men laughing, but neither laugh belonged to Dag or Will. The ring of hammer on metal continued unabated.

Hesitant to interrupt if Dag were conducting business, Clara paused outside the door.

"So ya picked the bitty gal from Norway up at the station like I tol' ya."

"Jude, what are you talking about?" Dag's voice held more than a note of exasperation. He spoke in English.

"Wal, looky here. My brother done learned to talk like ever'body else whilst I was gone."

Metal whanged on metal.

"So, did she think you was gonna marry her? Only the picture I sent didn't match what she see'd?"

Clara felt her eyes widen. She clamped her teeth on her lip to keep from crying out.

"You are not making any sense. I took Miss Johanson out to the Detschman farm like you asked and that was the end of it."

"But I sent'er a letter, with my picture. Only I signed yer name."

"She'da thought you was to marry her." The second man spoke up for the first time.

Clara listened to the two men laughing hysterically and thumping each other on the back. She could feel Dag's pain, emanating from the building like the tolling of the bell when a fire broke out.

"Jude, just get out of town." His voice sounded flat, beaten.

"You low-down, rotten excuse for a human being." Clara flew around the corner like a banty hen defending her brood from a low-flying chicken hawk. "Anyone who would do such a cruel and spiteful thing to another—least of all his brother. Why you ought to be horsewhipped." She stood toe to toe with the tall man and shook her fist in his face. "You think you're so smart. You don't know what it is to be a man. Even the lizards know more about human decency than you do."

Jude backed away, flapping at her with his hands.

Clara met him, stride for stride. "Dag Weinlander is one of the finest men in the country. And you have the nerve to make fun of him. Why he's worth ten of you. Twenty or forty!"

"Lady, enough. Back away before—"

"Before you what? You take to beating women, too? And children, I suppose. I pity your poor wife. God bless her to put up with the likes of you." She backed him all the way to his horse, which also shied away from the barrage of verbiage.

Jude and his cohort swung aboard their mounts and hightailed it out of there. Jude looked over his shoulder as they fled, as if afraid she might pursue them farther.

"Thank God I didn't marry him!" Clara stamped her foot and dusted her hands together, as if good riddance to bad rubbish. As the dust settled, the enormity of what she had done began to seep into her consciousness.

She turned around to find Dag watching her, the old spirit of unworthiness beating him into the dust.

"That's the way! Miss Johanson, you done good." Will leaped forward to grab her hand.

"Will!" The tone of Dag's voice stopped the youth short. He turned, caught the nod, and, after giving Clara a hint of smile for encouragement, left for the recesses of the livery.

Clara watched the lad go and wished she could do the same. What must Dag think of her? She left off memorizing the shoe and looked up to catch the sorrow in her friend's face.

"Clara, how could you... ?"

"How could I what?" She felt the force flow through her again.

He believed what his conniving brother had said. After all these months, the old Dag was just waiting to be beaten again—by his brother. "Dag Weinlander, I'm amazed at you! Don't you know what a fine man you are? Everyone in town says so. Mrs. Norgaard thinks of you almost like a son. God made you to walk tall like the man you are. He doesn't make mistakes. God loves you and—" She bit off the words. She put a hand to her mouth. She'd almost said, "And so do I."

"And...and He wants you to be happy." She stared up at the face above her, drowning in the eyes of mountain lake blue. Eyes that had once clothed her in warmth but were now rimmed with frost. What had she done?

Clara turned heel and strode swiftly down the street before the tears she fought could win the battle.

Go after her, man! screamed the voice in his head. But Dag stood, as if rooted to the spot like a century-old pine tree. What could he say? What could he do?

Clara, she was magnificent. He rubbed the inside of his cheek with the tip of his tongue. Never had he seen his brother back down and run off like that. Why, he'd been almost afraid to get in the way in case she turned on him. A chuckle tickled his ribs.

He picked up his hammer from beside the smoldering forge, but instead of cranking the blower to heat the coals, he slipped the sledge into its assigned slot on the workbench and sank down on an upturned bucket.

Why didn't he let Jude have it? Why couldn't he think of a thing to say? He scrubbed at his scalp as if to drive the ideas either into his brain or drag them out.

Jude hurt Clara! The thought flared forth in a burst of pure, red rage. His brother tried to make a fool out of the woman he loved. Dag ground his teeth together. Where could he find him? He rose to his feet and began pacing back and forth. What would Jude do? Go home to their mother? Dag shook his head.

Hide out? He nodded. One fist slammed into the palm of the other hand. The rhythm beat with each stride. Where would the dirty dog hide? Step, slap. Would Clara ever speak to him again? Step! Slap! What difference did it make? Who was he that she should care?

He leaned against the support post, barely restraining himself from pounding his head against the wood. *Dolt. Dag the Dolt.* He heard again the jeering voice from his youth. One tear squeezed past the power of his will and trickled down into his perfectly trimmed beard.

When Clara returned to the big house, she dropped the mail on the hall table and dragged herself up the stairs. Without speaking to anyone, she staggered into her bedroom and slumped on the bed.

Dag, her best friend, would probably never speak to her again. And his brother—oh, she could wring his neck with her bare hands, just like butchering a mean, tough old rooster. But Dag— how could she stay in the same town and not see him? Not talk to him? Not study with him, laugh with him, see the world through his magnificent eyes? Not tend the sick or visit the well?

Her hand over her eyes blotted out the sun streaming in the windows.

When Mrs. Hanson knocked on the door, Clara sent her away with a mumbled excuse. What kind of a woman was she to scream at a total stranger like that? But he—Jude—what a perfect name for him—the betrayer—he had laughed at Dag. Tried to make a fool of him. Treated him like pond scum.

She bit her lip so hard she could taste the blood.

"God, Father, what am I to do?" The tears trickled down the sides of her face and watered her hair.

This must be how a bucket feels coming up from the well, she thought, as she pulled herself hand over hand toward the light. A rapping penetrated her fog. And repeated.

She forced open her eyes. The afternoon sun had dimmed to

dusk. The thumping she now recognized as Mrs. Norgaard tapping on the door.

"Clara, dear, let me come in. I know you are in there." She tapped again.

Clara pushed herself up on her elbows. Had she locked the door in her anger? She shook her head. Waves sloshed from side to side within her skull. She groaned and flopped back down.

"Clara, please."

"Come in, it's not locked." She covered her eyes with one arm to still the pounding in her head. She must look a sight. She could barely open her eyes, they were so swollen.

Mrs. Norgaard pushed open the door and swept across the carpet. After studying the form crumpled on the bed, she sat down on the edge. "Is it really as bad as all this?" Her voice floated like dust motes on a warm and caring sunbeam.

Clara nodded. She clamped her fingers against pounding temples.

"I've taken the liberty of asking Mrs. Hanson to make you some sassafras tea. When she comes, I want you to drink it all. Better than laudanum to ease a headache." She sat there, not moving.

Clara lay there, listening to her own breathing and the blood pounding clear to her fingertips.

Even Mrs. Hanson was quiet, tiptoeing in and keeping her voluminous comments to herself. She set the tray down, light as a whisper and, after propping Clara against pillows stacked and fluffed behind her, left the room.

"Here." Mrs. Norgaard handed Clara the cup as soon as the young woman opened her eyes.

Clara took a sip and made a face.

"Drink it, its good for you." Clara obeyed, her thoughts and feelings in too much of a muddle to resist.

When the pain lines furrowing Clara's forehead relaxed, Mrs. Norgaard settled herself in a chair she'd pulled over to the bed.

"Now, my dear, I can't help you unless I know what terrible thing has transpired."

"I'm so ashamed." A sob turned into a hiccup.

"What could you have done to make you so ashamed?"

Clara waited, wishing the woman would disappear on one hand and that she were a mind reader on the other. Then she wouldn't have to tell the entire miserable tale.

"There I was, screaming like a fishwife, right out where all the town could hear."

Bit by bit, Mrs. Norgaard dragged the story from her sorrowing friend.

"And so, Dag will probably never speak to me again," Clara finished the tale on another sigh.

A tap sounded at the door. Upon Mrs. Norgaard's "Yes?" Mrs. Hanson stuck her head in. "There's a young man down here who wants to talk with Clara."

"See, I knew Dag has more sense than you give him credit for."

"No, I don't want to see him. Tell him I'm ill."

"You don't look so good, that's true." Mrs. Hanson withdrew her head and they could hear her thumping down the stairs. Silence settled back in the room.

"You have to see him again."

"I know. But not like this." Clara listened to the silence again. By now, peace had begun its gentle attack on her strident emotions.

"You know what I think?"

"No, what?"

"I think I see God's hand in all of this and He has a marvelous plan still to be worked out. But not all tonight." The older woman rose from her chair. "Would you care for a bit of soup or toast?" When Clara shook her head, Mrs. Norgaard just nodded. "All right then, let's get you into bed. Like the Psalm says, 'Weeping may endure for a night, but joy cometh in the morning.' And we want that morning to come soon."

Even after being tucked in and kissed on the forehead, Clara felt sure she'd never cut off the voices in her head long enough to sleep. But the next thing she knew, the rising sun tinted the curtains creamy gold.

The first thing she thought of was Jude on his fancy palomino, hightailing it out of town. She had to admit, it was funny. Like when the horse kept jumping around. She must have been something when even that big dumb, four-footed beast was scared of her. Anything that would carry Jude around had to be dumb.

She stretched her arms over her head and wriggled her toes. Somewhere a rooster crowed...and another answered.

When she thought of Dag, she remembered a dog she'd seen beaten one time. How it crawled away with its tail dragging in the dirt. How all his life this man had been beaten down by his conniving younger brother. The fire simmered in her belly again. What could they do to make Jude crawl like the worm he was? How could they get even?

Chapter 12

I could kill him!" "Dag, no!" Will shook his master's shoulders. "Wake up, Dag, you're dreaming."

Dag fought his way out of the fog and sat upright. He could feel his brother's throat clenched between them, his hands squeezing, squeezing the life out. "No!"

"It's all right, come on, everything will be all right," Will murmured in the soothing, singsong voice Dag had taught him to use with a skittish horse. "You'll never kill anyone, not even your brother, even if he does deserve it."

"He was going to use Clara to make a fool out of me again." Dag sank down on the crinkly mattress. "Why does he hate me so? All my life I tried to do as my father said, take care of Ma and my brother. All my life. I know I'm dumb, dolt they called me, and big and ugly, but Will, I tried." He sat up and grasped Will by the collar of his shirt.

"No, Dag, no, no, you're not dumb." Will reached for the massive hands of his master and friend.

Dag continued, not even hearing Will's plea. "I quit school so I could go to work and earn some money. They could have farmed, but Ma said the land was too poor. Even when I got my own forge, they called me dumb dolt."

"Dag, listen to me. They're just jealous. And lazy and mean."

"Dumb dolt and now I feel such anger I want to kill my brother.

My only brother." Dag rolled his head from side to side. After a time he began again. "And now Clara won't see me. After attacking Jude like that. Humph! No one puts anything over on my Clara. God, can't I do anything right?" He threw himself from his bed and thundered out the door of the soddy.

Dag ran as if pursued by the devil himself. As his bare feet pounded the mud of the road, his mind kept pace. *God, if You are really the God they talk about in church, take me away from here now. They say there's a heaven. It'd sure beat this life on earth.* He slipped in one viscous hole and fell to his knees. When he rose to run again, he caught himself slipping and sliding with fatigue.

The next time he fell, he lay flat out, face down in the mud. He raised his head just enough to breathe. "God," he panted at the heavens, "I give up! You hear me, I give up!" The words ended on a screech.

Dag lay there waiting for a lightning bolt to strike him. When nothing happened, he pushed himself to his knees and then his feet. When he staggered home, chills rocked his body, but he stopped at the windmill and, with one shaking hand, began pumping. After sluicing buckets of clean water and scrubbing with the bar of soap in the scrub bucket, he rinsed again and padded into the soddy. He rubbed himself dry with a coarse towel and fell back in bed. Clean, he finally felt clean. "Father, forgive me," he mumbled as he drifted off to sleep.

The rooster crowing from the farm across the way brought Dag bolt upright in bed. Had it all been a dream? More like a nightmare. He rubbed the top of his head. No, his hair was still damp. He had indeed lain in the mud and been washed clean. But now he felt . . . he felt like crowing as the rooster did. He began singing instead, "Onward Christian soldiers..." His rich baritone filled the soddy and escaped out the chimney.

Will stumbled from the other room, rubbing his eyes. Dag singing. . .in the morning? Dag singing. . .at all? "Yip-pee!" He dragged his pants from the end of his bed and staggered after Dag, pulling his pants on as he ran.

"I'll go see him as soon as he gets to the shop." Clara took another turn around her room. "He must open at seven." She glanced at the clock on her chest of drawers for the umpteenth time.

"I'll go see her as soon as it is polite." Dag brushed an imaginary piece of straw off his navy wool pants. He gave his hair another brushing.

They met halfway in the middle.

"I'm sorry," they both said at once. They looked at each other and laughed.

"Have you had breakfast?" Clara asked. At the shake of his head, she took his arm. "Good, Mrs. Hanson makes wonderful pancakes."

"I...I —" They both started to talk again at the same time.

"Ladies first." Dag looked down at the silly black feather bobbing almost at his shoulder. What was she doing wearing such a fancy hat this early in the morning?

"All right. Please forgive me for making such a fool of myself yesterday."

"The only one you made a fool of was my brother. Please, accept my apologies for the way he has acted."

"Of course. Now that that's out of the way, I have a plan. How would you like to get even with your brother? Turn the tables on him for a change?"

"And how would we do this?"

"Well, this way." They climbed the stairs to the porch as she talked. "Jude wanted you to feel like a fool when I learned of his treachery, right?" Dag nodded and opened the door for her. "What if he thought we were courting?"

"How could we do that?" He helped her off with her coat.

"The way everyone courts, silly. You could escort me to church, to the social at the schoolhouse, out for drives in your oh-so-shiny buggy..."

"It's too muddy to take out the buggy." He hung his own coat up.

"Dag, you know what I meant." Together they entered the dining room laughing.

"Now these are the faces I love to see in the morning," Mrs. Norgaard said as she winked at Mrs. Hanson. "I think you better go flip some more of those pancakes of yours and fry extra bacon. Dag looks like he could eat a whole ham."

She turned to the two young people. "Sit down, my children, and tell me what brings such smiles to your faces."

"We're going to get even." Clara plunked herself down on her chair. "With Jude. He's been mean to Dag for too long."

A slight frown marred Mrs. Norgaard's forehead. "Get even. You know, God says that is His job."

"I know. But we're going to help Him out." Clara explained the plan, totally seriously and in great detail. "What are you laughing about?"

"I'm not laughing." Mrs. Norgaard swallowed the chortle that belied her words. She sipped her coffee to stifle another giggle. When she had composed her mouth, if not her eyes, she continued. "I think that is a very good plan and you should begin immediately."

Dag looked from his young friend to his old friend and back again. There was something going on here that he could sense but not recognize. But then, how much had he ever tried understanding women in his monastic life anyway? He shrugged the thought away. At least this plan was better than the one he'd dreamed of during the dark hours.

The sun smiled on their plan as they walked through the town that afternoon. Dag recognized one of Jude's cronies standing by the train station so he knew word would get back to his brother. But as he and

Clara passed the church, he forgot his brother and remembered the song in his heart when he awoke. That night he walked with her to their English class at the church. Will accompanied them, hands in his pockets, whistling away. When Dag had shared a little of "the plan" with him, the young man nodded solemnly. "That'll get him for sure," was his only comment. But he didn't stop whistling.

When Dag walked Clara home, Will made excuses and went another way.

"But I don't know how to dance." Dag threw his hands up in the air, hoping to end the discussion.

"But if we are to do this courting right, you must take me to the box social at the schoolhouse on Saturday." Clara sat in the chair in front of the window in the sitting room. Late afternoon sunlight slanted in and set her hair afire.

Dag couldn't take his eyes off the golden threads.

"It's for a good cause. They are trying to earn enough money for a new roof." Clara laid her hands in hei lap.

"I'll put the roof on myself," Dag muttered in a voice Clara barely heard.

She wet her lips with the tip of her tongue. "You could leam to dance."

"I suppose you would teach me that, too." "My box will be the best-tasting and prettiest there." "Will and I do just fine at home. We aren't starving." "Maybe Jude will be there. This is a perfect opportunity to—" "Get even. Yes, I know." Dag dragged his hands over his scalp, mussing the hair he usually kept so carefully brushed. "All right. We will go. But we might leave early."

But they didn't leave early, and even though Jude never made an appearance, Dag and Clara had a wondrous time. Dag was blessed with the natural rhythm and grace sometimes given to big men, and once he learned the patterns of a dance or two, he couldn't get enough. He danced every dance, even those he didn't know.

He danced the waltz with Mrs. Norgaard and the polka with Mrs.

Hanson. His feet tapped out the reel with Clara, and they swung past each other on the round and square dances. If he made a mistake, he just laughed along with the others and went on dancing.

Clara sank down on a chair along the wall, next to Mrs. Norgaard. "I'm exhausted." She fanned her hot face with her handkerchief. She watched Dag swing Ingeborg past on another polka.

"I think we are seeing a miracle," Mrs. Norgaard whispered in Clara's ear.

"Dag?"

"Yes, Dag. I thank the good Lord every night for what He is doing with our young man."

"I wish—" Clara fanned herself again.

"What, my dear?"

"Oh, nothing. Would you like some punch?" At Mrs. Norgaard's nod, Clara pushed herself to her feet. What she wished was that Dag was truly her young man and that this courting wasn't just a sham.

"Think yer purty smart, don'cha." Jude strolled into the blacksmith's shop late one afternoon.

Dag ignored him, continuing to forge the point on a pickax.

"Well, she ain't for the likes o' you." Jude spit a glob of tobacco juice into the dirt. "You taken her out to see Ma?"

Dag thrust the heavy steel back into the forge and motioned Will to crank the handle on the blower. The whine of the machine overpowered any conversation. When the iron point glowed red, then white, Dag pulled it out and returned it to the anvil.

"Maybe I shoulda taken that little filly fer m'self after all."

"You have a wife."

"Don't remind me." Jude dug a kerchief out of his back pocket and blew his nose. "We're livin' out at Ma's now. To help her out some'at."

Dag returned the piece of steel to the forge. When he looked up, Jude was gone. Now he'd have to send more food and coal out there. He gritted his teeth and wiped the sweat off his brow with the back of his glove.

Knowing he would have a massive cleaning job afterward, Dag took the surry out on a Sunday morning to drive the household of women to church. Mrs. Norgaard still wasn't strong enough to walk the distance. When spring came to North Dakota, the frozen roads bottomed out with the thaw, but the streets in town weren't quite the morass of the country roads.

After greeting friends, Clara and Dag entered the sanctuary and sat side by side. Sharing the same hymnbook made them smile at each other. Singing together, her soprano blending with his baritone, made them smile.

Reverend Moen took his place behind the carved, white-and-gilt pulpit. He smiled at those before him. "Grace and peace from God our Father and our Lord Jesus Christ."

Clara settled back against the wooden pew. Today she could truly sense both the grace and peace. She felt it warm her from the inside out. She ignored the warmth emanating from the man beside her and concentrated on the sermon.

"Today's gospel is from the fifth chapter of Matthew, verse forty-three and following." He glanced again around the congregation and began reading. "Ye have heard that it hath been said, Thou shalt love thy neighbour, and hate thine enemy. But I say unto you, Love your enemies, bless them that curse you, do good to them that hate you, and pray from them which despitefully use you, and persecute you; That ye may be the children of your Father which is in heaven: for he maketh his sun to rise on the evil and on the good, and sendeth rain on the just and on the unjust."

He closed the Bible and then his eyes. "Father, teach us this day what You would have us to learn. Open our hearts and minds that we might indeed listen unto You. Amen."

The congregation responded with one voice, "Amen."

Clara argued with the verses through the rest of the sermon, only catching random phrases of Reverend Moen's message. *But I have been praying for him, from way back when I first received the letter. And right up until...*She tried a different tack. *I don't hate Jude...I...I'm just angry with him. Furious is more like it. I don't want to do good to him...I want to get even. He hurt Dag; there's no love in the way he has treated Dag all these years.* She groaned inwardly. *Yes, persecute would be the perfect word to describe the way Jude and his mother treated Dag.*

"Our Father so often gives us a promise along with the hard commands, for these words are truly a hard order for us to follow."

Clara covered her unladylike snort with a cough.

"Just think, that we may be children of our Father who is in Heaven, but who loved us so much He sent His Son to be persecuted and to die on the cross. . .for you. . .and for me." Reverend Moen leaned forward. There was not a sound from the congregation.

"He forgave each of us..." The pause stretched.

Clara's heart felt like it was being pulled in two directions and at any moment, it might rip in two.

The pastor continued,' And so must we forgive. Amen."

Dag kept his shoulders rigid through superhuman efforts. *Forgive! I've been forgiving them all my life. So they hurt me. That wasn't so bad; I got used to it. But now Jude has hurt Clara. Beautiful, innocent Clara, who he hadn't even known. All to play a trick on me, his ugly dolt of a brother. That I can't forgive!*

"As you were forgiven." The words chased each other through his mind and around his heart, stabbing him as they ran.

Am I really a child of God? He looked up at the shiny gold cross in front of the picture of Jesus tending his sheep. Dag stifled a groan that tore from his innermost hidden place.

"He died on the cross…for you…and for me."

For me. For Dag Weinlander. Dag swallowed hard against the moisture rising in his throat and blinding his eyes. He blinked furiously.

"Our closing hymn for today is number 360, 'My Jesus, I Love Thee.'"

As the organ wheezed into the opening bars of the song, Clara and Dag stood along with the congregation. The words poured forth. "My Jesus, I love thee, I know thou art mine. For thee all the folly of sin I resign…"

Dag quit singing. He bit his lip and let the words and music roll over him, bathing him in the healing Christ promised. He whispered along with the final line. "If ever I love thee, my Jesus 'tis now."

Clara struggled to reach the high notes—and gave up. Singing was impossible from a throat clogged with tears. Why did Reverend Moen choose such a sermon for today? Had someone told him about their game? Who would? And was it *really* a game? Was getting even ever a game?

Neither Dag nor Clara spoke a word on the ride home, until they arrived at the big house, and then it was only a polite good-bye.

The doorbell announced a visitor just as the grandfather's clock bonged six times.

"Come right on in," Mrs. Hanson said. "You're just in time for supper."

"No, I mean, no, thank you. I'd just like a few minutes with Clara, if I may." Dag gripped his hat in his hands. This would be the hardest thing he'd ever done.

When Clara came to the door, he stared into her eyes, then dropped his gaze to the floor. "Could you come out for a moment, please?"

She nodded, reached behind her for the shawl on the coat tree, and stepped outside, her gaze never leaving his face. "What is it,

Dag. What's wrong?"

Her soft voice tore his heart from his chest. "I…we…that is, I cannot play our courting game any longer." He took a deep breath. "And I cannot see you anymore." He turned and stepped off the porch, his long strides eating up the distance to the fence.

"Dag, what is it?"

He kept on walking.

Clara chewed on her knuckle for one brief moment and flew down the walk after him. When he didn't stop at her calling his name, she grabbed his coat when she caught up with him.

"Now, tell me what this is all about." She put all the force she could into her words.

"Nei, no. Just let it be."

"Dag, you can't run away from me now. Not now or anytime." Clara grasped his lapels with shaking hands. "You can't leave because I love you and you love me, if you'd just open your eyes. If you can't see it, maybe I should take one of your hammers and smack you over the head with it till you get some sense."

"You love me?" His voice squeaked.

Clara stepped back. She tipped her head slightly to the side and glared up at him. "I said so, didn't I?"

Dag grabbed her around the waist with both hands and whirled them both around. "She loves me!" he yelled to the robin who fluttered out of his nighttime perch at all the commotion.

He set her down just long enough to wrap both arms around her and lifted her for the kiss he'd dreamed of during the long winter nights.

Clara wrapped her arms around his neck and kissed him back. When they drew apart to breathe, she traced one slim fingertip across his full bottom lip. "I like kissing a man with a beard," she whispered and placed her lips on his again. "But only if that man is you." Her breathy voice tickled the soft hairs around his mouth.

Slowly, he set her down, never letting her move from the circle of his arms. "I feel like Jacob who stole the birthright," he confessed.

"No, you have it backwards. You're the older. Your brother has spent most of his life trying to steal the birthright from you. But now you know how much you are worth. And nothing, no one, can take that or me from you."

"Clara, my heart, I love you." There, he'd said the words. He couldn't remember ever uttering them before. Such simple words. He thought back to this morning. He had said them before. Today, in church. Only it was a different love song, "My Jesus, I love thee, I know thou art mine." He looked deep into Clara's eyes, searching her soul. "My Clara, I love thee, I know thou art mine." And thus he gave her his heart.

Epilogue

Clara rocked gently in the chair on the wide front porch. She could hear the canary singing from Mrs. Norgaard's room up above. He serenaded them from the first rays of sunlight until the golden ball sank in the west.

On the flagpole attached to the house, she could hear the Norwegian flag fluttering in the breeze. The seventeenth of May, Norwegian Independence Day and Clara and Dag's one-year anniversary.

She leaned her head against the back of the seat and closed her eyes. What a day that had been. No, to be exact, the celebration had begun the week before that, when Mrs. Norgaard called her and Dag into the sitting room one evening.

After they took their places on the brown velvet couch, a gentle silence permeated the room.

"I have something for you," she said, her face serious but her eyes sending messages of warmth and love. "I've put off telling you this because I don't want you to be burdened by an old woman's silliness."

"What is it?" Clara felt alarm leaping in her heart. Was something wrong with her friend? Something she'd not told them?

Mrs. Norgaard leaned forward and handed them an envelope. When Clara looked up in consternation, the old woman just nodded.

Dag slit the envelope open and removed a parchment sheet. Together, he and Clara read the formal words.

Clara felt her mouth fall open. She stared from the letter to Mrs. Norgaard and back to the paper in Dag's hands. "You mean, you—?" She couldn't get the rest of the words out.

"Yes, the house is yours, but only if you truly want it."

"Want it? How could you doubt something so wonderful?"

"But that means you will be burdened with me until the good Lord calls me home."

"No, not a burden." Dag shook his head. "You have given me a life." He clasped Clara's hand in his own. "And a wife, and now a home."

"Then I believe we have made a fair trade, for without Clara, I would not be here to rejoice with you." Mrs. Norgaard blinked rapidly, matching the motions of the two on the settee.

Clara crossed the small space and dropped to her knees in front of her mentor. "Thank you, from the bottom of my heart."

Mrs. Norgaard stroked back the tendrils of silky hair that framed Clara's face. "I have one more favor to ask."

"What? Anything."

"Just fill these rooms with laughing children as soon as you can, so I can enjoy them, too."

Clara, dreaming in the rocker, stroked her rounded belly. Little Lars or Lisa seemed in a mighty big hurry to make an entrance—or else the baby was practicing broad jumps.

She sighed. And the wedding had been magnificent. Her in her *bunad* and Nora in hers. Now neither of them would fit into their black skirts or sparkling aprons. Their babies would be born close together.

Dag had stood before the congregation after the pronouncement of man and wife. "I have something I'd like to say," he announced. He glanced at Reverend Moen for permission. At the preacher's nod, Dag continued. "Most of you knew me long before Clara came to Soldahl.

You brought your plowshares to be sharpened and your horses to be shod. But I was not one to talk and share the latest news."

A ripple of laughter spread across the congregation. "But you saw me then and you see me now. What happened to me was God's miracle. He took a bitter, beaten man and poured love into his heart, that love that Christ talks about. God used a young woman to bring life to many of us in this town and then He gave her to me. Can you doubt God's great love? If He could love me, He can love anyone."

There wasn't a dry eye in the place.

Clara straightened from her idyll on the porch. The familiar whistle announced the arrival of her beloved whisper. She watched through the breaks in the newly leafed trees for glimpses of his head as he strode the street for home. She rubbed her back again.

Dag took the porch steps in one bound. "Have you been resting like you were told?" he asked, his smile causing her heart to leap in response.

"I have. Resting and remembering." She laid her cheek against the back of his hand.

"Remembering?"

"Oh, about the wedding and the months before that." She kissed a spot on his hand that had gotten too close to the heat.

Dag sank down on the floor beside her, one arm propped on a raised knee. "I have a confession to make."

Clara's eyebrows traveled upward.

"Your present didn't come in on the train."

Clara rubbed her back again and this time squirmed a bit in the seat. "I think yours might be coming sooner than we expected."

Dag turned in time to catch a grimace marring the serenity of her forehead. "Are you all right?" A tinge of panic touched his voice.

"I'm fine. Or I will be after a few more hours." She stroked her fingers through the coffee-hued hair that waved back so richly from his face. She'd come to Dakota to find her dream and now they were living it.